The Hidden Druid

Book Two

The Innisfail Cycle

Angela Laverghetta

The Hidden Druid

The Innisfail Cycle / Book 2

eBook Edition ISBN: 979-8-9877260-3-7

Paperback Edition ISBN: 979-8-9877260-4-4

Hardcover Edition ISBN: 979-8-9877260-5-1

Dark Land Books

75 McCabe Drive Box # 19845

Reno, Nevada 89511

Cover Design by ANKBookDesigns

Editing and Formatting by Gail R Delaney Editing Services

Dedication

To Gail, who gave me a chance

Content Advisory

Minimal swearing
Depictions of bodily harm
Sexually suggested themes
Wildlife deaths
Human death
Depictions of slavery
Discussion of suicide

Acknowledgments

I wrote a second book!

I can hardly wrap my head around it.

When I published The Buried Knight, I couldn't believe I'd written 55k words and now I've written a 76k novel! I dedicated this book to Gail, my dear friend and editor, because she really did give me the chance to reclaim my dream of publishing a novel and I wanted to thank her in the best author way possible. But I also really need to acknowledge that The Hidden Druid wouldn't have been written without all the readers who wanted to know how the story ended. There were days I felt like giving up. It's incredible to create, and incredibly hard to do it consistently. In the end, I didn't want to disappoint you all, and I powered through. Your encouragement is woven into the pages of this book. Thank you for believing in me!

Shout out to my amazing critique group! This book is only as decent as it is because they pulled it apart and broke the bones open —in a good way! (Any lingering issues are all my fault and not theirs.) Kat, Danielle, Aly, Alyssa, Kevin, and Teresa, I couldn't have done it without you!

A special thank you to Angela Meyerhoff and Lynda Bailey for taking the time to read through the entire novel to make sure there weren't any glaring issues. I seriously appreciate the peace of mind. Lynda, I promise I'll go slower next time!

Large thank you to Cindy Joy for her incredibly discerning eye for detail.

And thank you to all those who have helped me market my novels by posting or reposting on their social media platforms. Your help has allowed me to get my book into more readers' hands, which is the goal of every author. You all are too numerous to thank by name, and the fact that I can say that makes me tear up with gratitude. Thank you from the bottom of my heart.

As always (and forever), I have to thank my husband for being my biggest cheerleader, my booth babe, and my muse. There is no one better to bounce ideas off of than him. Not only does he support my dream, but he also continuously gives me a leg up to reach the next level.

Cast of Characters

Imogen (Genny) Wylde—museum intern, inheritor of Wylde House Retirement Home, and current owner of Excalibur

Aengus — the "Buried Knight" and Lancelot of legend

Nibbleink—a Brownie and Genny's friend

Geoffrey Corbin—Genny's father and the Green Knight (formerly of the Unseelie Court)

The Leannan Sidhe—(also goes by Leannan) a fae who steals power and is accused of killing the god Danu who controlled the gate leading from faerie to the human realm, forcing the Seelie Court to close the veil permanently

Wylde House Retirement Home

Everett Sinclair—the Charge Nurse
Home Residents—Jane Carlson (deceased as of book 2)
Solomon Friedman
Judith O'Cleary
Alejandro Perez
Liu Chu Hua
Sissy Bell

The Seelie Court

Aurnia Honeythorn—Seelie Leader
Betty—her assistant

Theo (Theophilus) Honeythorn—her son
Gaius—Court wizard (deceased as of book 2)

The Unseelie Court

Saoirse Silfweed—Unseelie Queen
Dennriall—her seneschal
Other Fae
Trell—a race of fae that both courts use as muscle
Fola tráill—humans turned into vampire-like creatures and used by the fae
Ossorians—humans turned into wolf-like beasts and used by the fae

Caldonia 490 c.e.

She had betrayed them.

The knowledge stabbed Danu deep. If gods possessed hearts, theirs was surely pierced, shredded. They'd always known she might leave. She was bold, beautiful—terrifying. A firebrand of opinions and passion.

But betrayal hadn't ever crossed Danu's mind.

Limbs suffused with lethargy, hung limp and lifting hand to face required an immense force of will. Their fingers moved, but the motion felt distant, as if controlled by an outside force.

If only someone had taken the helm when the first waves of infatuation took hold. The other gods voiced disapproval. Even the fae called on them to reconsider. If the humans had any awareness, they would have raised alarms as well, but no one stopped them. No one took control and made them turn away from her.

And now they died?

Even as consciousness tumbled downward. Even as the ground rose to meet them—to swallow them whole—Danu loved her still. Their heart as much a betrayer as she.

The world darkened into a void, deep and endless. Their weakness deserved the dark.

But part of Danu wondered; was it truly weakness to love?

If only she had trusted them, though a god ancient and stuck amongst old ways, they could change—would have changed for her. If she had held on to her patience a little longer, there would have been a new world where they were together.

Warmth touched Danu's cheeks, and they knew she was near. Her intoxicating smell of smoke and peat overwhelmed them. Enveloped in heady memories, they tried to reach for her. Danu's arms refused to obey. Darkness pulled them deeper until all that remained was the crushing silence of their entire world shattered into nothing.

Chapter One

The wards protecting Wylde House Retirement Home were crumbling.

Recasting the wards should have happened by now, but Jane's death had stripped the coven of their strongest member. A weakened shield meant the coven remained vulnerable but to be recast, the spell needed a truckload of magic and an equal amount of control. For all the grand power I supposedly possessed, I was about as helpful as a fork without tines in the control department.

Yet here I was trying anyway. I believe the term is "glutton for punishment."

Three months ago, my life had been normal. Well, as normal as someone who can see ghosts and the fae can make it.

Until Aengus appeared. *Don't call him Lancelot, he gets snippy.*

Then a sword *chose* me. *Excalibur. You might have heard of it.*

And suddenly I could wield magic.

Although, as I said before, "wield" gave me a bit too much credit.

And where were all the players who'd dragged me into this drama of fae courts and *custos* and the end of the world as we know it? Radio silence.

It was only a matter of time before The Leannan Sidhe showed up to take what she wanted—me. Or, more accurately, the power I possessed.

I set my palm against the aged wood of the front door, smooth from years of diligent application of furniture polish. The scent of oil and mulled lemons brought flashes of my grandmother and a warmth pulsed beneath my hand. For a moment, breathing seemed impossible through the grief.

Behind me, Mrs. Liu smacked her cane against the floor. "Now this time focus, Genny."

I scowled over my shoulder. It didn't help that the petite, older woman had already dressed to start the day, gray hair smoothed perfectly to curl under her chin and pristine white canvas shoes on her feet. Honestly, asking me to do anything before 7 a.m. was an effort in futility. My thinky-thinky parts needed caffeine first.

Mrs. Liu smacked her cane again.

Despite feeling like I was experiencing the description of insanity —doing the same thing over again and hoping for a different result—I focused on the door. I didn't hold out much hope this time would break the cycle. Closing my eyes, I fell deep into the dark space, seemingly both existing within me and everywhere at the same time.

The wards shimmered before my mind's eye, flexible as a spider's web and just as strong. Usually. Most areas appeared whole, but in some sections small pinpricks of black spotted across the surface like mold. Holes in the fabric of the spell.

Before I could even try to plug the holes, my control faltered. The shimmer of the wards seemed to fall behind me as my consciousness reached outward. Seeking, almost hunting for what my magic desired.

"You're losing it," Mrs. Liu snapped.

"I know," I said through clenched teeth.

I needed to relax and focus on just the wards, but all I could see were tendrils of light twisting and twining around me. Their energy pulled at me, flirted with me. Each one represented a life and if I reached out, I would find the threads of everyone in the neighborhood, probably the entire population of Carson City—maybe even the state. I didn't know how far I could reach. But I was certain with a yank I could pull all the strands to me, snatch their energy, take their life, and wield power no one should have.

It was never meant for those with fae blood and those who possess magic to produce a child, yet here I was, and now both the witches and the fae considered me an abomination and their scared voices named me—Cailleach Fae.

My remaining concentration shattered, and with a violent heave, I pulled my arm from the door. The magic ripped away and punched a hollowness down through me. A hunger I had no way to sate. Or not any way I was willing to. Why did I do this to myself? I should have told Mrs. Liu *no* when she insisted I try again this morning. Now, for the rest of the day, I was going to be a hangry troll.

"You're not trying," Mrs. Liu chastised.

"I've done nothing *but* try," I all but snarled.

Mrs. Liu shook her head, and with a disappointed sniff, she toddled down the hall. With each step, her cane gave a corrective crack against the wood floor, which might as well have been across my knuckles. My head and shoulders slumped, and a sigh whooshed out in regret. She was only trying to help.

But the coven didn't need me. They needed another witch. A better one.

The residents assured me they were already recruiting, and "never I mind," they had it handled. It made me wonder how Grandpa, who was not a witch, but *custos*—someone with faerie blood in their veins—had pulled the coven together in the first place.

I shuffled down the hall after Mrs. Liu, ready to apologize and eager for the coffee denied me earlier.

At least I could hire an accounting assistant.

QuickBooks and I were still not on speaking terms.

Mrs. Liu had already headed up the back staircase when I entered the kitchen, so I made for the half-filled carafe steaming on the hot plate instead. It would probably be better to apologize when I wasn't having caffeine withdrawal anyway. On a positive note, an applicant was coming today, and I hoped I'd have more luck than I'd had the last two times. Thanks to my little Brownie roommate, none of the applicants had felt compelled to take the job.

On cue, Nibbleink trotted into the kitchen. I say trotted because the little foot-tall Brownie had somehow convinced one of the neighborhood cats to let her ride on their back. Or what was glamoured to look like a cat. Nibs called them kraggles, and they seemed to congregate around the house lately. Mrs. Liu was ecstatic to have more "feral cats" to feed. My neighbors—not as much.

Nibs wore one of her many outfits provided by my credit card. This one was an English riding habit, complete with a black plastic helmet between her long, ragged ears. With an overemphasized, "Whoa!" Nibs stopped her feline looking mount and jumped down. Hands on her hips, she stared up at me as I sat at the island sipping from my mug, the stolen wool tartan I'd left on the stool earlier over my shoulders. It's only technically stolen. If I could speak to Aengus, I'd have given it back.

I pulled it tighter around my neck.

The wool scratched against my skin and for a moment I was back in the room at the Seelie Court and Aengus had just called me "enchanting." The ghost of warm leather against my palm made me sigh, only to be replaced with the horrible memory of his blood leaking around the spear thrust through his abdomen.

My whole body shuddered.

My last view of Aengus had been when he'd turned away from me and followed Theo out of the Seelie Court basement. Head bowed and shoulders slumped. The desire to pull him back and let loose whatever power I had on Theo had been almost uncontrollable.

Every day I tried to remind myself that I was *not* a cartoon princess, and I was *not* in love with a man after three days.

Every day, the argument fell flat.

And now, months later, I still thought about him at least every other minute of my day.

Nibs tapped my leg as the cat/kraggle sat back on its haunches and proceeded to clean its face.

"Geoffrey says fix the wards now," Nibs ordered.

The Green Knight, aka. Geoffrey Corbin, was my newly returned-to-me father and currently an immovable topiary on my front lawn. No doubt the neighbors would have raised the alarm if they could see him in all his vine-encrusted glory with his human-sized double-headed axe with a tree sapling handle resting on his shoulder. Glamour to the rescue.

Nibs crawled up my pant leg, and I helped her onto the granite.

"You can tell 'Dad' I'm trying." Irritation from trying—and failing—just a moment ago spurred my next words, even though I knew very well that Geoffrey had lost his own magic when he became the Green Knight. "He's a witch. Why can't he do it?"

Her expression told me I was being dramatic.

The back door opened, and a gust of cold air proceeded Everett Sinclair as he entered to start his shift, puffy down jacket making him look even more like a football linebacker than the charge nurse. The winter breeze he'd let in rushed across my bare ankles. I shivered, pulling my feet up onto the stool and holding the tartan tighter. January—my least favorite month.

"You're upright early," Everett commented as he slid a beanie off his dark, bald head and removed his coat. He eyed Nibs warily, still uncertain about the fae world he'd only just learned about. He hung the coat, readjusting his scrub top, and made his way to the coffeepot.

"I've got another applicant coming this morning at nine," I explained.

"You might want to make sure you handle any possible issues before they get here," he said, indicating Nibs with his head. The Brownie paid no heed as she dipped headfirst into the sugar bowl and scooped out a handful.

"Agreed." I pinched the back of Nibs' clothes and lifted her out.

Having Nibs in my life resembled housing a permanent kitten. She entertained me with her antics and taught me what it meant to be responsible for a living being, but unlike a small feline, she also knew how credit cards worked and could exact revenge at the slightest provocation. Like a kitten, it was a good thing she was cute.

The doorbell rang exactly at 9 a.m. I'd convinced Nibs that we might have a moth infestation and she should check all her clothes to make sure they were free of lepidopteran munch holes. That should, in theory, have given me at least an hour to handle the interview.

I'm not for lying to Nibs, her revenge game was stellar, but I'd do almost anything not to have to tackle the retirement home accounts again. The end of the month drew quickly near.

Making my way to the door, I noted the absence of residents and the normal ambiance of daytime television. From upstairs, Everett's deep voice carried down the stairs and it sounded like things were running behind. Lately, we'd been surviving on one nursing assistant and one other additional registered nurse—of the expensive traveling variety. They usually left right after finally getting comfortable with our routine, leaving us to start the process over again.

I debated if I had time to run into my room, I'd showered and dressed, but my feet were still coved in narwal slipper puffiness. Instead, I just kicked the threadbare slippers behind the desk. I really needed to replace them, but that required time and money. Money I'd much rather spend on an accountant. In the end, I might have to give up my internship at the museum to search for an actual paying job. I wondered how many jobs were looking for an employee with a bachelor's in history, who was cursed to see the fae and ghosts, chosen by the legendary sword Excalibur, and could wield deadly magic. I'm sure the list would be very long.

The doorbell dinged once more, and I rushed to open it.

In the bright cold sunlight, I found Theo.

He leaned one hand against the doorframe, his ego rolling off him like a noxious fog. He smirked, dimples marking his flawless lavender skin, as his lazy gaze traveled slowly over my body like a baby-duck-killing oil slick. "I guess I can kind of understand what Aengus sees in you."

I wanted to hurl.

Staying safe within the wards didn't keep my toes from freezing. I alternated covering one foot with the other. "Unless you've brought Aengus, you're not welcome here."

"Gotten rather attached, haven't you?" he said, waggling his elegantly sculpted eyebrows.

Beyond the porch, pops and creaks like the bending of a massive tree broke the morning stillness as the Green Knight leaned far enough over to look beneath the overhang of the roof. His deep, living green armor contrasted dramatically against the surrounding winter trees and brown yards. He stared at Theo in a disapproving silence. I might have been projecting my own disapproval, but it's hard to read emotion through a helmet made of leaves. I liked to think my father would be just as disgusted at seeing Theo as I was.

"Leave," I said, keeping my voice flat. Theo was the type to feed off another's pain. I wouldn't give him any to feast on. But it wasn't fair. The first time anyone had made contact in months, and it had to be Theo. The Green Knight lifted his axe into view. Okay, it wasn't just me, he was definitely disapproving. I made a move to shut the door.

"Wait!" Theo cried, losing most of his bravado.

Curious, I paused and fought the urge to circle my arms against my torso to keep the chill away, worried it would look like I was anxious. Obnoxiously, Theo stood in short sleeves and no coat, seeming immune to the cold. He put up both hands in mock surrender, but the corners of his eyes pinched with irritation. "I'm in need of...help." The word *help* came out strangled. He straightened and pointed a finger. "And you owe me."

"I what?" I nearly stepped out onto the porch but caught myself.

"If it wasn't for you mucking up the sword, Aengus would be where he's supposed to be, and I wouldn't be cleaning up the mess."

With the veil still open, nothing stopped any fae—dangerous or otherwise—from popping over for a visit and possibly grabbing a tasty human treat. Someone had to stop them and the Seelie had stepped up. Nothing as bad as the wildlife munching snake fae from a few months ago seemed to have made the news, but Theo did look worn. His hair—not quite perfect. His shirt—slightly wrinkled. Good. After what the Seelie put Aengus through, he deserved to suffer a little.

No, he deserved to suffer a lot.

I shrugged. "Too bad for you. Maybe you shouldn't have locked Aengus in the dungeon. Maybe instead he could be figuring out how to close the veil and whatever it is you need help with." I gestured in the air dismissively.

Theo looked taken aback, his brow furrowed. "Aengus isn't imprisoned."

My arm dropped to my side as his words rattled through my brain like a foreign language. Aengus had to be locked up. That had to be the reason I hadn't seen him. It had to be, right?

Theo's eyes brightened, and he grinned savagely. "Wondering why he hasn't called on you? Thought you meant something to him?"

Aengus had been free this whole time? I took a shuddering breath that hurt as much going in as it did going out. My next breath seemed even harder to catch. Even if it were true, I couldn't know for certain why he had never reached out. But doubt screamed louder than logic as I reexamined all our interactions. Had I only imagined Aengus had reciprocated my feelings?

My gaze found Theo, and he sneered. The sob climbing up my throat paused. I certainly didn't need to be mocked by a spoiled fae prince. I stepped back to slam the door.

"Wait!" he cried again, throwing out a hand despite the wards. The spell sizzled and cracked when his fingers drew near and he pulled back quickly.

"What?" I managed to say around the lump in my throat.

"Can I at least ask him to help?" Theo said, pointing at Green Knight still looming under the eaves.

"I don't care. He does what he wants." And this time I slammed the door before he could say anymore.

Chapter Two

Shoes on and prepared to meet my accounting savior, I sat on the front room couch, scrolling through my phone, with my back to the large picture window. I had a rising suspicion she would never arrive the later it got. The urge to look over my shoulder pressed against every thought, but I refused to see if Theo had left. Just as I refused to think about what he'd said about Aengus.

Seriously, free this whole time?

Nope. I forced myself to focus on waiting for my interview.

At nine-thirty, a one-line text dropped down on my phone screen and confirmed it:

> Found another job.

Well, at least she'd had the decency to let me know.

I dropped the phone in my lap and sighed.

Absently, I spun the cuff bracelet around my wrist, rubbing the pad of my finger over the engraved words in Gaelic — *Tá mo chroí istigh ionat*. I'd googled the phrase, and it said something like "my heart is in you". Which could be sweet...but also taken literally, a little gross.

I'll probably never find out how the bracelet found its way into the Seelie dungeon and then to me, but somehow it connected me to my mother. Or it had. For the last few months, she'd been silent as well. Jane, before she'd passed on, was certain it wasn't a case of a haunted object. You'd be surprised how many ghost hauntings are because of purchasing a cool antique at a yard sale. Buy a mink stole and get Great Aunt Mildred for free. But if my mother wasn't haunting the bracelet, it still didn't tell me how I'd been able to see and speak to her. And why I couldn't now.

What if I never spoke to her again?

Sometimes it was very hard not to be upset with the coven for taking my memories before I was five, and maybe even more upset with Grandpa for making them do it. All those years thinking my parents didn't want me and no way for me to go back in time and let "little me" know it wasn't true.

The doorbell rang. Doubly irritated with where my thoughts had gone and convinced Theo was trying to get my attention again, I yanked open the door with a glare.

The delivery guy, lanky with patchy stubble, stumbled back a few steps. He held out a small box. "Your package...ma'am."

I tried to salvage the interaction with a smile and a thank you, but the moment I had the box in my hand, he dashed off toward his truck.

No one else stood on the porch—in fact, my father was not in his usual spot either. Curious, I stepped out onto the boards and leaned over the railing, looking in either direction, and saw nothing but the delivery truck driving away. Had Theo actually convinced my father to help him?

A flare of jealousy spread through me. As the Green Knight, my father was under the control of the Unseelie Queen. How a witch from England ended up as a nine-foot-tall walking tree was a story he hadn't been able to tell me. Nor had he explained how he'd broken free of the queen's hold, but by staying rooted in the front yard, he remained free of her influence. So why had he decided Theo's cry for help was worth the risk?

I mean really—Theo?

My earlier jealousy faltered. I had to be missing something. What had really made my father go?

I closed the door just as Mrs. O'Cleary stepped down off the last stair in pressed slacks and a blouse. Her red dyed hair had faded to a harsh orange, but her war era makeup remained perfect as always. "Oh good, my graveyard dust is here," she said, reaching for the box in my hand.

I fought the urge to drop it to the floor. "Ew, what?" I shoved it at her. "I think I liked it better when I didn't know any of this witch stuff." What kind of spell would require graveyard dust?

Mrs. O'Cleary pinched her lips, holding in a smile. "It's mullein, sometimes called graveyard dust." She and the box headed down the hall toward the kitchen. I followed. "I'm not sure why graveyard dust is any more distasteful than the fact that all dust is mostly human skin, anyway."

I'd known that fact, but somehow the reminder made my skin crawl and I looked around the hallway. When was the last time we'd dusted?

"Chu Hua told me you failed to reset the wards again this morning," Mrs. O'Cleary said as she set her mullein on the island and gazed at me. It's always weird to hear the residents use their first names. I've grown up showing them deference and even as an adult, it just seemed right to give them the added respect since they weren't given it often in the outside world.

"I tried," I said, flopping onto a stool and putting my head in my hands. For a moment, the hunger brought on by using my magic to try and fix the wards gnawed within me, whispering nothing bad would happen if I took just a little energy from those around me. I shook my head against the desire and fought to ignore it. "I need to apologize. She's just trying to help."

Mrs. O'Cleary nodded as she turned away and walked toward

the stove, the sharpness of her shoulders and the slope of her hunch now visible. No one would have guessed her to be over ninety. Her mind remained pin-sharp, and her grip only trembled a little as she filled her special battered kettle at the sink. She set it on the burner to boil. Mrs. O'Cleary loved coffee, but only the instant variety, which was all she could get as a young teenager during the war.

I pushed the package on the counter with my finger, making it spin in a circle. The hunger whispered louder. "The coven needs a proper witch, not a dangerous, useless one."

Mrs. O'Cleary turned and raised a hand at my words. "I won't hear nonsense in this house." She softened her next word with a warm smile. "Until you understand your magic—" I opened my mouth to argue, but snapped it shut when one of her perfectly arched eyebrows raised. "Until then, we've posted a request for another coven member on our Discord."

I laughed. "Wait, witches have a Discord server?"

"Yes, 'Witches Abroad,'" Mrs. O'Cleary answered as if it were obvious. She held her elbows as she leaned her hip against the counter. "We could use someone younger, at least compared to the rest of us. Jane won't be the last to leave this coven. Not a one of us is immortal and the wards need to hold."

The truth of her words seared through me. Which of my retirement home family would be next? Each of their faces raced through my mind. Now I let myself wrap my arms around my abdomen as my stomach soured. Despite never finding acceptance outside of Wylde House, I'd never felt alone on the inside. I'd always had elder aunties and uncles willing to listen and give advice to a lonely teenager and now a flustered adult. I didn't want to lose any of them.

A hostile face, bleached white as talc with pale eyes, filled my thoughts and seemed to open the door and let winter in, freezing me from the inside out. The Leannan Sidhe. She had made a business of killing and stealing power. If the wards fell, what chaos would she enact if she gained mine? As a Cailleach Fae, I might be the abomination, but she'd be Armageddon.

I didn't allow my mind to question why The Leannan had stayed away for three months as well. I needed to keep my fears at a level that allowed me to get out of bed in the morning.

Which left me to focus on losing a resident of Wylde House. I tried to breathe around the jagged lump in my chest, but the air felt thin. "I don't like to think about that," I barely got out.

Mrs. O'Cleary reached across the island and gently patted my hand. "But that doesn't mean we shouldn't." She reached into the cupboard to pull out her delicate floral teacup and set it on the island. She took out a tablespoon from the drawer as she slid the jar of instant coffee closer, dumping a heaping scoop of crystals into her cup.

Her steady movements calmed me, and the lump softened as if doused in hot water, allowing me to inhale fully.

"You've been thinking about your mother," she said, abruptly changing the subject.

Startled, I stumbled over my words. "How...how did you know?" She pointed to my wrist. A red mark circled my skin, where I'd worried the bracelet. I tried to smile. "Honestly, both of them." I glanced a moment down the hall. "Geoffrey left."

"Oh, really?" Mrs. O'Cleary asked as she returned the coffee to the cupboard.

"It would have to be something serious for him to uproot, right?"

One side of Mrs. O'Cleary's lips raised in a smirk. "I don't pretend to understand tree people."

I smirked back and crossed my arms in mock annoyance. "Yes, but he was a witch and you *do* know them."

The kettle screamed and Mrs. O'Cleary stepped back near the stove to lift it with a potholder. With the precision of someone conducting a Japanese tea ceremony, she poured the steaming liquid over the little brown crystals, sending the smell of coffee wafting around the room. "And your mother, you haven't seen her these last few months?" she asked as she set the kettle back down.

I shook my head. "Not since she helped me unlock my magic and save Aengus."

Mrs. O'Cleary looked contemplative as she took a sip of her coffee. The ceramic caused a bell like chime on the granite countertop when she set it down. "And now you're wishing you'd went with that fae back to court to look for them both."

I looked around as if I'd find something to explain her knowledge. Had the witches figured out a way to see through glamour? My gaze fell on my open bedroom door and I smirked. "Nibs."

With an amused smile, Mrs. O'Cleary nodded in agreement. "She saw the *Icky Prince* out the window. Her words, not mine."

I sighed. Geoffrey hadn't left the yard in months. His leaving now with Theo could only mean something serious had happened. And what if it had something to do with why my mom had stopped speaking to me? Or why Aengus hadn't made contact? Were all three of them in danger? "Maybe I should have gone, too."

Mrs. O'Cleary had lifted her cup but set it back down without taking a sip. "My very purpose, this coven's purpose, is to protect you. Encouraging you to put yourself in harm's way is not the best way to do that."

My shoulders drooped as my arms fell to my side. She was right. Nothing about going to the Seelie Court again was safe. It was the complete opposite of safe.

Mrs. O'Cleary came out from behind the island and gripped my arms, her expression caring. "But you're also a grown woman who knows her own mind. If you decide to go, just be safe." She pulled me into a hug. I felt the fragility of her body, as if one good squeeze would send her into dust. In that moment, I didn't feel like an adult. I felt like a little lost toddler.

But I wasn't a toddler.

My resume might not bring all the jobs to the yard, but I was a powerful badass woman and I was going to march down to the Seelie Court and join my dad for a long overdue "Take Your Daughter to Work" day.

Chapter Three

On the corner of West 4th and Carson Street, the three storied cube of cement and glass shadowed the asphalt below in all its utilitarian glory. The dull gray color of the building matched the bleak mood of January. From the outside, it appeared quiet, boring, devoid of magic.

Liar, liar, pants on fire.

Unlike the Unseelie, who had made their court in an abandoned mine far from humans, the Seelie enjoyed being in the middle of everything. They also liked to hold—and pull—all the strings. In fact, the second story constituted mostly cubicles filled with fae employees handling everything from fae emergency services to customer support for fae run companies. The Seelie loved money almost as much as they loved laws.

On the roof of the nearby hookah bar, a dramatic caw broke the late morning stillness. Light glinted off a black marble eye as a crow twisted its head to stare down at me. Corvids are smart, but there was something about the way this one scrutinized me that felt almost human. I squinted up at it, trying to get a better look. With a croak, the crow flapped its wings, and flew off, leaving an ominous weight over the returned quiet.

I turned toward the Seelie building and scowled, twisting my bracelet. Over the last couple of months, I'd often wanted to stomp my way to the Seelie Court and pound on the door, demanding to go down into the basement levels to visit Aengus and possibly make contact with my mother again. A desire squashed immediately by the fragility of the wards at Wylde House. Poking the fae hornet's nest would only put the residents in danger and allow The Leannan Sidhe to gain my magic. And if there was anything I'd learned from personal experience recently, it was—the fae were dangerous.

My father knew all that, too. The Unseelie had forced him to become the Green Knight in a kill or be killed fight, where winning meant he was stripped of his free will and his humanity. What nightmare would I find inside if my father felt it dire enough to put himself in harm's way again? A dark thought took hold. What if Theo had found a way to *make* my father go?

Both scenarios seemed highly dangerous. I required a better defense guarantee than my unstable magic. My first stop needed to be the catacombs, not just to see if I could speak with my mother again or even to ask Aengus why he'd ghosted me, but I needed Excalibur. I knew bringing a sword to a potential magic fight probably wasn't the best idea, but it wasn't like good ideas were springing eternal in this situation.

The glass front door glinted from the shadow of the entryway.

What would I even say if I found Aengus beyond that door?

Nope. I needed to put him out of my mind. My parents were the most important part of this visit. I needed to keep my priorities aligned with the adult woman I was, not the lovesick teenager I was in danger of behaving like. I rushed to the entrance, afraid I'd fail to keep Aengus out of my mind if I didn't.

As the door swung shut behind me, I stopped and stared at the chaos.

The foyer looked unrecognizable compared to my visit three months ago. A jungle of plant life covered the gray walls, the stiff modern shaped waiting room chairs, and much of the low pile carpet. Leafy vines drooped and dipped from every available surface, almost appearing to sway purposely, as if conscious and searching for its next thing to smother. A seedpod, resembling a viper's head, cracked open and menacing, peeked out from under plate-sized leaves near me. I cradled my hand to my chest, rubbing the months old bite scar near my thumb where one of those very same seedpods had bitten me.

One step at a time, ducking and weaving around the predatory plant, I made way in hopefully in the direction of the front desk.

Betty, the assistant I'd met previously, was not present. Instead, a petite young fae with overly large circular glasses nearly falling off her tiny pink nose handled reception. Or more like helmed it. She sat cross-legged atop the large gray boat of a desk in a sea of green, a book in her lap. Her tall, pointed ears swayed like antennae, especially when a vine swayed close and she absently hit it away with a fly swatter She didn't acknowledge my existence until I was directly in front of her, then she blinked as if having a bit of trouble focusing on something other than her reading.

"How can I help you?" she asked, her tone much friendlier than Betty's had been.

"Ummm," I croaked, and the young fae cocked her head. "I'm here..." I started again and faded off as my heart thudded loudly in my ears. Talking to new people—one of my least favorite things to do. I needed to calm down. On my periphery, a vine shifted and I just barely hopped out of the way of a darting seedpod aimed at my ankle.

The receptionist frowned. "It's madness around here, sorry."

"What happened?" I asked, my voice still weak, but the adrenaline was helping.

She smacked the fly swatter against another attacking seedpod. "Apparently, some girl a few months ago let the fallrot plant bite her. I guess she was special, magically speaking, and this is the result."

I rubbed the scar on my hand again, reeling. I had caused this? Was this what Theo had needed my help on? Was my father right now hacking away at this plant in another part of the building?

The receptionist eyed me questioningly, and I realized I'd been silent for an unusual amount of time. I smiled awkwardly. "What happens if it isn't stopped?"

She shrugged. "Well, the last time in 1666 they had to light a third of the city on fire to destroy it, so...nothing good, I expect."

A third of the city? Carson City's historic district surrounded the Seelie Court. All that history burned to the ground? And it would be all my fault. I needed to get down in the dungeon and grab Excalibur. The Green Knight with his deadly axe might be able to handle the "veggie-cide", but I wasn't going to let him clean up my mess alone.

I tried using the truth, after all, Theo had come to my house requesting assistance. "Good thing I'm here to help with the plant situation." I smiled and gestured around at the blanket of fallrot.

The receptionist closed her novel and set it on the desk, using what I assumed was a dried fallrot leaf to mark her spot. I could finally see the cover. A very buxom blue alien woman almost popping out of her leather corset, held a very tiny woman in Victorian garb swung over her shoulder, the skirt riding up to her hip and giving a peek at her heart-covered panties. "Until Lady Aurnia returns, I'm not allowed to let anyone through," she said, her tone still friendly, but unwavering.

"I'm here with Theo," I clarified. She looked around me to exaggerate the fact that I was alone. "He's already here, with the Green Knight. I'm back up." I added. The young woman blinked in stoic silence. Was Theo's plan even court sanctioned? Did she know what was going on?

"Theo asked you to help?" the receptionist asked, clearly disbelieving.

I'd either have to stand in the middle of the Seelie Court and claim I was a powerful magic wielder who couldn't safely wield her power. Or if I wanted to get in and down to the dungeon, I'd need to change my tactic. My gaze fell on the book on the desk. I forced myself not to shudder. "Okay that's a lie, I'm here to *see* Theo." I smiled wide and looked away shyly to really sell the role.

"I'm sorry. Only essential personnel are allowed into the building. I'm only here to direct people. And they only picked me because plants listen to me." A vine slithered across the desktop, knocking off a pen and a block of sticky notes. The receptionist pushed it away and a seedpod mouth hissed. "Sort of listen." The young fae gestured toward the front door. "You'll have to come back another day."

Then she dropped her gaze dismissively and grabbed up her book.

If my ruse was going to work, I needed to go all in. I turned back toward the receptionist and tried to giggle, it came out more like a disturbed clown. She looked up. "Oh, I know he's not here. He told me to wait for him in his room while he handled the plant problem. You know how he gets after a fight. All hot and eager." I tried not to gag. There was also no way I was winning any acting awards. Would this fae girl really buy it?

She looked up with a dead stare. "I can assure you I have no idea how Theo gets." She squinted, eyeing me up and down. "Odd. He usually doesn't like women so..." she trailed off.

"Adventurous?" I supplied.

"Willing," she finished.

This time I did gag and hid it behind my hand with another forced giggle. I tried to look coy and cocked my hip. "Theo told me where he keeps the chains."

She raised her eyebrows, but didn't respond. The young fae seemed nice. I decided to play to her kindness. "If I'm not in his room when he's done, he'll get really upset..." I trailed off, hoping she'd take pity on me.

"Whatever. You do you. Third floor, fourth room on the right. You'll have to take the stairs. The plants" —she gestured to the wall of green around her— "have jammed the elevators." I took a step toward the stairwell, but the young woman called out. "Wait." I glanced over my shoulder. "No kink shame, but if things get a little rough knock the phone off the hook and demand a trell."

Wow. I hadn't expected that. Betty would certainly not have cared. My esteem for the young fae grew. "Thanks, I will," I said genuinely. She shrugged, swatted at a vine, and dropped her nose back in the book.

I wished her happy smut.

The receptionist hadn't lied. No guards. No fae. The entire building felt like a forgotten place, made worse by the hanging vines of fallrot. I made my way down the stairs, stepping gingerly. My blood had caused the plant explosion, and I didn't want to face what would happen if I let the fallrot bite me again. I pushed open the heavy steel industrial door out of the stairwell and into the basement.

Or what would be a basement in a normal building.

The vines had likely tripped all the motion sensors. I could clearly see the chaos. The fake torches, their little motor whirring, were all on in the large circular room and also down all the branching corridors. To be honest, the theme park style dungeon Lady Aurnia had created appeared a little more legitimate now with the addition of a carnivorous plant. Unfortunately, this also meant Excalibur, driven into the cement floor of the main room by my magic, was barely visible beneath a mound of foliage.

I moved closer.

A bit of the hilt poked up above the greenery and I reached toward it, only to snatch my hand away before a seedpod mouth could latch on. I tried one more time, but when I almost failed to get my hand away in time, I knew it was hopeless. There was no way I could grip the sword long enough to release it with so many angry mouths near.

How was I supposed to help my father if I couldn't pull Excalibur free? Without a sword, all I had left for a weapon was magic. With how unpredictable it was, and how dangerous my hunger could be, I'd label it more a liability than a weapon. The only time it had worked as intended was with the help of my mother and Dennriall.

I glanced up and found the spot on the wall where The Leannan Sidhe had created a portal last fall. She'd disappeared through it, Birga the spear of Fiacha in hand and dragging Dennriall with her. Out of all the fae I'd interacted with, I could honestly say Dennriall was almost nice, possibly even friendly, even if he had spider legs and three eyes. With his ancient strength—he wouldn't tell me how old he was, which definitely meant very old—and my mother's guidance, I'd been able to heal Aengus.

Dennriall was gone, possibly dead, but maybe my mother could still help. She'd been nearly solid one more level below. The level where the Seelie hid their dark secret.

The catacombs.

This was probably a bad idea, but honestly, it wasn't like I was making good life choices today.

Oppressive silence filled the very bottom of the Seelie Court. The fallrot plant had only made its way halfway down, leaving the rest of the stone staircase clear. My way might not be hampered by vines, but each deliberate step I took down brought Underhill closer.

Running deep within the earth, Underhill pulsed. A corridor of magic that traversed the globe as it branched out from the very first fae realm gateway, opened centuries ago in Ireland. It was why the humans had called the fae realm Innisfail—Ireland's original name. Years passed, the island changed and more doorways opened, but the name remained. Then the veil fell, closing all the doorways and cutting off the flow of fae magic. Those fae left behind followed Underhill through the centuries, setting up new courts only to move each time the magic river below depleted. Finally, they'd ended up in the new world, lingering along the old mountains of Appalachia and then the steep Rockies into the wild west.

Standing in the catacombs, I felt the golden heart of Underhill pumping magic in all directions, strong and constant. The reopened veil had renewed the magic and I wondered if the courts would eventually leave and return to those first courts across the Atlantic.

What would my life be like without the fae?

An electric hum raced up my legs as I stepped off the last stair and I gulped back a surprised cry. The intensity of the magic below me had my thoughts swimming. What was going on? It hadn't been so powerful the last time I'd visited the catacombs.

The glowing mushrooms along the wall cast the subbasement in a blue light as I made my way down the narrow corridor. The cerulean-rimmed stones made me think of aquariums I'd gone to, but instead of fish, this place held slaves of the blood—the *fola tráill*.

Or had.

Confused, I paused. Gone were the moans and whimpers. All the thick wooden doors yawed ajar, giving full view of the shadowed cells within.

What had happened?

The Seelie and Unseelie weren't allowed to create any more *fola tráill* or *ossorians*—humans turned into werewolf-like creatures— since the veil closed, but that really didn't help those who'd already been turned before and kept since. Fourteen hundred years of slavery was a fate I couldn't even begin to comprehend.

I stepped toward one of the open doorways; what had been Aengus's cell. I needed to be sure he wasn't there. The chamber swam in darkness, but for a moment the memory of Aengus was so visceral I saw him hanging from manacles and speared through the abdomen. A dark spot on the stones still marked where he'd nearly bled out, but the coppery tang had faded. Now I only smelled stone and damp. The cell was empty.

Relief flooded through me for a moment, eclipsing Underhill's thrum. Theo had not lied. Aengus wasn't locked away.

But why then hadn't he reached out this whole time?

I placed a steadying hand on the door frame. Splinters from deep grooves on the inside pricked my hand. Leaning closer, broken fingernails were visible within the channels. Someone had tried to rip through the wood with their bare hands. I pulled my hand away as if singed by the knowledge.

I searched the other cells and found them empty as well.

Where was Aengus?

And where were the Seelie slaves?

I couldn't focus on that now. Without Excalibur, I needed to control my magic to help my father. My mother had been instrumental the last time I'd successfully used it. I stepped back into Aengus's former cell. My mother's presence had felt almost solid this close to Underhill.

"Mom?" I called as I touched the bracelet. "Mom, can you hear me?" Although the metal felt warm beneath my fingertips, my call was met with silence.

Absently, my fingers ran the length of my forearm. There was no scar, but the memory remained of The Leannan Sidhe nearly killing me to release my magic. I'd only survived because my mother guided me. Maybe I needed to reach out, just a little, with my magic. Maybe then I'd reach her. I closed my eyes.

The golden river rose up to swallow me.

The force of Underhill drove the air from my lungs, expelling it out of my mouth in a huff. When I tried to inhale, magic flowed down my throat and filled my lungs.

I was drowning in power.

Mom! Mom, please! I gaped like a fish as every part of my body swelled taut with golden light, ready to burst.

"Imogen!"

Through the roaring in my ears, I heard my name. Not my mother's, but still familiar. "Aengus," I mouthed, but only magic answered.

Chapter Four

Magic replaced the blood in my veins; replaced the air in my lungs. I no longer felt like a physical being, but one entirely made of golden light. An all-consuming light, devouring everything within and without; leaving me gutted. Underhill roared beneath my feet and urged me to consume, to take it all. I would. I could. All of it would enter me, become me.

I fought the desire. Deep down beyond the hunger, I had a vague awareness that ruin would follow if I gave in. Underhill had no limits. No finite amount. If I tried to consume it all, there would be nothing left of me. I may have raised my hands as if to push the flow of Underhill away, but my arms seemed separate from my body. Acting autonomously.

"Imogen," Aengus called my name again. My eyes flickered open. A vague shape wavered above me. When had I fallen to the floor?

"You need to let go of Underhill," Aengus said, his voice closer. "Hold onto me."

I opened my eyes, unaware I had closed them again. Aengus crouched near, his arm cradled around my back, lifting me to sitting.

His face swam beneath the haze of golden mist before my eyes. "Can't." I barely got out the word. I tried and failed to move away.

My resolve weakened as every second Underhill battered my senses. If I let go of such an immense source of power to grab ahold of Aengus's dangling life thread, I couldn't guarantee I wouldn't take it all and kill him. "Don't...Don't want to hurt you."

"You will not," he assured me as he laid a hand against my cheek. I felt more than saw the flash of brightness that coalesced into his distinct separate thread of life. One long bright beacon in the deluge threatening to pull me completely under.

"Let go of Underhill. Hold on to me," Aengus urged again.

I tried to shake my head. I could only manage a jerky twitch. "I'll kill you."

"Please, you must."

Magic pulled like a tide within me, threatening to pull me apart. Why was this happening? For a brief moment, I wondered what was different this time. What had changed? Three months ago, Underhill had felt powerful, dangerous, but distant, contained even.

Darkness hovered at the edge of my vision, and I knew I wouldn't remain conscious for long. Desperate, I did as he asked and reached for his life thread, pulling it close like a drowning victim clutching a tossed floatation device. I heard Aengus gasp. His whole body tensed, and I knew I was hurting him.

No.

There had to be another way.

Holding onto just one golden thread allowed me to gain a tiny bit of focus. Other strands clarified around me, separating into their individual parts. One of those separate strands spider-webbed across the others—interconnected and growing. The fallrot plant.

I arched away from Aengus, releasing my hold on his life and falling back to the floor. I let out a cry that sounded distant to my own ears, as I snatched for as many parts of the fallrot plant threads as I could reach. I yanked them to me. Voraciously, I reeled them in, winding them together to settle deep in my core, pushing

Underhill out as I filled every part of me with the fallrot's life energy.

My eyes closed. Through my ragged breaths, I heard Aengus. "Imogen?" He placed his cool hands against my heated face; his thumbs rubbed along my cheekbones. "Imogen?" he repeated, his words tinged with a touch of panic. Before I could answer, the hunger inside me ripped the last of the fallrot plant life into me and pulled me under.

The sensation of movement, a gentle swinging from left to right, woke me. Soft, warm fabric cushioned one side of my face and I rubbed against it, realizing quickly it wasn't a blanket. I looked upward and the V-neck of the sweater came into view, followed by the dusky olive skin of his neck, until I could make out the profile of Aengus's face.

I had literally fainted like a damsel in distress and now was being carried off like an injured princess. I'd felt so confident when I'd left the Seelie Court a few months ago, with my newly claimed title as *custos* and a determination to learn my magic to help close the veil—be a hero. But I was the same weak and useless hazard, needing others to save me.

I fought the urge to cover my face in embarrassment and looked outward instead. We had left the catacombs and now made our way through the basement dungeon. Only the whirring of the little fans under the fake flames in the sconces competed with the shush of Aengus's footsteps in the quiet. The near hush amplified my thoughts, giving them space to echo around me. I spoke, trying to drown them out.

"Aengus?" My voice sounded strange in my ears, warbly and weak.

Aengus jerked and shifted me in his arms. He gave what he probably thought was a comforting smile but looked more like an uncomfortable grimace. No doubt he felt just as disappointed with my severe lack of usefulness. "You're awake."

I nodded. "How did you know I was here?"

"You passed my room..." He hesitated, tilting his head and looking everywhere except at me. "And I smelled you."

"Oh...umm...that makes sense," I said, unsure how I felt about being located by smell. Effectively being hunted. What did I smell like? I contemplated lifting an arm to take a whiff, but then the other part of what he said registered. "Your room?"

Aengus glanced down. "Gaius's former chambers. I was reading."

The odd slide of his footsteps punctuated his words, and I leaned back, peering down past his arm to see loose sweatpants resting low on his hips and hard soled slippers on his feet. My brain conjured an image of him lounging in a plush chair, a leg outstretched, a book held in one hand. I might have let out an appreciative hum.

But the sexy image quickly gave way to reality. Staying in Gaius's chambers meant Aengus hadn't been locked in a cell. He hadn't been tortured or starved. Just as Theo claimed. Aengus had been free this whole time.

And yet he hadn't reached out, letting months pass.

Was it possible I misunderstood? Had the attraction been one-sided?

Great, now I was a distressed damsel *and* a lovesick teenager pining over a literal stranger. I was really failing at being a strong, independent woman today. And yet I needed to know the answer. Had I truly misread the signals?

Slowly, I lifted my hand, raising it higher until I rested it under his ear, along his neck. He almost imperceptibly leaned into my hand as I let my fingers wade into his blonde curls and he briefly closed his eyes, his breath leaving in a soft shudder.

I pulled my hand back down to my chest. My fingers tingling from the touch.

I had my answer.

"It's been months. Did the Seelie keep you away?" I asked. He refused to look down at me and gave an infuriating shake of his head. What did that even mean? "What kept you away?" I pushed.

"My duty." His words strained to get free of his tight jaw.

Right. Duty. "You mean being buried alive?"

His fingers tightened against my side and then released. Maybe he wasn't so calm about returning to his tomb to re-close the veil as he'd like to appear. How had it felt to be trapped under stone and earth for centuries? I shivered, imaging the perfect dark and for a moment the air in my lungs felt thin. Even dreaming of the changing world, how had he not gone insane?

Aengus didn't answer but pulled me closer. Pressed between his arms and chest, heat radiated off him, thawing the chill of my wayward thoughts. The fae magic flowing through his veins burned, altering what had once been human. I'd always thought vampires were cold, but he wasn't quite what the stories claimed. Nothing about him was.

Pretending how tightly Aengus held me wasn't a distraction, I concentrated on the hallway, seeing for the first time heaps of dark, oily dirt running along the walls. And how had I not noticed the smell? Old feet coated in sunbaked sauerkraut.

No, not dirt—the fallrot plant—dead and already decayed.

I'd killed it. I'd pulled all of its life into me. Dark, oily veins stretched out across the floor and up the walls. Rotting leaves hung wet and limp from the shriveled vines, and the smell smothered the oxygen in the air. How had I destroyed so much of it? I was well aware I couldn't keep a houseplant alive, but this was going a bit too far. I guess I'd ended up helping Theo after all.

The magic within me pulsed, racing along my nerves, crackling under my skin, testing the prison walls. *Let it go. Set it free.* The magic whispered, urging me to throw open the gate and release what I'd captured. The desire gnawed at me until I gasped and Aengus, hearing my distress, tightened his arms further.

Inside, my body caged the power, and outside, Aengus's arms caged me further.

Suddenly, everything was too much. The magic. The claustrophobic dungeon walls. The smell of the rotting fallrot plant. The heat of Aengus's chest. My heart stuttered and I couldn't seem to grab a full breath. Like a frightened animal, I flung my limbs out without thought of where they would land, fighting to get free. Aengus let go and I fell to the stone floor, hip hitting first, exploding with pain bright and distracting,

Aengus dropped to his knees. "Imogen?" he said, alarmed.

Through quick shallow breaths, I tried to assure him. "I'm fine. I'm fine." But I also held out a hand, urging him to stay back.

"Clearly you are not fine."

I let out a sharp laugh, nearly a sob. "No, I'm not."

Hesitant, he reached toward my raised hand and engulfed it with his own, like he held a baby bird, protective and gentle. "Breathe," he whispered.

I almost asked him how a guy from the fifth century knew about mindful breathing, but realized he meant for me to take an actual breath because I was holding mine. I let it out slowly. As I inhaled, I focused on the cool of the stone beneath me, the dull throb in my body from the fall, and the rhythmic circling of Aengus's thumb against the palm of my hand. By inches, the tightness in my body eased, but the magic inside me still ached, resting heavy as stone in my chest.

I looked up, and our gaze locked.

Aengus was here. He was hale and whole. Not under Merlin's spell, not dying impaled by the Spear of Fiacha, not a blood starved beast. He was just Aengus, holding my hand.

We stared as the circling of his thumb in my palm pushed away the panic. Soon even my chest eased and the tightness in my shoulders released. The hunger of the magic faded almost to the background, replaced with a different kind of craving. My fingers twitched at the desire to grab Aengus's sweater and pull him to me. So shocking was its intensity, I forced myself to look away.

We were near the end of the corridor, nearly to the main room where Excalibur stood.

Aengus broke the silence, clear frustration in his tone. "Why are you here?"

I bristled. "What do you mean?"

Aengus pulled his hand away and ran a hand through his hair. The blond curls bounced and fell over his forehead. "The fae are dangerous. You should have stayed with the coven."

Who was he to tell me where to stay? He'd ignored me for three months. I gave him a withering look. "I'm dangerous," I reminded him, gesturing toward a nearby stinky lump of rotting fallrot. Sure, I was technically the distressed damsel in this scenario, who'd just had a mild panic attack, but I had skills. Skills I would certainly master... someday...maybe. "Why are *you* here? The fae upstairs said everyone was gone."

"Gaius's room is well warded, and I did not wish to interrupt my research."

"Right. Wouldn't want anything to get in the way of your duty," I grumbled.

Aengus arranged himself more comfortably on the flagstone floor. It looked like he wanted to touch my knee but stopped himself. "I am pleased to see you."

His words made me wish I could raise one eyebrow to really emphasize my disbelief.

"Truly," he added.

"I'm here because of Theo," I said, answering his earlier question.

Aengus's whole body tensed and he leaned forward. "Theo brought you here?" Menace hung on every word.

I thought of the night Aengus and I were locked in a room upstairs. How Aengus had responded to Theo knocking on the door and how glad I'd been to keep Theo out. "No," I assured him and he calmed slightly. "He came to the house and wanted my help with,

I'm guessing, the fallrot, I wouldn't go, but then my father did. And when I found out, I followed."

Aengus nodded. "But why were you in the catacombs?"

"My mom. I wanted to try and reach her."

Aengus sighed clearly frustrated but nodded.

I shifted to get my feet under me. Aengus looked like he wanted to stop me, but he pulled himself up first, before reaching down to help me stand. He didn't let go when I finally stood.

A clump of dead vine slid down the stone and plopped to the floor at our feet, drawing our gaze. I'd pulled so much life energy, what if it wasn't only the fallrot. In fear, I looked at Aengus. "Did I hurt anyone else?"

He gave my hand a light squeeze. "I do not know."

The slamming of the stairwell door and running feet in the distance had us both turning our heads toward the end of the corridor. Theo jogged into view. He threw up his arm, pointing aggressively. "She said someone was here for me. I knew it had to be you. And now look what you've done. I'm not getting blamed for this!" He whined as he skidded to stop next to us.

"Didn't you want my help?" I asked. I'd thought he'd be pleased.

"This isn't my fault." He tried to grab my arm, but Aengus pushed it away. Theo narrowed his eyes first at Aengus, then me. "You're going to come with me now and fix this or you're confessing to my mom how you killed the Green Knight and started a fucking war."

My heart didn't start pounding at Theo's words. It stopped dead.

Chapter Five

The room Theo led us to had boxes stacked like pixelated mountains, nearly reaching the high ceiling on both sides of a narrow walkway. The dead fallrot oozed down the walls and over the cardboard, oily residue spreading out beneath like grease stains. Some boxes had tumbled to the floor and cracked open; their spilled contents unrecognizable beneath the sludge. In the back, a loading dock bay door remained rolled up, letting in the late morning light and the January chill.

Within the square of daylight, my father kneeled, head bowed, axe lying before him.

Even kneeling, his massive frame towered. An oily web of rotting fallrot covered my father, weaving deeply through the vines that created his armor, and bursting out along the floor in a mockery of what his roots had done when he'd planted himself in front of my house. The foliage making up my father's armor had lost all color. Each vine and leaf had grayed to ash with fissure lines where they threatened to crumble. What would be left behind if it all disintegrated into dust?

"How did this...I don't..." I began but lost the words to finish. I stumbled forward, my legs as jumbled as my thoughts. I felt the steadying pressure of Aengus's hold on my elbow.

Theo glared. "You tell me." Stepping close, he gave my father a vicious kick. Like a falling tree, the Green Knight fell forward, crashing to the floor and sending a cloud of gray ash into the air.

The magic inside me roared, my heart a war drum, and I lunged toward Theo, my fingers curved like talons. "Asshole!" If I'd kept my head and grabbed Excalibur instead of racing up the stairs without it, I'm pretty sure his chest would've sported a new sword ornament. Aengus's grip tightened on my arm. I tried to pull free, but he held firm.

"Imogen, stop," he urged. I only yanked harder. "Imogen, look," he said sharply, pointing with his other hand toward the Green Knight.

I saw it then. One of the Green Knight's arms lay stretched out to the side. Beneath the destroyed armor, I caught the barest hint of healthy flesh.

Not green and plant-like. Pink and human.

I pulled again, and this time, Aengus let go. I ran to my father, dropping to the floor beside the crack in his facade.

The black fallrot clung to his body even as the armor disintegrated. I pushed my fingers through and the moment I touched his skin, I could feel it. A thin golden strand, nearly a breath away from shrinking into nothing, reaching out from the orb at his core, its light flickering and sputtering. My breath whooshed out in a surprised, "Oh."

"What is it?" Aengus asked, crouching down beside me.

"He's alive," I whispered, as if speaking louder would whisk away what was left of my father's life.

"Can you save him?"

At his words, the magic I held inside beat at the walls and nearly pushed free. I skittered back from both Aengus and my father. When I'd healed Nibs, innocent bystanders had died. Theo had spoken to the smut-loving receptionist in the foyer before finding us in the dungeon which meant I hadn't harmed her earlier with my magic, but I feared using it now would, as well as anyone else left in the building. "No, I can't."

"You saved me." Aengus laid a hand where the spear had pierced him months ago.

I shuddered at the memory of Aengus bleeding out on the stone floor. I had saved him, but not without help. Dennriall had survived me pulling energy from him, no worse for wear, probably because he had been ancient. If I pulled from Aengus or Theo or even both, could they handle the loss? And without my mom this time, I had no help with control.

Aengus lifted some of the oily dead fallrot off the floor, letting it slide through his finger and plop to the floor. "What about all the magic you pulled from this? Could you transfer it to your father?"

The magic burned up my spine, snaking toward my extremities, reaching for freedom. The effort to not just release it in that moment added a growl of frustration to my words. "You act like I know what I'm doing."

Theo leaned in, his pointed finger poking into my shoulder. "Fix this, Wylde. Aren't you supposed to be some powerful witch everyone's so scared of?"

Aengus shoved him back away from me. "You will not touch her."

Theo snatched a fist full of Aengus's sweater and yanked him close. "You've gotten awfully disobedient this time around. Once you're back in your tomb, and Mother isn't trying to keep you happy, maybe I'll just decide to make the witch mine."

I felt more than saw Aengus flare with anger as he ripped Theo's hand away. Panicked, I jumped in between them. If I'd ever imagined two guys fighting over me, Theo certainly wouldn't have been one of them, and I wouldn't have been standing over my dying father's body. "Do you want me to fix this or not?" I snapped at Theo.

He sniffed and backed off, kicking at a pile of fallrot. The puddle didn't move, but a clump stuck to his boot and he frantically rubbed it across the cement floor, trying to scrape it off.

The light in my father sputtered again and nearly went out. Panic drove me back to his side, and Aengus followed. I couldn't watch him die. I had no memory before five years old, and no knowledge of my father outside of his current existence as a walking tree. But now, after my inability to reach my mother in the catacombs, he might be the only family I had left.

No, I refused to believe she was truly gone.

I spun the bracelet, feeling the skin-warmed metal. I had no control without her. But if I didn't try, my father would die. Maybe just her memory would help. Removing the bracelet, I set it into my palm and placed my hand against the only visible part of my father.

Eyes closed, I sank until my consciousness floated within the darkness. Two floors below, Underhill rushed, powerful and alluring. The self-preservation part of me urged me to pull away. A louder desire lured me to dive deep into the broiling magic. This time I managed to keep my head above water. Barely. The magic inside me vibrated, flinging itself frantically against my bones, clawing its way to the surface, trying to rip free. Pain flared in my joints, burning with intense heat.

My breaths were labored and fast against the pain. I followed the sharp heat down my arm out to my fingertips and the sensation of the metal bracelet that bit into my palm. With a shudder and cry, I released the magic, willing it into the human part of my father.

A hurricane level blast exploded out from me, ripping through the remaining crumbling armor, scattering ash and dead fallrot in all directions. Aengus dived behind me just as the force sent me flying backwards. He grunted as I slammed into his chest, but he braced and held as the concussive wave ripped through the surrounding boxes, hurling them against the wall, bursting their contents like shrapnel. Theo screamed.

My head dropped to my chest, too heavy to hold up. Gone was the pain, replaced with a hollow emptiness and an expanding weakness. Where I touched Aengus, I could sense his enticing gold strand of life energy and it beckoned me to refill my now empty well. Teeth gritted. I fought it.

My father lay still and fragile on the floor, naked with bones jutting beneath his skin like branches threatening to break through. His hair and scraggly beard looked dull and held more gray hairs than I remembered from when the witches had removed his helm before. The Green Knight had survived for centuries, passing his mantle to the next victim through combat and death. But I had stripped my father, the Knight's last host, of the enchanted armor. Was he free? Or had I taken the last of his life by removing the spell?

I couldn't make myself move away from the support of Aengus's chest against my back. He felt solid and real, when doubt was making everything seem uncertain.

I stared at my father, unblinking, willing him not to be dead. Seconds passed that seemed to stretch into an incalculable measure of time, dragging my fear with it. With a jerk, my father curled into a fetal position and his barely covered skeleton seemed to rattle with spastic coughing.

My breath left me with a whimper and I crawled forward on weak limbs. "Da—Geoffrey?" I said, stumbling over what to call him. He groaned in response and coughed again. "How do you feel?"

With one last cough, he rolled his head, gazing up with glassy eyes. "Like I've fallen off my mount and subsequently trampled," he wheezed.

I marveled at his cultured British accent. Not the accent itself, but at the improbability that somehow my small-town mother had met him. Would I ever get to hear that story? I realized I still gripped the bracelet in my hand and forced my frozen fingers to release so I could put it back on.

Theo stumbled toward us. "You're a menace," he growled. Ash and black fallrot ooze covered him completely and blood ran down one side of his face from a gash near his hairline. He noticed Geoffrey lying on the floor and pointed. "Is that the Green Knight? What did you do?"

Before I could answer, my father braced himself on an arm, thankfully showing no parts I didn't need burned into my retinae. "Where am I? Who are you all?" he demanded.

He didn't remember us? Memory loss? I hadn't expected that. I nearly rolled my eyes at my own thought. As if I'd done this before and knew what to expect. Seriously, we were lucky the room was still standing! I held my palm out in pacification. "I'm your daughter, Imogen, remember?"

My father dropped his brow and frowned. "I don't believe I do."

It shouldn't have hurt. To be fair, I had no memories of him either, but after speaking with Geoffrey for that brief spelled moment months ago I'd held onto hope. My mom and dad had seemed within reach, and now I felt like I'd lost them again. And the worst part was they were real people to me now, not just insubstantial place holders.

Theo reached down between us, jarring me out of my thoughts, and grabbed Aengus viciously by the shoulder, yanking him backwards. "Leave. I'll deal with you later." Surprised and unprepared, Aengus flung his arms out but could not keep himself from landing on his back.

I stumbled to my feet, my knees wobbly. "No, he stays."

Theo stabbed a finger toward me. "Do you know what you've done?"

Aengus leaped to his feet, fists clenched and his face a deep red. He angled his body in front of me, causing me to lean around him to yell at Theo. "Fixed it, like you demanded."

"No, you stupid bitch. The Unseelie Queen has nearly joined with The Leannan Sidhe. This will drive her the rest of the way." He swung his pointed finger in Aengus's direction. "I told you to go. Unless you want to see how long you can go without my blood before you go mad."

Anger leached out of Aengus, and his shoulders sank. How many times had Theo and Lady Aurnia withheld their blood to control him? I shifted until I stood in front, my own blood pounding in my ears. The last time Theo had taken Aengus away, I hadn't seen him in

44

months. No way was I letting that happen again. "And I said he stays."

Theo's lip went up in a snarl. "He's going now, and you're staying here to explain to my mother how you caused all this." He moved to grab Aengus's arm.

I locked eyes with the arrogant prince. "You won't touch him," I said, my voice flat and emotionless.

The empty well where I'd held all the magic ached with hunger. This time when the desire to consume whispered in my ear, I didn't push it down; I set it free. A tiny voice inside told me what I was doing was wrong. I told it to shut the hell up. With an invisible grip, I snatched at Theo's life strand, gulping his life energy into me. In that moment, I didn't care how much I took.

"What are you doing?" Aengus questioned me.

I pulled harder. Theo let out a faint cry as his eyes rolled back into his head and he crumpled.

The hollow sound of his head hitting the cement floor rang in my mind, shaking loose my rage.

I needed to let go. If I kept pulling on Theo's life force, he would die. And as much as I knew the world wouldn't mourn the loss of another bully, making an enemy of the Seelie didn't seem like a brilliant idea. But it was like whispering near a waterfall. I was beyond hearing reason. I'd let my magic flow and there was no hope of a dam.

"Let go, Imogen." Words reached my ear, low and calming. "Let go, *cor meum*." It was Aengus, his lips brushing my ear. Desperation in every word. He held my arm, pulling it to his chest. Electricity rippled over my skin and I shuddered, breaking eye contact with Theo.

Instantly, my mind felt clearer. Another shiver raced over my scalp and down my back, and I trembled. Aengus, his eyes pinched with concern, lifted his other hand to my cheek. "Let go," he urged.

With a heave of mental energy, I released my hold and gasped, falling against Aengus's chest "I nearly...I almost...I..." I mumbled incoherently against him.

"Shhh," Aengus said softly, running his hand over my hair as he held me close.

I peeked down at Theo lying like a cast-off marionette. His chest rose and fell as he breathed. He was fine—I hadn't killed him—he'd be fine. But a small, terrifying part of me felt irritated that Aengus had stopped me from stealing every last drop. I shook the thought from my head and turned away, instead gazing up at Aengus.

"Thank you."

His lips twitched into almost a smile. "My pleasure."

He didn't drop his arms. I didn't step back.

I hadn't taken nearly enough from Theo to satiate my hunger for magic and he lay at my feet, vulnerable. I could easily reach down and take the rest.

No. My muscles vibrated with tension. I wasn't a murderer.

Aengus tightened his hold against my back, pulling my thoughts away from my need for more magic and replacing them with different ones. I reached up, gripping Aengus's neck. As I dragged his face closer, I silently asked him to give me what I needed. His eyes widened for a moment, then brightened with heat as his lips met mine. A blast, not unlike the one that had destroyed the room earlier, seemed to explode inward, sending heat to every corner of my being until resting heavily in my core. Aengus pulled me tighter, his hand diving into my hair, as he pressed his heated lips harder against mine. I opened to him as our tongues and hands explored frantically. When he groaned, I melted against him.

Someone cleared their throat.

Startled, Aengus and I leaped apart, panting.

My father looked up at us from the floor. "Very sorry to interrupt, but would you either of you happen to have a pair of trousers?"

Chapter Six

The weight of my father draped across my back and shoulder nearly took us both down when I fumbled for the doorknob. I swung in the front door and heaved us over the threshold. For once, the television wasn't blaring and the scrape of my father's borrowed slippers against the wood floor seemed loud in the space. The entire coven sat in the front room as if waiting for us; all eyes turned our way.

We shuffled toward the nearest wingback chair. My father reached out to grip the back and fell against it, letting out the barest groan. Sissy looked up and blinked, eyes huge behind her thick glasses. Her hooks moved in her hands as if working independently, and her feet bounced, hanging a good distance off the floor.

"Apologies, ma'am," my father croaked, one hand holding tightly to the sweatpants that threatened to fall off his emaciated frame.

Aengus's sweatpants.

The image of Aengus stripping down to his navy boxers to help cover up my father sprang to my mind, and I pushed it down quickly. I hadn't wanted to leave him. I still felt the tingle on my lips from our kiss, but he'd convinced me that if he didn't stay and explain, especially concerning Theo, Lady Aurnia would think the worst. A war with the Unseelie would serve no one. Was it bad that I probably wouldn't care if it meant I could kiss him again?

But what he didn't have to say, and what made me actually leave him behind, was if he didn't explain, Aurnia might withhold her blood. And I did care whether Aengus became a mindless, feral beast.

Everett had jumped to his feet when we'd shuffled in. Now he grabbed his stethoscope from the desk and rushed over. He eyed me critically, and finding me whole, turned his attention to my father. Before I could open my mouth to introduce him, Nibs streaked across the floor screaming, "Geoffrey! Geoffrey! Geoffrey!"

Mr. Friedman, sitting between Mrs. Liu and Mr. Perez on the couch, grabbed his walker in front of him and heaved himself upright, swaying for a moment. The tufts of what was left of his white hair, stuck out over his ears like wings. Mrs. Liu reached out and put a steadying hand on his leg.

"Geoffrey?" His voice cracked on my father's name.

Nibs used the chair leg and climbed from the floor to the top, leaping straight at my father's neck. He swayed as he caught her and Everett and I both braced him on either side. "What's this?" he asked, startled.

"It's a Nibbleink, silly," she said, patting his cheek affectionately.

"A Brownie, correct?" Geoffrey eyed her like a zoo specimen.

Nibs shot a confused look at me. I reached out for her and reluctantly she left Geoffrey's arms for mine. "He doesn't remember us," I explained.

"What does he remember?" Nibs asked, her eyes watery and large.

Geoffrey gave a wan smile down at Nibs. "As I told Miss Wylde on our walk here…" He paused, taking a large breath. "I remember who I am, a reasonable amount of my childhood, and I have a memory of boarding a plane for the States."

Mr. Friedman looked shocked. "You remember nothing else?"

"No."

From the other wingback chair, Mrs. O'Cleary stood up. "Spell amnesia. Very common." She walked close and gestured for me to step aside. "May I?" she asked. Geoffrey nodded.

Everett pulled the stems of the stethoscope from his ears and let the drum fall away from Geoffrey's back as he held out an arm as a barrier. "This man needs medical attention. Not woo-woo witchiness."

"Everett—" I started, but Mrs. O'Cleary cut me off.

"Young man," she said as she laid her delicate hand on Everett's arm, her papery, veined complexion standing out against his satiny dark one. "He needs both. I'll be done in a jiffy, and then you can do your work." A tension filled second ticked by before Everett stepped back.

First, Mrs. O'Cleary looked into my father's eyes—leaning very close. Then she grabbed his wrist, almost as if she were taking his pulse, and placed her palm against his chest as she closed her eyes. She let out a low, "Hmmmm."

"Is it bad?" Mr. Friedman asked.

"Sit down, Sol. Of course, it's bad," Mrs. Liu snapped, grabbing Mr. Friedman and pulling him back down onto the couch. Mr. Perez hid a chuckle behind his hand and salt and pepper mustache.

Mrs. O'Cleary opened her eyes. "Well, it's not the worst." She looked at me. "How did you remove the Green Knight spell?"

I told her what had happened, leaving out the part where I'd wanted to murder Theo. And the kiss. I didn't want to be reminded of either incident for completely different reasons.

She nodded. "I could be wrong," she paused. "But by the state of you, Geoffrey, I'd say the magic that made you the Green Knight was less a mask and more a rewriting of your entire being." Geoffrey bobbed his head at her words. She turned to me. "When you ripped the spell away, I believe some of what makes up your father ripped away with it. Time will tell if he will reclaim that missing part or if it's gone forever." Mrs. O'Cleary smiled gently at Geoffrey. "Just know you are among friends."

Nibs froze in my arms and squeaked. "He might not remember us, ever?"

Mrs. O'Cleary moved away so Everett could continue his examination. "It's one of those 'wait and see' kind of things."

Pressure built up behind my eyes. Having no memories before I was five and now with my father's memories taken as well, was I doomed to never fill in the parental void I'd lived with all these years? Seriously, kind of a dick move, universe.

My father seemed to melt, his legs giving out beneath him, and only Everett's strong arms kept him upright. "I apologize, but I'm feeling a bit tired. Is there somewhere I might have a lie down?"

Everett leaned closer. "I'm going to pick you up, if that's okay Mr—"

"Corben," I supplied.

"Mr. Corben?" Everett asked.

When my father nodded, Everett swung my father's arm over his shoulder and slid an arm behind his knees. "Please, just Geoffrey," he said, his voice more air than sound.

Everett turned to me, "I'm going to run an I.V. but he should go to the hospital."

Mrs. O'Cleary shook her head. "Nothing they can do. He either heals or he doesn't. This is magic, not science."

My father's head fell to Everett's chest. His sunken and shadowed eyes closed. I felt a twinge of guilt at my relief at handing him off to someone more capable. Honestly, unpacking my feelings about everything that happened today was going to be messy and right now, avoidance seemed the better choice.

"Just do the best you can to make him comfortable," I said. Everett wanted to argue. I could practically see him fight back his words until he sighed deeply and carried my father down the hall toward the infirmary.

Nibs urged me to put her down, and when I did, she scurried after them.

"Will he make it?" I asked, and I knew everyone could hear the childlike tone in my voice.

Sissy spoke, her voice hoarse and weak. "For now."

Out of everyone there, I would never have expected Sissy to answer. And I didn't think anyone else expected either. The entire room froze.

A few months after I'd started the second grade, a petite woman with an enormous suitcase arrived. Jane had told me Sissy didn't speak, which wasn't completely true. Sissy used expression and gestures to get across most things. But I'd always assumed for whatever reason Sissy couldn't speak, not that she wouldn't.

Mr. Perez leaned forward. "Have you seen something, *chiquitina?*"

What did he mean by, had she "seen something"? Did "for now" mean she knew what would happen?

Sissy set her crochet hooks down, her fingers disappearing into the puddle of knotted yarn.

"It's alright," Mrs. O'Cleary said gently.

Sissy tipped her head to the side like a bird. "Since the release of her magic, I've had flashes. Nothing definite."

The residents clearly seemed to understand what she meant. I did not. "What do you mean flashes?"

Mr. Perez took pity on me. "Sissy is a seer. She sees important moments from the past, the future. But they are very difficult to understand."

Sissy smiled with a wink.

"Do you see them all the time?" I asked her and Sissy shrugged. "Is that why you don't..." I trailed off not wanting to be rude.

Mr. Perez smoothed his mustache. "Being a seer *es arriesgado*—is dangerous. Not everyone who holds power does so for good."

And asking someone if they were "a good witch or a bad witch" probably didn't get accurate results. I turned to Sissy. "You don't have to tell me anything. I want you to stay safe."

She squinted, pushing her thick glasses back up off her nose and smiled wide. "I'm safe here. Not talking is mostly just a habit."

Mrs. Liu sniffed loudly. "This is taking too long. Tell us what you've seen, some of us need to eat."

"Chu Hua!" Mrs. O'Cleary admonished.

But Sissy didn't seem upset. In a deeper tone and a lilting cadence, she spoke, "There is a creature large and many tentacled. She crawls from the water, becomes a woman, and a man holds out a sword. It's Excalibur. He asks for a spell to find someone like him. Someone not yet born." Sissy blinked quickly, pulling free of whatever her mind showed her. "That's all that's clear right now," she said in her regular voice.

I opened my mouth to ask Sissy what the woman and man looked like when the front door burst open and crashed against the wall.

It was The Leannan Sidhe, the fae who murdered Cailleach Fae like me to steal their power, who nearly killed me three months ago, the very reason the wards needed to remain strong. That Leannan Sidhe stood in the doorway flanked by two drooling and growling wolf-creature *ossorians*.

The universe wasn't pulling any punches today.

Chapter Seven

A damp chill settled over the living room and the fug of wet dog, mixed with the smell of smoke and an earthy scent reminiscent of band aides, clung to my nose.

The Leannan Sidhe stood just outside the doorway, her booted feet so close to the edge of the ward they created ripples. Her ice white hair intricately braided against her head accentuated the sharp angles of her pale face and her clothes, ancient in style, shimmered and flowed unnaturally. In her right hand she held Birgha, the unmistakable spear that had killed Gaius and nearly Aengus as well. The two *ossorians* at her side whined and snarled, their fearsome teeth on display.

The scene made me feel everything I'd done today had been merely a side quest and now I'd made it to the boss battle. Any minute, the eight-bit musical fight score would start. I'd have laughed if the danger wasn't so real.

Behind me the coven shifted, trying to move closer, Mr. Friedman's walker squeaking. I looked back at them and noted the fear in their wide eyes. They shouldn't be able to see any of it, but clearly, Leannan was not bothering to hide herself or her wolf creatures with glamour.

Reverberations like bass thumps echoed through the house, and I turned back toward the doorway. Leannan held the spear close enough to the ward it gave off tiny angry sparks. She gave a sharp tap of the triangle blade against it again, the bass thump warping the sound once more. The magic shuddered, and I felt it nearly extinguish. There was no way the wards would hold out against another push.

Leannan smiled like the Mona Lisa and I knew she knew it, too.

"You're not welcome here," I said firmly, as if stating the obvious would somehow help. Both Mrs. O'Cleary and Mrs. Liu moved to stand at my side. I wanted to tell them and the coven to leave and get somewhere safe, but nowhere was safe.

Not even by my side.

The adrenaline coursing through me made it almost impossible to stay unaware of the coven's life threads dangling enticingly around me. The hunger inside me wanted to refill the well. I dug my fingernails into the palm of my hands and fought the desire.

Leannan touched the side of her nose. "A little birdy told me you made a trip to the Seelie Court today."

A birdy told her? What bird? Then I remembered the unsettling crow on the roof of the hookah bar. It seemed my instincts about it had proved correct.

Heavy steps thundered up from the back of the house as Everett rushed into the room, no doubt hearing the slam of the door. "Everyone all right?" He barely gave Leannan a passing glance as he visually took in his charges. Before I could tell him to stay back, a shrill whistle from Leannan's lips froze him. His dark eyes shifted and locked onto her pale ones.

"Large one, leave the witches and come to me," Leannan ordered. Without hesitation, Everett did as she commanded, his expression unnaturally blank. Leannan twisted her lips into what could have been described as a smile but seemed more like a predatory show of teeth. "Humans are always so pliable."

I grabbed Everett's arm as he stepped past me. There was no way I had the strength to hold him, but at my touch he seemed to come back to himself. He moved his head side to side as if shaking it clear.

"I'm good. I'm good," he assured me.

I didn't like the way Leannan still eyed him. "Don't look at her. Go back to my father and make sure the other nurses and Nibs stay clear of this room."

He opened his mouth to argue, but I stopped him. "I'll handle the weird stuff, remember?"

"I'm going to keep listening. You call me if 'Braveheart Barbie' takes one step inside."

"Go," I urged again, and this time he listened. I didn't want to tell him that if Leannan got inside, we wouldn't even get the chance to call out.

Leannan clucked her tongue, clearly disappointed I'd stolen her opportunity to do whatever it was she wanted with Everett. Her gaze drilled into me. "I see your hunk of wood is missing."

It took me a moment to realize she meant the Green Knight—and I never wanted to associate those words with my father again.

Wait. Was that why she had chosen now to show up? Could my father really have been the reason The Leannan Sidhe had stayed away? Something about that explanation didn't seem right. "He's not missing," I said, which wasn't technically a lie, and followed it up with, "Why are you here?" hoping to distract her.

Leannan laughed, and the *ossorians* shifted, growling low enough I felt it in my chest. "Wondering why now, aren't you? Wondering why I left you alone for so long?" She ran the spear tip along the ward again. The smell of heated metal filled the air. "Although not my first choice, letting you simmer and grow has certainly paid off. Now when I take all that delicious power, it will be a meal and no longer a snack." She touched her fingers to her lips and let out an appreciative hum.

"Is that really your end goal? Take my magic and watch the whole world burn like some lame comic book villain?" I asked, unable to hide my frustration.

A flash of pain flickered in her expression before it disappeared. "Don't speak of things you don't understand. You *custos* should have fought alongside me, and yet you chose their side," Leannan snarled.

Their side? What did she mean by *their side?*

A hum vibrated in the air, drawing both Leannan's and my attention. The six coven members had situated themselves into a circle, hiding their intent by continuing to face the open doorway. Their mouths now moved nearly as one as they chanted. The last time they'd chanted in a similar way they'd pushed back the Green Knight's spell long enough for my father to speak to me. What spell could possibly help this situation?

Leannan's nostrils flared, and a vein pulsed on her forehead. "Witches," she snarled. "Their magic reeks of the peasantry." With a thrust reminiscent of her murder of Gaius, Leannan drove the spear head directly into the ward. I cried out as the magic let out a resounding pop and the barrier disintegrated.

The witches yelled out, "*Murus!*"

Liquid silver rolled down like a falling curtain, halting Leannan from stepping over the threshold. Through the ripple of silver waves, I could make out her furious expression.

"It's a mirror spell," Mrs. O'Cleary said, and the frailty in her voice had me spinning around toward her. "We recognized the spear and knew what she planned. Any magic she casts will bounce back on her, but it won't last more than a few minutes," she added.

My gaze crawled over the coven as they hung on each other and the furniture in exhaustion. Three months ago, Jane had expended too much magic and died. Would it happen again? I harshly pushed the thought away. I couldn't think about it now. The Leannan Sidhe still stood at the door and I was the only one left with power.

I really didn't want to be anyone's "only hope".

When I reluctantly touched my magic, a dark whisper rushed through me, tingling beneath my skin, and urging me to take what was left of the coven's power. I stumbled closer to the mirrored doorway and away from them. Never! I'd never hurt them! "How do we get her to leave before it falls?" I croaked, fighting to push down the villainous hunger.

Through the spell shimmer, Leannan pushed at the mirror spell, no doubt waiting for the moment it fell. The *ossorians* behind her had dropped to their bellies on the porch, their drooling snouts between their paws.

They had yet to stand on their back legs or speak as I'd seen them do a few times before. Did Leannan keep them from acting more human?

Just like the *fola tráill*, the *ossorians* were slaves. Surely, they didn't like the fae who had tricked them into giving up their human forms forever. Yet they still fought for them. The *fola tráill* were connected to the fae by blood. Aengus couldn't leave the Seelie Court, because he needed the blood of the line that created him, or he'd turn feral. But how were the *ossorians* dominated?

And could I break it?

I closed my eyes and hesitantly let my consciousness tip toward the magic cliff. Having a goal seemed to keep my hunger at bay, as I fought to focus on the wolf beasts. They had a golden thread that looked the same as any other, but twisted around it, not unlike the fallrot, was a black vine that ran directly from them to The Leannan Sidhe.

"It's beginning to fall," Mr. Friedman's voice reached me.

We all knew, once the mirror spell fell there was nothing to stop Leannan.

"I think I have a way," I whispered. "And I need you all to move as far back from me as you can."

The space helped, but I still fought the hunger, my breathing sharp and fast. Hesitantly, I closed my eyes and reached out with my mind to grab onto the black cords twined around the *ossorians'* golden ones. They slithered, twisting to get free, and I gritted my teeth against the force I exerted to hold on. If I could disconnect the cords from Leannan, then the *ossorians* should be free. I hoped they'd take out their anger where it was deserved. My plans depended on a lot of "ifs" but it was the only one I had.

I gripped the black snaking magic tighter and yanked. With a snap, they broke away from Leannan. The two ends flew up, coiling in the air, but instead of disappearing, they spiraled toward me, slamming into my chest. The ends burrowed like worms deep under my skin.

I jerked open my eyes and the *ossorians* on the porch leaped to their feet.

As if gazing into another room through an open door, I felt their surprise.

The mirror spell fizzled.

Leannan stiffened, and her gaze jumped from the *ossorians* to me. "What have you done?"

"I took them from you," I said, honestly leaving out the part where it definitely hadn't been my goal. In my mind, I kept repeating, "I'll let you go, but you have to help," hoping the *ossorians* would understand.

The one closest to Leannan finally reacted. With a snap, its jaw came down around the spear and it leaned back, pulling and tugging, but Leannan managed to rip the spear from its mouth.

"I think you should leave," I said, taking a step toward Leannan, hoping to intimidate her. I wasn't certain the *ossorians* could really stop her, but she backed up as they growled, their ears pinned and their lips curled.

Leannan reached out to the side and slowly circled her hand, fingers moving as if plucking strings. A portal appeared like a viscous oil slick, expanding until the size of an average person. The same type of portal Dennriall had been lost through.

My bracelet warmed to the point of almost burning, and for a moment a whisper rushed past my ears. Before I could understand, Leannan disappeared through the portal and it snapped shut, leaving us and my new pair of pet werewolves behind.

Chapter Eight

The place where The Leannan Sidhe had stepped through the portal sizzled with dissipating energy and steamed against the cold air. I stepped over the threshold onto the porch, wincing against the fear and anger, emotions that were not mine. Emotions drowning out everything else—even the hunger.

Even that positive outcome didn't change the fact that I'd accidentally bound two werewolves and I now had the pleasure of experiencing canine emotional oversharing. I took a step closer. The *ossorians* growled low and crouched, tails tucked, their bear-like claws digging deep groves in the wood of the porch.

The coven crowded in the doorway, but I held out a hand for them to stay back.

"Let uth go," the larger one lisped.

"Believe me, this isn't what I want, either. I'm going to get you free and out of my head as fast as I can." I tried to smile, but the moment my lips pulled away and revealed teeth, they growled again, so I stopped.

I didn't even know what kind of magic had been used to create the link in the first place, and now it was attached to me. I felt the tiny hooks digging deep into my skin, just like the mouth of a leech. Oh god, why had I given myself that image? I fought the urge to viciously scratch at my chest.

"I don't know what to do." I turned to Mrs. Liu standing closest to me.

She reached out and gently squeezed my arm—gently for her meant I probably wouldn't bruise. "What does the spell look like?"

Closing my eyes I focused on where the black cords originated from in the *ossorians*. They weaved around the golden thread and then tangled around their core. "It's like a leash wrapped around their life strands," I answered, my eyes still closed.

"Can you pull them loose?" Mr. Perez asked. There was a hint of chattering as he shivered in the cold doorway.

I visualized gripping both dark threads and gave them a hard yank. The *ossorians* yipped and hot, sharp pain ripped through my chest as my heart skipped more than a couple of beats. With a gasp, I released my hold, my eyes springing open. The two wolf-beasts cowered at my feet. "Oh no, I'm so sorry." They snapped their jaws, teeth clicking. "I won't do that again, I promise."

Gradually, they rose and sat back on their haunches, waiting. "I'm going to try just one," I informed them. The large one lifted his jowl. "Gently," I assured him. Reaching inward and taking ahold of just one of the black strands, I started the lightest, slow pull. The smaller *ossorian* lifted a lip and lashed its tail. With a sigh of defeat, I let it go.

What was going on with this spell? I took a harder look. The black chords did not reflect light, instead, they seemed to pull it into them like a black hole. Where they attached to the *ossorian* again, the black interwove with their golden life strand, but now I could see they weaved together more like a basket of gold and black straight over the heart with each side fused to the other. There was no pulling one strand without pulling it all.

I opened my eyes. "I can't remove the spell, not yet."

Anger flared like a flame in my mind, and my brain swelled with heat. With a wince, I glared at the wolf-beasts. "I don't want this," I said, gesturing between us to mimic the black chord.

"Let uth go," the larger one repeated and the smaller one dragged one of its clawed paws against the wood, making it squeal.

"I don't think I can. Not right now. If I try to remove it, I'm pretty sure you'll both die."

"Lies!" the larger one cried.

"I'm not lying!"

Behind me, Mr. Friedman cleared his throat, drawing our attention. He pushed his glasses up from the bottom of his nose. "Maybe if you can't break it, you can alter it," he offered, and the rest of the coven nodded in agreement. They all huddled close for warmth.

The *ossorians* cocked their heads. The smaller one took a step closer. "What do you mean?" Each word came out wet and drool filled.

Mr. Friedman shifted and rubbed his arms, partly to warm them and partly in obvious discomfort. "Well, if we can change the spell, it would still be there, but maybe it wouldn't affect you the same way— for the better," he quickly added.

"I can't do anything right now. I can't control my magic. Not enough." I said. The *ossorians* took a menacing step toward me, their lips curled and their tongues flicking between their canines.

"I believe they need more assurance than just our word," Mrs. O'Cleary said, rubbing her own arms against the chill.

Mrs. Liu leaned around her, a look of joy on her face. "Yes, a Blood Vow, perhaps."

The *ossorians* jumped up and yipped, the tone not of pain but excitement.

I definitely didn't like the word "blood" as a descriptor. "I thought witch magic didn't deal in blood?"

"There are always exceptions to the rule," Mrs. O'Cleary said.

My gaze returned to the two sets of yellow eyes, feeling the eagerness flow through our bond. I looked back at the witches. "How dangerous is this vow?"

Mrs. Liu waved her hand dismissively. "Oh, it's not dangerous."

"Unless you don't complete the vow," Mrs. O'Cleary clarified.

"Which Genny won't do." Mrs. Liu's words sounded more like a command than a statement of fact.

The vow sounded ominous, but I truly did want to release the *ossorians* from me. I couldn't see myself not finding some way to do that. Decided, I looked hard at the wolf beasts. "If I take this blood vow, you two must then protect this house until I can complete it." They bobbed their blocky heads in agreement as drool dripped, making dark circles on the planks.

"Okay, what do I have to do?" I called over my shoulder.

Mrs. O'Cleary clapped her hands together. "Everyone inside where it's warm. We haven't had a blood vow since the eighties." She called into the house. "Sol, grab the wine. Alejandro, please find the scrying bowl. Sissy, we'll need one of you tapestry needles."

Sadness flickered through me and I focused on the smaller one. "Otherth," it lisped.

"Others?" I repeated, and it nodded. I didn't know how many *ossorians* were held captive. I'd only seen a few at a time. "If I can save them too, I will," I assured.

What's another task to add to my list anyway?

The forefinger on my left hand stung where I'd jammed a two-inch tapestry needle deep into the pad. I rubbed my thumb against the bandage, unable to leave it alone. At least the amount of blood needed for the vow was less than I'd imagined. Just a few drops spread around the bottom of the scrying bowl, which happened to be the bowl we ate salad out of on any other day. How long could you soak ceramic in bleach before it disintegrated?

I didn't feel any different after taking the vow, but the coven assured me it was binding. I would have done all I could without the magic promise, but because of it, the *ossorians* were willing to keep the home safe in the meantime. Their dark forms now lay like furry hillocks on the ground before the front steps.

I walked through the kitchen and poked my head into the tiny infirmary. My father lay curled up in a fetal position on the hospital bed, his form beneath his borrowed oversized clothes, frail and frightening. One of my father's thin arms, skin pulled tight against bone, lay outstretched with an IV line running from his hand to the hanging bag of fluids. Nibbleink sat cross-legged near his wispy and unkempt hair, her gaze focused, her little fists clenched on her knees. Everett sat close, almost comically large on a metal folding chair, scrolling on his phone.

"Should I bring him a blanket?" I asked quietly.

Everett dropped his phone into his scrub pocket and heaved to his feet. "He's barely allowing the clothes to stay on. Says anything against his skin feels like vines." He glanced behind me. "Mr. Perez said 'she' is gone? And what was with the bowl?"

I lifted my sore finger. "Don't ask. And yes, The Leannan Sidhe is gone." I glanced back over my shoulder. "The nurses?"

Everett let out a deep sigh. "Sent them home. We'll see if they come back tomorrow."

I sighed, magic hat off and business hat on. "Speaking of going home." It was almost five in the evening and near the end of his shift. "I don't see Lucrecia." I had a feeling I wasn't going to like what he said.

"Quit. Sick momma out in Denver." His "what are you going to do?" expression said it all. There really wasn't much we could do, but it didn't help my frustration that my friend was stuck with a double shift.

"Go take a few hours in Jane's old room."

Everett glanced down at my father.

I wouldn't want to leave him alone, either. His life seemed fragile, balancing on the proverbial pin head. "Just tell me what to do if things go wrong and everything starts beeping and I promise I'll wake you." He gave me a hard look and I raised my hands in defeat. "And I'll call an ambulance."

Nibs jumped to her feet. "Things won't go wrong!" She squeaked, finally seeming to acknowledge our presence.

"Of course not," Everett said very gently and even gave Nibs a smile. Clearly, some bonding had gone on while they were both together, taking care of Geoffrey. Everett turned his attention firmly on me. "But wake me up for anything." I nodded as I made an X over my heart. That seemed to mollify him and he stepped out into the hall, his heavy tread up the staircase following moments later.

I turned back to Nibs and Geoffrey. Watching her try to pat down his rumpled hair. "Thanks for taking such good care of him," I told her, sitting down on the folding chair Everett had vacated. Nibs nodded, but didn't stop fussing. "Do you mind if I stay here with you both for a little bit?"

Nibs looked up and squinted her eyes with mistrust.

"Just to sit." I assured. "You're doing a fantastic job, I wouldn't want to get in the way."

Nibs puffed up her chest. "Damn straight," she responded in a tone that sounded an awful lot like Mr. Friedman's and I had to lock my jaw, trying not to laugh.

Chapter Nine

Geoffrey stirred around midnight. Startled, my phone tumbled to the floor. When I straightened after grabbing it, he was staring silently at me. He looked nothing like the man I'd first seen under the Green Knight's armor three months ago. His hair had thinned to the point where his bold widow's peak was now barely visible, and his beard looked thin and patchy. But his stormy gray eyes were the same, even sunken deep into the shadow of his skull.

At the end of the bed, Nibs leaped to her feet. "Do you remember me now?"

He shifted, trying to maneuver himself to sitting, but only managed to bring his head up a few extra inches. "Not as yet, little one," he said gently. She sighed loudly and curled back up against his blanketed leg, her expression full of disappointment. Exhausted, Geoffrey flopped his head back down in my direction, his eyebrows drawn together, creating a crease in his pallid forehead. "The wards I felt before, they're gone."

His words caught me off guard, but of course he'd noticed the wards. I'd gotten my witch side from him, after all. Even though logically we were a couple of strangers, lacking the years that created a true connection, just having him exist in the father space that had always been empty filled me with joy.

"The Leannan Sidhe was here. She tore them down," I told him, trying to keep my tone light. Geoffrey's eyes widened, and he shifted weakly, as if trying to get out of the bed. "She's gone now," I said. He stopped struggling, but he didn't look reassured.

"How long has she been in this realm?" he asked, his voice noticeably weaker.

"I don't know, a few months, maybe a year. You should try and sleep. You've been through a lot."

He dragged his arm across his chest and gripped my arm, the bones in his fingers almost creaking as they applied only a weak pressure. His flickering lifeline swam in my vision, fragile and barely strong enough. My father's eyes widened as he stared at where his hand touched my arm. "The wards need to be recast." His voice barely rose above a hoarse whisper.

"The coven is trying." I cringed inwardly, knowing if only I had the least bit of control, the wards would be up again already. "You really should sleep."

Geoffrey's gaze found mine, and I knew he'd felt the power barely controlled within me. I could see it in his eyes. "You said you were my daughter." I nodded. Somehow, I'd managed to ignore my worry that I'd have to tell my father I was a Cailleach Fae before he remembered himself. "Your mother—"

"Had fae blood," I finished.

He didn't pull his hand free, but I felt him tremble. "Why would I..." He trailed off. His eyelids stuttered up and down. He was losing the battle to stay awake.

"I don't know. Maybe when you remember you can tell me," I said in a playful tone.

"I'm sorry we did this to you," he whispered as his lids fell again and stayed closed.

Everett switched with me around 2 a.m. No alarms had gone off, but Geoffrey hadn't stirred for the last couple of hours. He lay so still, in fact, for much of the night I'd focused on the slight rise and fall of his shoulders, making sure he kept breathing. Before I left the room, I asked Nibs if she wanted to come to bed too; she looked at me as if I'd asked her to set her wardrobe on fire.

Point taken.

I shuffled off alone. Lying in bed, my body ached with exhaustion, but my mind raced. Full of alien emotions emanating from the *ossorians* outside and my own jumbled emotions. In the dark silence, my thoughts reviewed every action I'd taken over the last twenty-four hours and picked them apart. Had I really done the right thing with the *ossorians*? They had to be better off with someone on the less evil side, right? But they were still slaves, and that really bothered me.

As much as I worried about them, another memory kept surfacing—the kiss. What did it mean? I'd already given up talking myself out of caring for Aengus. That was a done deal now. But I also knew for Aengus, nothing was more important than returning to his duty and closing the veil. What was a fling compared to the fate of the world? But he'd kissed me back, like really kissed me. Maybe he thought we could be something more, too. Ugh!! Why was this just as difficult to navigate now as when I was a teenager?

My eyes closed just as the sky lightened, only to have my alarm for work go off at eight. I rolled over, marking how spacious the pillow was without a Nibs-sized body stretched out over it, and reached across to my desk chair serving as a bedside table to tap "stop" on my phone.

My "do not disturb" switched off, lighting up my phone with notifications. I glanced and immediately swiped to read one of the emails. My supervisor, Diana Wovoka, had taken a leave of absence. Until another supervisor could be arranged, my internship had been placed on hiatus. As someone who'd loved many a television show put on hiatus, I knew it was hardly ever a good thing.

Odd that Diana hadn't mentioned leaving for an extended period. I'd spoken to her last week, and we'd talked about the script for the tours in the new year and her excitement about possible expansions for some of the exhibits. She was a grown-up; she didn't have to tell me anything, but I'd thought we were becoming friends. I'd even made it to the bar a few times for drinks. I might have even given her a teeny bit of information about my home life, which was a big deal for me.

I opened up our most recent text conversation and typed.

> Hope everything is alright. Talk when you get back?

When Diana didn't respond right away, I closed the screen, set the phone back down on the chair. With a flop, I landed on the pillow. Well, if I didn't have to go into the museum, a few more minutes' sleep couldn't hurt.

A siren of howls reached me even through the closed bedroom door, just as a burst of anger, red hot and intense, ripped through my mind from the *ossorians*. I lurched upright with a gasp. From the kitchen, pottery crashed and Everett swore loudly. I flung off the comforter and dashed out.

Everett looked askance at me as he bent over, picking up the remains of a large mug from the floor. The howling continued. "What the hell is that?" he grumbled.

"I think our new guard dogs are sounding the alarm," I said, concern rising as the tone of their howls increased. The neighborhood dogs had now added their barks to the cacophony. Had The Leannan Sidhe returned? I took a step toward the hallway but looked back at Everett. "Is Geoffrey..." I couldn't finish my question.

"He's the same," Everett said.

Before I could thank him, from outside Aengus bellowed, "Imogen!"

I rushed through the house and out onto the porch. Morning winter air attacked me from head to bare toes and I found Aengus held at bay by the two *ossorians*. He'd gone back to wearing what I'd first seen him in—a long black trench coat and a beanie, his blonde curls smooshed against his forehead. He saw me and tried to take a step closer, a touch of panic in his eyes. "Is Leannan here? Has she hurt you?" The *ossorians* snapped their jaws and the large one swiped a paw, not unlike a bear, forcing him to jump back.

Aengus bared his teeth, showing his normally unnoticeable extended canines.

I thundered down the front steps, relieved months hadn't gone by before I saw him again, but not if it involved a werewolf vs. vampire death match. I stopped between the *ossorians*, my toes tingling against the frozen cement. Hesitantly, I laid a hand on the small one's shoulder, fully expecting the wolf beast to turn its head and snap off a finger. Its stiff hair poked unpleasantly against my palm, and I fought the urge to pull my hand away. To my relief, the *ossorian* quieted instead of attacking. So I placed my other hand on the large one and he quieted as well.

I smiled at Aengus. "You're here," were the only words I could find to say. It was then I realized I stood with no bra, dressed in my pajamas, and with no doubt epic bed head with no way to fix it.

"Get away from them," Aengus shouted, directing me back toward the house.

I froze at his guttural tone, and the *ossorians* rumbled beside me. I curled my fingers deeper into their fur. "I can't—well, I can but—I'm sort of connected to them. Honestly, it's okay."

Aengus narrowed his eyes. "Explain."

"The Leannan Sidhe destroyed the wards." Aengus's entire body stiffened. "I'm fine," I rushed to remind him, "but the only way to stop her from getting to us was to steal her connection to the *ossorians*. I'm kind of in charge of them—just these two I mean—but I've promised to figure out how to set all of them free."

Aengus scratched his hairline where the beanie rested and sighed deeply, his entire body drooping as if only the fear that I might have been in danger had kept him upright until that point. "Are you truly well?" he asked, his voice cracking.

I noticed then how exceptionally pale he looked this morning, with dark circles under his eyes as deep as bruises. Lifting my hands from the ruff of the fae beasts, I stepped toward him and stopped without touching him. Why did I feel more awkward now after we'd kissed? It made no sense. Putting all the assurance I could into my words, I repeated, "I'm fine."

Before I could truly register what he was doing, he pulled me close, my arms instinctively snaking around his middle as the trench coat wrapped around me, protecting me from the cold. Even with my feet frozen, I probably would have lingered in his embrace for much longer, but an annoyed barking whine echoed in the morning air, starting up a few of the neighbor dogs again. We had an audience, and they weren't amused. I glanced over my shoulder.

The *ossorians* had laid down, the smaller one had buried his nose beneath his front paws and closed his eyes. The larger stared unblinking, with a lip curled. Irritation ran along our bond, splashing cold water on the mood. I stepped away, instantly bombarded with the cold, and fought the desire to dive back within Aengus's trench coat once more.

Aengus pointed to the house. "We should go inside. Your teeth will break from all that chattering." I was shaking and my toes had gone from tingling to numb. Aengus's eyes glazed, and he rubbed a harsh hand over his face.

"You're out in daylight," I burst out. How could I have forgotten? Without Merlin's spell, the sun drained Aengus like any *fola tráill*.

"The winter sun is weak, and it is early," he said, trying and failing to brush away my concern.

I grabbed onto his arm and pulled. Aengus gave the wolf beasts a wide berth but followed.

As I closed the door, Everett called down from the top of the stairs, "Everything all good?"

"Yes. Crisis averted," I yelled back.

"My ass is tired. Can we hold off on any more weird shit until I've had a full night's sleep?"

"No weird stuff. Got it!" I assured him, even though we both knew I had no say whatsoever in the chaos that was my life.

I led Aengus to the couch, and he sank down, boneless, his head rolling to rest against the back as if too heavy to hold up. Clearly, the sun had affected him more than he'd let on. I ran to put on a bra, clean my teeth, and hastily drag a brush through my hair, throwing it up in a ponytail. I hurried back to the front room and dropped down beside him, grabbing a folded blanket off the arm of the couch to wrap up in, pulling up my feet too.

We stared at each other in silence. When I couldn't take the awkward pause any longer I asked, "Why did you come?" Realizing how it sounded, I added, "I'm glad you're here."

He didn't answer right away, instead he pulled my feet out from under the blanket and started to rub them, massaging away the cold. "I find myself reluctant to share," he said, finally looking up.

Tingles rushed over my skin at his touch, and it took a moment for my brain to register what he'd said. "It's obviously important if you're out in the sun."

"Hmmm," he answered, still focused on my feet.

I wanted to let him continue to avoid the topic and keep rubbing my insoles, but with a sigh I asked, "What is it?"

Aengus dropped his hands away. "I found an enchantment. One that can return Excalibur to me and also enough of Merlin's spell to recast."

"Oh." I pulled my feet in and hugged my knees. Tingles of pleasure were now drowned out by a sour stomach. Merlin's spell.

The one that makes it impossible for us to touch. Neither of us spoke. Aengus refused to meet my eyes.

I dove against his side, burrowing under his arm. Aengus tensed, but finally looked at me. I smiled up at him. His lips slowly rose to mirror my own. This was the very reason Aengus had stayed away for all those months. The closer we became, the harder it was going to be to say goodbye.

Out of obligation, I asked, "How does the spell work?"

Aengus shifted so he could see me better, but didn't remove his arm from around me. "There is a druid in the vicinity. Or there was. Gaius's notes mention him. We will need a druid for Excalibur's spell."

"I'm still not in control of my magic. There's no way I can cast Merlin's spell yet." I tried not to let my relief show on my face. We had time. The veil needed to be closed, but I wasn't ready to lose Aengus. Not now. Not ever. I needed to find another way to close the veil, and I needed to find it quickly.

From the hallway, a weak voice spoke. "I think I may have a solution."

Followed closely by a happy cry from Nibs. "Do you see? He's awake. Genny, do you see?"

I jumped to my feet as Geoffrey shuffled down the hallway toward us, using the wall to keep himself upright. Nibs stood by his leg, confident in her ability to catch him if he fell. Her clothes were rumpled and creased from holding vigil all night. Aengus moved quickly, his earlier exhaustion gone, and helped Geoffrey into one of the wingback chairs. Geoffrey fell into it with a humph. Nibs crawled up and sat proudly on the armrest.

"What are you doing up?" I demanded, scanning him for additional damage. The thinnest green line snaked over his skin, down his arm, and stopping at his wrist. It hadn't been there last night.

Geoffrey pointed a trembling finger at me. "I've been mulling over the predicament we have with the wards." He took breaks between every few words to breathe. "A witch draws power from the earth, and the fae use blood magic. As a Cailleach fae, you are receiving too much magic input. It's no surprise you are finding it difficult to focus."

"Are you saying I have like 'witch ADHD?'" Why not? I already had anxiety; what was one more.

Geoffrey let out a laugh that sounded like a wheeze.

"Oh! I can bring you pills," Nibs said brightly. "I know where they are."

"No, thank you Nibs," I said, fighting the urge to go check the lock on the controlled substances—again. We didn't need another incident like we had a few months ago. "And remember, we talked about this, you aren't allowed to handle the meds."

Nibs rolled her eyes and angled herself away from me.

"You don't have an attention disorder," Geoffrey clarified. "More like sensory overload. If you were just fae, the magic from Underhill would be, for lack of a better word, filtered through you before you accessed it. But your witch abilities are letting you bypass that and go straight to the source. It's too much power all at once. I believe you need a cynosure," he said, confidently as if I had any idea what that was.

"A what?" I asked.

"An item that allows you to focus your power."

Aengus, who'd sat back down on the couch, leaned forward. "Yes, you might be right."

"How can I find a cynosure?"

Geoffrey opened his mouth to speak, but coughed instead, his hand flying up to cover it. Were there more vein-like green lines than there had been a few minutes ago? He smothered the last of his coughing and dropped his hand to answer weakly, "it has to be an item your magic recognizes."

"Excalibur," Aengus blurted out, and both Geoffrey and I turned to him.

Excalibur made sense. The sword was linked to me. I

remembered about how it felt to hold the hilt in my hand. The rightness. The completeness. I smiled. "I think you're right."

"Do you have a way to obtain it?" Geoffrey asked.

Aengus and I shared a look. Why hadn't I grabbed the sword when I'd had the chance? I scratched my head and sighed. "Yeah, but I'm definitely going to need to have a cup of coffee and a shower before we tackle it."

The intro music to one of the residents' beloved shows was turned up loud enough to shake the walls. Mr. Friedman really needed to use his hearing aids. Aengus sat with his elbow propped on the arm and his head lying in his hand, asleep. Mrs. Liu sat nearby, dividing her attention between the television and eyeing him suspiciously.

Mr. Friedman had angled his chair to better ramble off plot points to Geoffrey as he tried to explain the episode. Geoffrey gamely nodded along.

Within the time it had taken me to shower and change, already new green veins had stretched up his neck.

"Genny!," Nibs squealed when she saw me, jumping to her feet on Geoffrey's lap, her long ragged ears bouncing. "Geoffrey remembers!" A smile stretched from ear to ear.

Geoffrey turned as I took another step closer and his lip trembled, his eyes damp. "Part of me had hoped that seeing you all grown up had been a dream."

I reached for the television remote and clicked it to mute. Aengus lifted his head at the absence of noise, and Mr. Friedman and Mrs. Liu turned to me and glared. I reminded them that one, they'd seen this episode more than once, and two, there were subtitles. There was still a lot of huffing.

Unsure what to say to Geoffrey, to my father, I just asked the obvious. "You remember now?"

He nodded as he absently scratched at the green lines on his arm. "It's returning to me, slowly."

Aengus and I found each other's gaze, and I wished we could speak mind to mind. Did he have the same dark feeling about why my father's memories were returning as I did? I looked back at Geoffrey. "Were you aware the whole time you were the Green Knight?"

He gave a halting head shake, his body too weak to do it correctly. "Mostly, I was unaware of anything, just emotions. I knew you were in trouble, so I focused on wanting to help you."

"You did," I assured him.

"But so many years—"

"Do you remember, why you left...I mean left my mom...me? What happened?" I asked, needing to know. This grabbed everyone's attention, the show forgotten. The entire coven had helped Jane and Mary lock away my magic and take my memories.

Geoffrey stopped rubbing the green veins and touched a white outline on his left hand. A place for a wedding band. "Your mother, she's gone too? You said that before."

"Not long after you did."

"I told her not to follow me." Frustration and pain filled his voice.

"Well, she did. You both left." I couldn't hide the twinge of anger.

"We didn't leave you, Genny. We were trying to protect you. The memories are hazy, but I know that to be true."

"By disappearing?"

"The Queen's Glamour," he said abruptly, not answering my question. He rubbed the side of his head as if trying to scratch out more memories. "Your mum and I wanted to hide you from fae." He paused. "You're special. They would have stolen you. Used you..." He didn't have to add murder me.

The Queen's Glamour? I remembered Brona had placed one on

me when she'd forced me to go to the Unseelie Court. "How would that help? It doesn't hide you from the fae."

Geoffrey coughed roughly, his face flushing red. When he spoke again, words barely left his chest. "I studied fae artifacts at university. The Queen's Glamour hides the wearer from whatever the person placing the glamour wants. We could have hidden you, and the fae would've never found you." He lifted his hand and scratched at the scraggly beard. "I should groom," he said absently.

"You should rest," I disagreed.

He nodded as his eyelids dropped and his whole body relaxed in the chair like a discarded doll. I thought about moving him, but he'd have more people watching him if he stayed.

Mr. Friedman and Mrs. Liu gave me a guilty look, but I just clicked the sound back on the television.

Aengus heaved to his feet and placed a hand on my shoulder. "Do you see?"

I knew what he meant. He'd noticed the same thing I had. The green veins.

"See what?" Nibs asked, looking from me to Geoffrey and back again from the arm of the chair.

"Yes," I said sadly.

"What do you mean, yes?" Nibs demanded.

Aengus set a comforting palm against the back of Nibs' head and confirmed my worst fear. "The spell is returning."

It made sense. As the spell returned, so did his memories.

Nibs ducked away from Aengus' touch and patted Geoffrey's arm. When my father didn't wake, she looked at me with big wet eyes. I reached out for her, and she climbed into my hands. I cuddled her to my chest and felt her little body shudder. "I need to get Excalibur so I can focus my magic and find a way to fix this permanently."

Aengus nodded.

Logic said showing up at the Seelie Court's front door two days in a row was asking for trouble. But doing my best King Arthur impression and pulling the sword from the flagstones had now become my highest priority.

Chapter Ten

I'd driven us in the van so Aengus wouldn't have to walk in the sunlight, but he still swayed from exhaustion as we stood in the Seelie office foyer. Instead of the smut reading fae I'd spoken to yesterday, Betty met us at the entrance with her familiar haughty stare and bright red lipstick. Her super model body, sheathed in a little black dress, towered over us in three-inch heels, blocking us from moving further inside.

What is the point of heels if you're already a bazillion feet tall?

Behind her, workers in white hazmat suits scrubbed the dark stains on the walls and were rolling up strips of carpet, revealing oil-stained cement beneath. A sauerkraut smell still hung in the air.

Betty flicked her gaze to me, her lip curled.

I tried very hard not to press my arms against my puffy winter jacket to make it look more form fitting. As it was, I couldn't help readjusting the strap on the bag holding Nibs and rewound my scarf to have it drape nicer. If only I had grabbed Excalibur yesterday, then I wouldn't be subjecting myself to unobtainable Seelie beauty standards today.

She turned her attention to Aengus. "The Lady might forgive you for sneaking off, now that you've returned with Theo's attacker," she said.

Aengus wrapped his fingers around my wrist and pulled us both past her. "We do not have time for your interference, Beaticola." Betty's eyes narrowed at what must be her full name, but she stepped out of the way.

Her cultured voice carried down the hall as she alerted Lady Aurnia over the phone intercom. "Sorry to interrupt, but I'm sure you would want to know that Aengus has returned," she paused, "along with the witch girl."

"*Oblatratrix*," Aengus hissed under his breath. Name calling in Latin. Aengus was definitely frustrated. Nibs leaned over the lip of the purse and threw up her middle fingers behind us and I barely stifled a laugh. Where had she picked that up?

"We can't just grab Excalibur and leave now, can we?" I whispered at Aengus.

He stopped and pulled me close, his lips brushing against my ear. I shivered as his warm breath caressed my neck. "When we go in, reveal nothing unless I do so first. Do not speak unless she asks you a direct question. And agree with all that I say."

I pulled back and Aengus released my arm. "That's asking a lot."

A crease formed on his brow as he scowled at the door at the end of the hall. "Trust me," he said, his voice firm yet still quiet. "Oberon will have left her agitated."

Nibs pulled a disgusted face and dipped back into the recesses of the bag. I gazed down the hall at the closed door and then back at Aengus. "As in, King Oberon of the faeries?"

He nodded, "And Aurnia's husband."

"What about Titania? Isn't that his wife?"

"Yes, she is. The fae do not follow human conventions. Wife and husband are not even terms the fae use amongst themselves. Innisfail cannot be without a reigning queen. When Aurnia was forced to remain in this realm, Oberon claimed another wife."

"And Aurnia went to visit Oberon and his new queen? Yeah, I can see why that would put her in a nasty mood," I agreed.

Aengus reached toward me and I placed my hand in his.

Dark oily patches where the fallrot had clung surrounded the now tarnished gilt name plate beside Aurnia's office. Aengus raised his hand to knock, just as Lady Aurnia pulled open the door with an aggressive whoosh.

When last I'd seen her, Aurnia had been draped in faerie ceremonial robes of magenta, today she was back to her pant suit, albeit a bit more rumpled and her makeup smudged. What did it mean that an ancient fae that could control her appearance with a wave of her hand had smudged eyeliner and wrinkled clothes? She eyed both of us shrewdly and without surprise. "Well, isn't this perfect? Two volunteers."

I blinked in confusion. Aengus visibly straightened and shifted so that I was farther behind him. "Volunteers?" he asked, his voice a low rumble.

Lady Aurnia swept her arm out to the side, directing us into the room. Aengus hesitated. She twisted her lips into a dark smile. "Theo is under the weather. Someone will need to take his place." The look she leveled on me nearly sucked out all the air in the room.

Aengus dipped his head, "Of course." He stepped into the office, and I followed.

With the door shut, Aurnia moved around us and grabbed at Aengus's chin. "I can always count on you, Anguselus."

Jealousy fast and hot ripped through me at her use of Aengus's Latin name and my magic flared at the reminder Aurnia had been his lover. She let go before I lost control and either stole her life force as I had Theo or ripped her hand away. Honestly, what had Aengus seen in her?

The office looked mostly the same since I'd been there three months ago. But the massive, cherry wood desk that took up much of the room no longer appeared clean and organized. Now teetering stacks of folders covered the surface, threatening to fall to the floor. I stepped close and looked at the labels, but I couldn't read the language. Aurnia walked around the desk to take her spot behind it. She didn't sit down but continued to stand, her fingers drumming discordantly against the wood. "Another incident has been reported."

"Incident?" I jerked my head up and asked, unable to stop myself.

Aengus gave me a pointed look. I scowled, not liking this plan to stay quiet at all. He touched my hand and leaned in. "She means fae from Innisfail that have entered this realm."

"Fae who won't follow the Seelie rules," Aurnia added.

The way she said *Seelie rules* made me wonder if the Unseelie had their own set of different ones. Nibs shifted at the bottom of the bag. I squeezed the top closed to keep her hidden. I hadn't wanted to bring her, but she insisted on helping Geoffrey. I'd thought we'd be in and out quickly. Ha! What had possessed me to assume anything with the fae would be easy?

Aurnia resettled a shifting pile of folders. "I would normally send *Theo...*" Her voice put emphasis on the name as she glared at me, twisting her lips tight.

She definitely knew it had been me who injured Theo. Maybe Aengus was right about staying quiet. Quiet and invisible sounded like a good plan now.

"I will go," Aengus offered. "But Imogen will only impede my quest. She is untrained and still has no control over her magic."

Wait! I mean I knew it was true, but—

Aurnia lifted her arms, gesturing widely. "So, this mess isn't of her making?"

Aengus dipped his head and sighed deeply before looking back at Aurnia. "She did indeed destroy the fallrot, but as I told you, in so doing nearly killed the Green Knight and your son. She is a danger to herself and others."

My jaw ached with how hard I was biting down, trying desperately to remain quiet. Nibs shuffled in the bag again and this time popped out before I could stop her.

"You take that back!" she raged at Aengus. "Genny's not dangerous. She saved my friend. She's gonna save the oss—"

I cupped my hand around her face, stifling her before she could finish. I had a pretty good notion, Aurnia should not know about the *ossorians* or that I'd somehow bonded with them *or* our deal for me to set them free.

Aurnia ignored Nibs. An instance where Seelie chronic elitism would save our ass. If she didn't think a Brownie would say anything of consequence, we were better off. Her arms crossed over her wrinkled blazer, she shook her head once. "No. You'll both go. And you'll also use this time to figure out how to transfer Excalibur. Have you discovered anything useful among Gaius's books and papers?" She pinned Aengus with a pointed look.

He shook his head. "No, not as yet."

Would she be able to tell he was lying?

Aurnia tilted her head. "My patience is coming to an end." Luckily, she sounded frustrated and not angry, proving her belief in Aengus's lie.

He gave a small bow. "I will look harder."

Aurnia turned from him to this time skewer me with her sharp gaze. "Saoirse threatens war unless the Green Knight is returned to her. What exactly did you do?"

"His name is Geoffrey," Nibs yelled from the bottom of my bag.

We needed Aurnia's help to close the veil, just as she had over a thousand years prior. Whether it was a matter of "keep your enemies closer" or "the enemy of my enemy is my friend", the wellbeing of this realm required Aurnia's trust, so I gave her the truth. "I stole the life energy from the fallrot and I pushed the spell back." Aengus stiffened, but I kept going. "It's not something I could do again, and it's not permanent. The Green Knight will return."

Aurnia appeared relieved, although I wondered if I imagined that she seemed a bit unnerved by my ability. "I'll speak with Saoirse. And Theo?"

"An accident." Aengus chimed in and I nodded in agreement,

even though part of me wanted to tell her I'd almost sucked him dry on purpose. But friends, and certainly frenemies, don't like it when you suck the life from their children, even if their child is a serious douche canoe. "What happened with Theo proves Imogen's magic is too unreliable."

"The welfare of wayward fae is of no concern to me," Aurnia said without compassion. "Therefore, she seems like the perfect choice to go with you."

Aengus scrubbed his hands over his face, letting out a guttural complaint, before he seemed to resign himself to my going and asked, "And where was this incident?"

"Pyramid Lake."

Chapter Eleven

The landscape rushed past the windows as I drove east on I-80, steep stark hills of striated colors on the left and the lush green of the Truckee River's valley below on the right. Overhead, a dome of gray clouds threatened snow, but the weather app claimed it wouldn't fall until tomorrow morning.

Not wanting Everett to be without the van, Aurnia tasked a trell to drive it back to the retirement home, and then handed us the keys to Theo's truck. For being a lifted monstrosity with wheels the size of ponies, the cab felt cramped. Aengus took up all of the passenger side and some of the middle as he leaned against the cab door, his trench coat pulled up and over his head like a cape and cowl to hide from the daylight, his face just peeking out from under the heavy fabric, his lashes resting against his cheeks. I'd almost mentioned his seatbelt when he'd first settled in, but realized that a 1400 year old vampire didn't need me as a helicopter parent.

Although, part of me wished I could have forced Aengus to accept Lady Aurnia's offer of blood before we'd left.

There was certainly an ick factor surrounding the thought of him drinking blood, and nothing made me happy about his reliance on that family, but I'd rather him take a bite of her wrist then go all wild beast while we were out in the middle of nowhere. Aengus had waved away my concern, saying he was certain he'd be fine for another day at least.

I looked up at the cloud cover again and frowned.

Despite Aengus curling up to sleep through the trip, it was anything but quiet. My patience flagged the longer Nibs sat on the dashboard, pointed out things we passed. We were at ten red-tailed hawks, three coyotes, and one frantic jack rabbit. She even made me stop, with cars flying by at eighty miles an hour, when a herd of woolly mustangs stood along the roadside munching on scrub grass.

It took many promises of future clothes shopping trips and sugary confections to convince her that one, we had no way to bring a horse home. And two, we had nowhere to keep it either.

It took all my self-control not to snap at the Brownie, whose only fault was her unrelenting excitement regarding new things. I sighed in relief when she curled onto my lap to nap.

Miracle of miracles, she even stayed asleep when later the stiff suspension had us bouncing like we'd traveled over a boulder instead of a small pothole. Excalibur, propped up between Aengus and I, clunked against the back window. If it was anyone else's vehicle, I would've worried the glass would break. Since it was Theo's, I secretly hoped it would shatter. All the dead fallrot had been scraped from its surface, but the aroma of rotting plant still clung to the metal and scented the trapped air in the cab. My palms smelled awful from carrying it, and I feared it would never go away.

Just as I took Exit 43 towards Wadsworth, Aengus shifted in his seat and let out a long sigh. I glanced over. His sleep-heavy golden eyes and gentle smile gave him a peaceful look I'd never seen him make before. My cheeks flushed as I smiled and I looked back at the road to hide it. "Will you be okay? We still have a little ways to go."

I heard him shift his coat away. "I have rested and the sun is behind clouds."

"No sparkling today," I teased, shooting him a quick glance.

When he looked confused, I shook my head. "Don't worry about it. Silly joke."

He squinted out the windshield and pointed at the passing landscape. "This is the reservation where those who lived on this land first were placed?"

"Forced not placed. And yes."

"Your country's destruction of its native people reminds me in a small way of what Gwynevere's ancestors endured under the legions," Aengus said.

"Really?" My curiosity piqued.

"Her mother was Pict. Or at least that is what the Romans called them."

"Gwynevere was Pict. I always liked that theory, I'm glad to know it's true."

"Yes, her mother was sister to kings."

I wanted to ask more questions, but in the distance, a sliver of blue twinkled across the horizon. We were nearing Pyramid Lake.

Turning off the main road, the growl of the grated road beneath the wheels made any further talking impossible. The clouds sank closer and darkened as wind whipped up the dust from the surrounding scrub and slammed grit and tumble weeds against the side of the truck. I held the wheel with white knuckles, hoping a gust didn't flip us.

Sandhole Beach was easy to spot with all the vehicles. Lady Aurnia said we'd be met by the tribal police, but I hadn't expected what looked like a full-on murder investigation with police tape cordoning off most of the waterfront. A blue tarp, covering a section of ground, flapped against the large stones placed to hold it. Four figures stood near, three appearing to be in uniform.

Nibs woke up and balanced herself on the wheel to look out as I parked the monster truck off to the side next to a marked vehicle. She hopped onto my lap and started to make her way down off the seat to the floorboard. I opened the cab door and pointed to the three-foot drop. "How do you plan to get down?"

Nibs rolled her eyes. "You'll help."

"Okay, but how do you plan on not getting snatched up by all those hawks and coyotes you saw on the way here?" I pointed outward, partly joking, but also kind of worried a tasty Nibs treat might prove too irresistible to the local wildlife.

Her little ears twitched as she scanned the skies. "I will ride in your bag."

"Good idea," I said hiding my smirk.

As I helped Nibs into the bag, Aengus opened his door and stepped down from the truck. I followed a moment later. The wind that only moments ago might have flipped a semi, dropped away suddenly leaving the air heavy and still. Weather app, shmeather app, the storm was coming much quicker than tomorrow, but since we had already arrived, there wasn't any harm in seeing what we could do. We would just need to leave before the snow started to fall.

Before I closed my own door, I reached behind the seat to pull out an umbrella I'd snatched from the foyer coat stand at the Seelie Court. I met Aengus as he stepped around the tailgate. "Here, this might help." I held it out, and he hesitated before slowly reaching for it, confused. "It's like a tent you carry around. To protect you from the rain or the sun."

He chortled as he looked up at me. "I am familiar with the device; I have just never had someone anticipate my needs before."

"Wait, no one? That can't be right." I stared at Aengus. He came from a harsher past, but everyone had someone that took care of them. Parents. A friend. A lover. Could he really have been so alone?

"Genny? What are you doing here?" someone called my name.

I turned as my boss Diana dipped under the police tape by the shore of the lake and strode toward me. I rushed to meet her halfway. "What are *you* doing here?" I echoed her words back.

Diana had traded her stilettos for boots with a wider heel and her skirt and blazer for jeans and a thick jacket. She eyed Aengus with a narrowed gaze, but turned back to me to answer, "I'm here to help my grandfather."

I looked past her toward the water and noted one of the uniformed was an older gentleman with long gray hair in a low ponytail that reached midway down his back.

Diana gave a weak smile. "Normally, I'd love to see you, but we have a situation."

I wasn't sure what to do. Lady Aurnia had ordered us to the lake and yet I couldn't go off spouting about the fae and how there was an open veil between the human realm and faerie letting in dangerous creatures. For one, Diana wouldn't believe it and second, I really wanted to keep my internship. Trust me, talking about things that "aren't there" erodes confidence in a person's mental stability. "We're here to help." That seemed safe enough.

"How did you even know to come here?" Diana warily eyed Aengus again.

I tried to smile. "We were sent." Staying vague.

Diana pinched her nose and sighed. "I'm not going to try and figure out why you and your boyfriend are here, but you're going to have to leave."

"Oh, he's not," I quickly pointed at Aengus and then myself. "We're not. I mean who wouldn't want to, he's you know, but we aren't together. We're not?" I looked over at Aengus suddenly unsure of what I was saying. He raised an eyebrow and smirked. I felt heat rise from my toes to the top of my head, my cheeks hot with it. I took a deep breath, straightened my shoulders, and turned my gaze back to Diana. "What I mean is, please trust that we're really here to help."

Diana let her head slowly tilt in confusion.

From under the police tape, the man I'd assumed was Diana's grandfather exited and moved toward us. "Who do we have here, *to go'o?*" he called.

When he reached us, she pointed at me. "This is Genny Wylde. She works at the museum and this is..." She trailed off as she pointed to Aengus.

Aengus brought his fist clutching the umbrella to his chest and gave a slight bow to them both. "Hail, I am Aengus"

Nibs, finished rearranging the items in my bag to her liking, poked her head out. "I'm Nibs!"

Diana took a large intake of breath, but her grandfather just chuckled and said, "Pleasure to meet you Nibs."

"Nibs!" I hissed. "What have I told you about showing yourself to people?"

"She did nothing wrong. We can see her just fine," Diana's grandfather said.

I blinked, letting his words repeat in my head. They could see Nibs? Diana could see Nibs? My boss, the person I'd been lying through my teeth to from the moment I started at the museum, could see Nibs? Why was I the last to know everything? I flung my arms out wide and sighed in annoyance. "Is anyone who they say they are? Well, I guess I can tell you why we're really here then."

Diana and her grandfather, named Eugene, led us to the edge of the tarp.

Eugene crouched and drew the edge back to reveal what lay beneath.

For a moment, I couldn't understand what I was looking at. A small body lay on the rocky beach, its form plump and round like a toddler, but its face appeared lined and weathered, with dark hair draped down its form like strips of seaweed. One arm lay out away from the body, displaying a raised welt like symbol—a spiral with a straight line starting from the middle and traveling down past the last circle.

I'd seen that mark before. On Aengus.

Nibs sighed deeply. "Poor water baby."

Anyone who'd lived in Nevada long enough knew about "water babies." Campers and hikers claimed to have heard their mewling, infant-like cries while staying near lakes, especially Pyramid. They were even said to pull the occasional swimmer down beneath the water to drown them.

Eugene noted my expression. "The symbol is familiar to you?"

I looked to Aengus who nodded and dragged up the sleeve on his own arm to show off a matching branded scar.

"That you both should have this mark—is it a message? A warning, maybe even a threat?" Eugene asked as he slipped on a blue glove and ran a finger over the mark on the water baby's arm.

"I do not know," Aengus answered. He yanked back down his sleeve. "The only message in this mark is ownership."

From the clouds above, fat, cotton ball shaped snowflakes started to fall, quickly building up upon the shore. Eugene stood up, removing the glove. He motioned to the two other officers that stood off to the side. "You two, go back to the station. This is faerie business. I need you to call this in as a false alarm. I'll take the body with me. I've got someone I want to have a look."

The two men didn't argue. One lifted a radio from its holder on his shoulder and called in a code. From his wrist, dangled a leather thong bracelet with a charm—a *sul aos si* talisman. I looked for another on the other officer and found it as well. At least that explained how they could see everything. The two men acknowledged us with a nod and then both trudged through the falling snow and got into one of the marked vehicles.

Eugene pulled the tarp back over the body and rose haltingly to his feet. I heard his knees cracking from where I stood. Diana and Eugene wore no obvious bracelets or necklaces, I wondered what fae blood was in their past?

I shook the wet blanket of snow that had already built up on my head. Aengus popped open the umbrella and held it over me. "I brought that for you," I said.

He shrugged. "And I am using it."

Diana leaned toward Aengus, scrutinizing him again from beanie to boot as snow settled on her like falling ash. "We've never met?"

"No, my lady."

Diana rolled her eyes and huffed. "My lady is it?"

I laughed. "Trust me, he's being genuine for a guy from his time."

Diana stiffened and looked concerned. "His time?" She narrowed her gaze on Aengus. "What have you pulled Genny into?"

"Nothing of what she was not already aware," Aengus answered calmly.

I gave him the side-eye. "Maybe not completely aware. I was doing a pretty good job of not getting neck deep in crazy before you showed up."

At least he had the decency to look guilty.

Diana smirked. "You did still have a reputation, but you were very good at avoiding. I took a chance that you were more than that."

"Wait, did you hire me because of the fact that people said I was weird?"

Diana shrugged. "Partly, but I also thought you were perfect for the internship."

I thought back to our previous conversations with new knowledge. Open-ended questions. Leading topics. Dozens of opportunities I could have given more and I always evaded. Well, the Nibs was out of the bag, now. I smiled at Diana. "So, you're *custos*, too?"

Eugene scoffed, his words hardened with old anger. "No. We would never claim that title. We aren't the ones who make a habit of taking children from their families."

I shivered both from the cold and the sickening reality of what his words represented. Suddenly, I wondered how many families had actually wanted to send their half fae children off to be *custos*.

His expression lightened as he explained further. "That I have the sight is rare, that my granddaughter has it too, is rarer still, but the fae have been known to us for centuries."

"But the sight is inherited, right?" I looked at Aengus for assurance. Why would it be rare?

Diana brushed the collected snow from her hair and shoulders.

"As enlightening as this discussion is, we should all head home before this storm gets worse."

Eugene pointed to Aengus's arm where the mark lay beneath his sleeve. "Indulge me a moment more. I have questions."

I agreed, the matching brand was odd and concerning, but there would be no way we'd outrun the storm if we didn't leave now.

A cacophony of splashes pulled our attention toward the lake. From the water, through a curtain of snowfall, a very large horse-like creature thundered onto shore, letting out an inhuman scream.

Chapter Twelve

The corpse-gray horse creature steamed in the cold air as snow landed and melted upon its hide. A steady plop of water fell from its mane like a drippy faucet. With a snort, the creature pawed a ragged hoof against the stony beach, knee joints green with mold. Then it raised its head, opening its mouth, showing off pointed teeth made for tearing meat gleaming like polished bone as it screamed again, the sound filling the air like tiny sharp daggers scraping over the eardrum.

All four of us froze.

"A kelpie," Eugene whispered in awe.

Not taking my eyes off the creature, I slowly leaned close to Aengus and whispered, "Kelpies eat people, right?" I'd read about kelpies at some point. I remembered the salient details. Namely, if someone touched a kelpie, their hand became glued to the hide and the kelpie would drag them under the water to drown and then eat them.

I looked down at the tarp. Not too unlike the legend of the water babies.

"Usually," Aengus agreed absently. He cocked his head to the side as he stared at the kelpie. "But maybe not this one." He threw a mischievous smile my way and pushed the umbrella handle into my hands. Before I realized what he planned, he'd already jogged off toward the pawing and snorting murder horse.

"Wait! What do mean not this one? How do you know that?" I called. He didn't answer. "Aengus what are you doing?"

He paused a foot from the kelpie. Well within striking range of teeth and hoof.

"Son," Eugene called out, "this is not how you want to die."

"Bad horse!" Nibs screeched, her body hanging half out of the bag.

Aengus held out his palm. The kelpie shuffled its feet nervously. Its head bobbed twice, letting out a snort before shaking its entire body, water droplets flying in all directions. Aengus stayed perfectly still. With a final snort, the kelpie placed its muzzle into Aengus's waiting hand.

No one moved.

Diana, Eugene, Nibs, and I all sucked in a scared breath, holding it tight as Aengus raised his other hand and rubbed the kelpie's forehead. Instead of dragging him to his death, it nickered, the soft sound muted in the snowfall. We all expelled the air from our lungs in relief.

Aengus turned to walk back toward us and the water horse followed like a Labrador, lipping its wet muzzle against Aengus's fingers. Aengus smiled like he'd been given the very best gift at Christmas. "This is Amicus. We met a very long time ago." He placed his hand on the kelpie's damp neck, the mane dripping water onto his sleeve.

Eugene spoke first. "Why has your dangerous friend come here?" he pointed at the tarp. "Was it your friend who harmed our spirit?"

Aengus stared deeply into the kelpie's closest inky, black eye. "Amicus, what happened?" The kelpie snorted and pawed at the ground. He dropped his head away from Aengus's gaze then lifted it again. Aengus softly patted his neck. "All is well," he whispered.

Aengus pointed to the tarp. "He says that smells like a carnivore, almost like dog, but different. Not like one of your spirits."

Diana lifted the tarp off the body once more, her expression one of disbelief. "A dog?"

The body of the water baby still lay there unchanged. I glanced at Aengus and then down at Nibs. "Is there a glamour on it?"

Nibs leaned forward, squinting her eyes. She nodded as she settled back into the bag. "Very strong."

Aengus rubbed his chin, shocked. "Damn my eyes, whoever created the glamour was truly powerful. We all missed it."

"But why? For what purpose?" Diana asked what I considered the right question.

Eugene hummed and tapped his thumb against his leg in contemplation. He looked at Aengus. "It seems who I really must speak to is not you, after all."

Aengus eyed Eugene curiously. "You know who would do this?"

The old man's shoulders drooped and he sighed. "Yes, but we won't make it to their ranch with this storm."

Diana touched her grandfather's arm. "*To go'o?*" Her tone was unsure and questioning.

He reached over and patted her hand. "Besides, the druid can't stay hidden forever," Eugene answered enigmatically.

Diana frowned.

The kelpie screamed, startling everyone. We slapped our hands over our ears against its piercing volume.

"Yes, yes, go back in the water," Aengus said, waving the kelpie towards the lake. "We will speak again, my friend." The kelpie pushed his head into Aengus's chest and he stumbled, scratching between its wet ears with a laugh. With a pivot on its haunches, the kelpie spun away to gallop back to the water. Its feet kicking up pebbles in our direction, causing everyone to move from protecting their ears to protecting their faces.

"Bad horse!" Nibs screamed after it.

"What was that about?" I asked, dropping my hands from my face when the kelpie disappeared below the lake's surface.

"The desert air starts to dry him out," Aengus explained.

The snow which had been drifting down like graceful white feathers, began to fall harder and faster. The wind from earlier returned, causing a white curtain to obscure everything beyond a foot in front of us.

Eugene pointed at Aengus. "Son, would you put the body in my truck bed?" Aengus dipped his head, then bent to wrap the body in the tarp like a burrito, lifting it into his arms. He pushed into the wind toward the general direction of where everyone had parked. We all followed close behind him.

After he set it down, Eugene slammed the tailgate closed. "Let's get to my place before we're stuck out here. We've got plenty of food and beds. Tomorrow we will take a drive."

Chapter Thirteen

My stomach warm and full of Eugene's wife's homemade chili almost made up for fact that we were snowed in and unable to go home. Already, over a foot of snow covered the ground, and the storm didn't appear to be stopping. It had taken an hour just to get a few miles down the road.

I eyed critically the travel trailer Aengus and I had been led to. Definitely not what I'd imagined when Eugene had claimed they had "plenty" of beds. He and his wife lived in a small two-bedroom house. Their second bedroom was currently being used by Diana and by their blue heeler, BeeBee and her new litter of seven day old puppies. That second bedroom was also Nib's current location. She'd waved us away as she'd crawled into the whelping box and waded into the cuddle puddle of puppies who whined and rooted around her.

The travel trailer on Eugene's side drive had two full tanks of propane in the front and an extension cord plugged into an outside outlet for power. Diana had turned the knobs clockwise on the tanks outside, releasing the gas, and then led us inside to light the furnace pilot. The tiny trailer had a full bed on one end and the bathroom on the other, with a minuscule kitchen and table in between. Diana pointed to the table. "That turns into a bed, too." She squeezed past us to leave, but paused, giving me a look. "I've slept on that table bed, it's barely better than the floor. I've got a queen size if you don't want to stay out here. Plenty of room for both of us."

I thought about hearing whining puppies all night and glanced at Aengus trying to turn on the overhead light and failing. "No, that's okay, but thanks." Diana nodded. She reached up and switched on the light for him and wished us "goodnight" before she headed back to the house, her footprints already disappearing as the snow filled them.

Now alone, I turned and nearly ran into Aengus's chest.

"Tight quarters," he said smiling.

I turned sideways, moving past him to take a seat on the edge of the bed. "Very cozy," I agreed. Aengus didn't sit down next to me but settled onto one of the table benches. I pointed. "Should we convert that to a bed?"

Aengus looked at the table dubiously.

"Not actually sure how it works though," I admitted with a shrug.

The furnace continued to blow out hot air, quickly heating up the one room. I removed my coat and Aengus did as well, heaping them onto the tabletop. I imagined a large clock ticking away minutes as we both sat in uncomfortable silence. At the same time, we both blurted out a sentence.

"We should talk about that kiss—" I said.

"Do you believe Excalibur should be left in the truck—" Aengus asked.

I answered Aengus as if I hadn't spoken. "It's fine. No one's looking in car windows in this weather." Truthfully, I wasn't 100% sure no one would try to take it, but it would be super heavy for them and if the weight didn't deter them, the smell would. It's the main reason I didn't want to bring it into the trailer.

"And the kiss?" Aengus prompted when I continued to pretend I hadn't spoken.

"Right." I took a deep breath. "About that, I'm sorry I just grabbed you. My magic was really overwhelming, and I needed a distraction...which is not an excuse. I should have controlled myself. So, I'm sorry."

Aengus raised his eyebrows and gave me the oddest look. "Do you believe you made unwanted advances?"

"Maybe? I certainly didn't ask," I answered, feeling uncomfortable and a little queasy.

"There was nothing unwanted." His eyes darkened, and my entire body zinged with electricity, then he looked away. "Just impossible," he whispered.

"Impossible?"

He ran a rough hand through his curls and turned to me. "I will not, I cannot abandon another."

When he didn't continue, I softy prompted, "Is that what happened? With Elaine?"

Aengus clenched his jaw and his hand gripped the table tight enough that I feared he might actually break it. "I knew of her sadness and yet I left," he said, barely getting his words out. "When Gwyn and Arthur called for aid, I abandoned her without hesitation. Part of me even felt relief at being free of her melancholy." His eyes found mine. "I will not do the same to another."

I stood up. "Wait. Are you saying you won't get close to me because you think if you return to your tomb I'll become so distraught I'll do something drastic?"

"No if—when."

I threw my hands in the air. "I call bullshit!"

Aengus blinked.

I held up a splayed hand and tapped my forefinger. "First, your girlfriend didn't end her life because you left. I'm not going to lie and say she wouldn't have liked you to stay. Of course, she would, but suicide? That's not a reasonable response. Elaine needed a healthy dose of therapy and likely medication, the kind that wouldn't exist for over a thousand years. You are not responsible for her death. But second," I tapped my middle finger before I placed both hands on my hips, "you don't get to make decisions for me based on your trauma."

"My trauma?"

"Yes! What you went through was horrible, but that doesn't mean you get to project what happened to Elaine on me. If—and I still want to believe we'll find another way—but if you have to return to that tomb with Excalibur, I'll be upset. I'll scream. I'll cry. Dishware may be thrown, but I won't break." I dropped down on the edge of the bed and the whole trailer shuddered. "You can stay away from me because you need to protect yourself, or you don't feel the same, but you don't get to make decisions for me."

Seconds, ticked by like hours. I refused to look Aengus in the face until he stood up, his whole body leaning toward me. "You believe I hold back because I do not desire you?"

"I don't know what you feel."

He leaned in closer, his knee lifting to rest next to my leg, the feel of the fabric of our pants rubbing sending shivers up to the base of my skull. He lifted his hands to cup my face and heat like a flash bomb raced outward from every point of his touch. I sucked in a breath as his lips parted and his pupils widened, becoming dark pools. Slowly, he leaned down, only closing his eyes right before his lips brushed mine. I closed mine a second later.

His dry, soft lips lingered and his warm breath mingled with my own when we pulled back, staring into each other's eyes.

"I will leave you." Aengus rested his forehead against mine.

I arched my back and lightly grabbed his bottom lip in my teeth, giving it a light tug. "Well then, wouldn't you like something to dream about in that musty old tomb?"

Aengus groaned. "You steal my willpower."

I reached up and wrapped my arms around his chest pulling him closer. We fell back against the bed. Aengus dropped his hands from my face, one falling beside my head to prop him up and the other skimming down my body to grab my knee, pulling my leg up against him. Aengus captured my moan with a deep kiss, his tongue dancing with mine.

Fumbling, I pulled up on his shirt, my fingers finding warm skin beneath. His whole body shivered as my fingers skimmed along his abs. Breaking away from my lips, he reached over his shoulder and yanked his shirt up and over his head, tossing it back toward the table. I grinned as I ran my hands up the plane of his chest and over his shoulders, remembering his almost comedic lack of shirt when we'd first met. Desire punched through me, stealing my breath as I touched him the way I'd wanted to do then.

Out of the corner of my eye, the angry red brand on his arm caused me to pull back. I lightly ran my fingers over the welted skin. Aengus reached over and placed a hand on top of mine, halting my movement. "No harm will come to you," he assured me, not understanding my hesitation.

"It's not that," I said, pulling myself up to sitting. "Before you mentioned your body not being your own. I know I was pushing about not letting what happened to Elaine stop you, but if you have other reasons why you don't want to do this. I understand."

Aengus drew my hand to his lips, kissing it gently. "Seeing to my needs once more," he said with a smile. "But what I need," he paused and ran his gaze along the length of my body and when his eyes found mine again, they were filled with hunger, "is you."

A flame ignited my own furnace pilot within me. I yanked at my shirt, pulling it over my head. With a look of awe, Aengus marveled at my completely boring white t-shirt bra. Delicately, he ran the back of two fingers down my strap and over the cup. I bit my lip as my whole body shivered.

Knock! Knock!

At the sound of the knock at the door, Aengus and I leaped apart, Aengus hitting his head against the low ceiling over the bed.

"Genny?" Diana called from outside. "There's been an incident."

An incident? Like a dangerous fae coming through the veil incident? I grabbed my shirt, pulling it on, Aengus doing the same. I moved to the door and opened it. Diana stood in the snow with a sobbing Nibs cradled in her coat. Her eyebrow quirked, and I wondered if she knew what she'd interrupted. My face flushed.

"What happened?" I asked, reaching out for the Brownie. Nibs scrambled into my arms and I instantly noticed she wasn't dressed in the same outfit she'd had on. Instead, she wore what looked like a sock with a head and arm holes cut out. Oh dear. I had a feeling I already knew what Diana was going to say.

But before Diana could speak, Nibs screeched, "They pooed on me!"

"The puppies?" I asked. Nibs sniffled and nodded. I tried not to laugh.

Diana zipped up her now empty coat. "I scrubbed her outfit and hung it to dry, but she wanted you. Sorry." She looked between both Aengus and I when she apologized, her expression blank, but her eyes danced with withheld laughter.

She definitely knew.

The top of my head felt like it was on fire. "No, I'm glad you brought her, thanks."

"Okay," she said with a wave. "See you in the morning."

I closed the door and turned back around. Aengus's shirt was on inside out and backward. Diana was a saint for not saying a word.

Chapter Fourteen

Nibs squealed in excitement as Eugene slowed his police truck and snow cascaded down from the roof over the windshield. She clapped her hands together when the wipers swished and pushed it off to the side. "Again!" she cried. "Do it again." Her clothes, a pink sweater and pants made of fabric printed to look like jean material, had successfully dried, and the poo incident appeared forgotten. She'd even given each of the seven puppies a kiss goodbye.

Aengus, seated on the passenger side, looked over his arm stretched across the back of the seat and winked.

From the back seat, I smiled and hoped it didn't look weird. I didn't know what to do with this whimsical side of Aengus. I'd gotten used to the stoic and driven Aengus. But since this morning he'd woken and without hesitation, he'd leaned over the sleeping ball of Nibs between us and kissed me good morning as if we'd been waking up next to each other for months. The smile stretching across his face as he pulled back had squeezed the air from my lungs. Was this the Aengus that Gwynevere and Arthur knew? Carefree? Before everything happened?

We hadn't planned on not returning to town last night and I worried maybe he suffered from a lack of Honeythorn blood, but he'd waved it away, even declining to take the backseat to hide from the sunlight and sleep. I tried not to let it worry me.

Leaning forward, Excalibur slid down toward my knees. Thankfully, the smell had lessened considerably. "Who are we seeing again?" I asked.

Diana wasn't even allowed to come. I'd heard her question Eugene about it as we'd gotten our boots and coats on. Her voice tight, she'd asked, "How is staying here helping? I thought you were retiring?"

"You are and I am. I will speak to them. These things take time. The druid can't be rushed," Eugene explained in a voice that told me they'd had this conversation before.

When Aengus heard "druid" he'd stood up straight. "We shall bring Excalibur. I have questions, and this druid may help."

"Fine. Fine." Eugene answered.

And that's why the sword was with us and Diana wasn't. Eugene chanced a quick glance over his shoulder at me as he drove before he answered my question. "It's best if I let the two of them explain. It's not my place to tell their secrets."

I sat back and ran a hand over the blade. Would a druid truly be able to help return Excalibur to Aengus? For a moment, the memory of Aengus's hand across my skin from hip to neck made me shiver. Would anyone notice if I tossed the sword out the window and pretended I had no idea what happened? I desperately needed another way to close the veil.

Another mile down the road, we pulled up to a gate with barbed wire fencing stretching out into the distance on either side. Beyond the fence, snow-covered mountains edged the view and smaller hillocks, drifts covering their sagebrush like white mushroom caps, dotted the landscape.

The pristine snow covered road stretching out past the gate could only be distinguished by the dip of the ditches on either side. Eugene took the truck straight down the middle, barely going above fifteen miles an hour, and we could all feel the wheels occasionally slip and lose traction.

Parallel lines of lonely vehicle tracks stretched out behind us as we neared a large Spanish hacienda looking house, with red tile roof and stucco siding and two substantial livestock paddocks on either side of road. Three black cows, a llama, and a donkey munched on a mound of hay on one side and on the other, a herd of horses varying in size from only a few feet tall to massive draft size mingled on the other. Their dark tracks in the snow giving the illusion they walked on a floor of cookies and cream ice cream.

At the end of the drive, Eugene parked the truck directly in front of the house. A red barn rose out of the white just beyond the hacienda and off to the right stood a greenhouse with a foot deep drift covering the roof.

Even through the closed windows of the truck, I clearly heard music blaring across the property. We opened our doors, and the sound intensified. Nibs pulled her long ears in against the side of her head. "What is it?" she whined, as she slipped into one of Aengus's deep trench coat pockets to hide from the sound. Aengus placed a hand against the pocket to secure the Nib-sized lump. He then stepped down out of the cab onto the packed snow.

"I think it's disco," I answered, slamming my door and resting Excalibur's blade flat against my shoulder. "Really bad disco."

Behind us, an unknown voice yelled over the music, "I personally miss his obsession with jazz."

We all turned.

A man, pointed ears visible on either side of high cheekbones, pulled his hand out of the pocket of his puffy winter jacket and waved. "Hello. Welcome."

A fae? I don't know why I was surprised. But what struck me more was his resemblance to Lady Aurnia. If he took his long chestnut braid and wound it into an updo, they'd look similar enough to be twins. I moved to Aengus's side and leaned close. "He looks like—"

"I know," Aengus agreed without needing me to finish.

The fae moved toward the house's main entrance, bounding up the icy stairs like a ballet dancer. "Come inside where it's warm. Dan should be in from the greenhouse soon." He paused at the door. "That's who you came to see, correct?"

"Yes," Eugene answered. He pointed to the back of the truck. "We have something I want him to take a look at. But the young lady with the sword should probably speak with you, Cathal."

"Me?" The fae, Cathal, sounded completely dumbfounded.

"Her last name is Wylde," Eugene said, clearly knowing it would mean something to the fae.

Cathal's eyes widened, and he stared at me hard, a ghost of a smile on his face.

I, Aengus, with Nibs in pocket, and Eugene gingerly made our way up the steps. Cathal opened the door, ushering us into the foyer. When the thick wooden door closed, the disco music finally faded to a low hum. "You may hang your coats here," Cathal said, pointing to an antique hall tree with empty hooks.

Shrugging Excalibur off my shoulder, I looked for a place to rest it, finally plopping it into the attached umbrella basket. After removing my coat and scarf, I reached out to Nibs, pulling her from Aengus's pocket, so he could remove his trench coat, too.

Holding the Brownie, I peered into the room off to the right. Large, mismatched furniture, draped in quilts and crocheted blankets, filled the space. Dim winter sunlight shone through the windows, making the nicked and rubbed wood glow. An open, tattered leather book lay face down on the couch, waiting. I desired to go pick it up, snuggle into the cushion, and never leave such a cozy room.

The moment Aengus dropped his trench onto a hook, Nibs reached out her arms toward him. With a bemused expression, he obliged.

"A Brownie," Cathal said, his tone not censored but definitely surprised. He pointed to Aengus. "Is it yours?"

Nibs dropped her ears straight behind her like an angry cat and glared, "Nobody owns Nibbleink!"

"Yeah, Nibs is her own—" I was going to say person but landed on, "being. She doesn't belong to anyone."

"Of course, my apologies. I've been secluded from court life for," Cathal paused, eyeing Aengus before turning his gaze back to Nibs, "a very long time."

Nibs huffed and shrugged. This Cathal would have to do a lot more to win her over. From experience, Nibs was a champion grudge holder.

"While we wait for Dan, can I offer anyone some tea or coffee?" Cathal asked, leading us toward the back of the house.

Four mugs of freshly made coffee steamed before us on the table nestled in the kitchen alcove. Just like the front room, the kitchen felt more suited to an English cottage than a modern home complete with a wood stove radiating heat. Above the U-shaped butcher-block counters, pots and pans hung like a musical instrument waiting to be played and below numerous open jars of utensils and canisters of unknown food stuffs ran along the backsplash.

I paused with my mug halfway to my mouth and stared aghast at Cathal, unable to comprehend what he'd just said. "Wait. You're my great-great-grandfather?" I finally croaked.

Nibs rested the spoonful of honey in her cheek Cathal had given her as an apology and scrunched up her face as she looked from both me to Cathal.

Cathal counted on his fingers. "One more "great", I believe."

Aengus lowered his mug from taking a sip and leaned close to me. He'd picked the chair farthest from the morning light. "That explains where your sight comes from."

I frowned, ignoring him, and stared at Cathal. "When? How?"

The fae pushed wisps of curly chestnut hair away from his face, as he looked out the bay window behind us. His lips raised in an almost smile, but his eyes appeared glassy with a hint of tears. "That is a story I lack the courage to tell."

Eugene laughed, breaking the heavy mood. He placed a hand on my shoulder. "Don't feel bad. Cathal has yet to tell me the story of my ancestor and he loved my grandmother nearly a thousand years ago."

Cathal rubbed his nose and sniffed as he turned away from the window. "I'll not apologize for keeping my stories."

I wondered if that was why the sight was rare in Eugene's family. Maybe the magic was too far back.

The front door banged open, and a voice called out. "Hally, do we have guests?"

"In here," Cathal answered.

Footsteps echoed through the house until he reached us. From his scraggly gray stubble to his threadbare khaki cargo pants, he looked nothing like any druid I'd have ever dreamed up.

Cathal pointed to me, then Aengus, "Dan, meet Imogen Wylde and Aengus. The Brownie is Nibbleink," Nibs saluted with her nearly empty spoon, "and you know Eugene."

Dan removed his dirt caked gloves and slapped them on the counter. He wiped his palms down his chest before reaching out to shake hands. "Pleasure," he said, his voice jovial and deep. He gave Cathal a friendly elbow in the side. "Got any more of your kids out there to show up at our doorstep?"

Cathal huffed, "To be fair, I only had two children. I had no control over what they did with their life after."

Dan grinned, clearly satisfied with his goading. They were like an old married couple. I got the impression they'd known each other for quite some time. "So, what can I do you all for?"

Eugene stood, and we quickly followed him to our feet. Eugene pointed toward the front door. "It's best you see for yourself."

Leaving Excalibur resting in the umbrella rack, we all bundled up in our coats once more. Nibs elected to stay on the table with another spoonful of honey. She was going to milk Cathal's guilt for all the sugar he was worth. We stomped across our previous footprints to the back of the truck. Dan and Cathal leaned over the side as Eugene pulled back the tarp.

"A water baby," Cathal said in surprise.

Aengus stepped close, dragging up his sleeve to give a full view of his arm. "Yes, but why is it branded with the sigil of House Honeythorn?"

Cathal looked from Aengus's mark to the matching one on the small, gray corpse in shock.

Dan, however, seemed pleased. "Worked like a charm, or in this case, like a glamour."

Chapter Fifteen

Eugene stared wide-eyed in disbelief at Dan. "You had something to do with this? But why?"

Dan laughed, seemingly oblivious to the older man's reaction. "Oh, it's not a water baby, I'd never hurt those adorable menaces." He pointed at the body. "It's just a bit of razzle dazzle." Dan looked exceedingly pleased, as he leaned against the side and waved a hand over the body. The illusion dissolved like a ripple over a still pool, leaving in its place a very dead coyote. "Infection got this one. Poor thing."

Aengus pointed down at the half-desiccated canid. "We knew it was glamoured. What we want to know is why?"

Cathal slammed a hand down on the truck bed wall, stunning all of us into silence. "For what purpose would you do such a thing?"

In an instant, Dan's face went from pleased to serious. "Because it's time, Hally." He reached out and gripped Cathal's shoulder. "You've served me well for millennia, but now there's..." the druid looked at the ground with a pinched expression. He seemed to fighting to find the right words. "Well, there's just something different. I think you need to go home."

Cathal sighed deeply and looked toward the sky. "Not this again," he mumbled.

"What do you mean 'again'?" Eugene asked as he pulled the tarp back over the body, which I appreciated. Where the glamour had made the water baby seem merely sleeping, the rictus grin and nearly empty eye socket of the actual animal was upsetting.

Cathal opened his mouth, possibly to answer Eugene, but Dan interrupted, pointing to Aengus and asking loudly, "Why do you have that mark?"

Cathal reached for Aengus's arm, who reluctantly let him pull it closer to look at the mark. "You are *Fola Tráill*?"

Aengus nodded. When Cathal let go, he hastily pulled his sleeve down.

"Was it my mother or my brother?"

"Theo?" Aengus scoffed.

And Cathal laughed darkly. "Ah, my mother then."

Suddenly, it clicked into place, and my mind tumbled into a spiral. Cathal not only resembled Lady Aurnia, but she was his mother. But Cathal was also my ancestor. Wait! Did that make me related to that horrible woman? Was I now part of that whole screwed up family? Ugh, would I now have to acknowledge Theo at family events? Abso-fucking-lutely not happening!

Eugene made a noise in the back of his throat and this time everyone acknowledged him. The old man's weathered, bronze skin had grayed. "A vampire?" He narrowed his gaze on me, his eyes filled with accusation. "In my home?" His quiet voice didn't hide the betrayal.

I held up my hands as if to push his words back. "You and Diana seemed to know more than me. I just assumed you could tell. And he's not dangerous." I thought about what had happened three months ago. "Well, not all the time."

Aengus looked at me quizzically.

"What?" I mouthed.

Cathal pressed his palms together and pointed them toward Eugene. "Peace, Grandson. No malice was intended."

I shook my head in emphasis.

Eugene gazed out toward the far mountains, his jaw tight, but finally nodded at the fae in acceptance. Part of me wanted to apologize again, but the other part wanted Eugene to realize there was nothing to fear with Aengus.

Dan scratched his nails against his stubble. "I hope you didn't come all this way for my help. I can't change what's been done to you."

Aengus shook his head. "No, we require help with Excalibur."

Dan pointed at me. "Your sword?"

"Yes," Aengus snapped, "and therein lies our trouble. I was charged with keeping the veil closed. It is my duty. I must have Excalibur returned to me. The human realm remains in grave danger the longer it remains open."

I noticed the harsh edge in his voice and frowned. A tiny inner voice wondered if I'd spoken too soon about Aengus not being dangerous.

Dan blinked. His eyes went from bright to unfocused and his posture hunched as his shoulders caved in. One hand rubbed the back of his neck and the other twitched at his side. I'd seen that exact loss of awareness before, in Jane, with her dementia. One moment she'd be herself and the next it seemed the very essence of her had been stolen away.

Cathal let out a sigh, but didn't seem surprised. He put a directing hand on Dan's elbow. "There's to be more snow tonight. Why don't you go check on the plants once more before we lock up." With a slight push toward the greenhouse, he sent Dan on his way. He looked to Eugene, "could you follow him? Make sure he is well?" Eugene eyed Aengus like he didn't want to let him out of his sight but gave a stiff nod and followed the druid.

"Come," Cathal commanded us. "We must talk."

Back at the kitchen table, Cathal peppered Aengus with dozens of questions about the first time the veil was closed. Aengus answered them all, even as his voice tightened with frustration with each response. Finally, Cathal paused his barrage. He held a hand against his lips as if afraid his words would escape before he was ready. In the silence, I reached towards Nibs lying in a sugar coma in the middle of the table, her small hands wrapped around the spoon like a life raft. She snorted and curled up tighter as I pulled it free, her lips smacking.

Cathal laid his palms against the tabletop. "So, my mother helped Arthur to close the veil. I had wondered how it all happened."

"Why were you here and not in Innisfail?" I asked.

Cathal pressed his lips and didn't answer. Almost like he couldn't answer.

"Does it have something to do with Dan?" I pushed. Cathal let out a noncommittal hum, and I took it as an affirmative.

Aengus rubbed the mark under his sleeve. "Neither of you has yet to answer. Why did he create this whole elaborate scheme?" Each word came out clipped and sharp and I was definitely beginning to worry.

Cathal rubbed his chin. "If it helps, your connection to this seems purely coincidental. Dan often gets confused. He doesn't remember that I cannot go home. I have a duty."

Cathal's words seemed to calm Aengus and when he spoke again, the aggression had faded from his tone. "As you say, I too have a duty."

Cathal nodded and hummed his agreement.

I fought the urge to roll my eyes. What was it with these men and their duty? And why would Cathal have to stay with a druid for over a thousand years? It made no sense.

Aengus tapped a finger against the table. "Will he be able to help us with the sword? The veil must be closed."

Cathal didn't respond right away, his expression introspective. "The veil used to remain open."

"You mean when Danu controlled the gate?" I asked, and Cathal nodded.

"But the god is dead. Will the druid help, yay or nay?" Aengus demanded, the edge returning to his voice.

Cathal lifted his shoulder in a slight shrug. "Hard to say, but his disorientation will only last a short while. He'll return from the greenhouse unaware anything happened. I just ask, if you want him to remain cognizant, you should not mention the veil or closing it again."

Thirty minutes or so later, Dan stepped into the kitchen, Eugene following behind. I jumped to my feet. Excalibur nestled in the crevice of Dan's arm. "How are you holding it? Isn't it heavy?"

The druid held out the sword as if testing the weight, then brought the hilt close to his jaw, closing one eye as he gazed down the blade. "We came to an understanding."

"You talk to swords?" Nibs asked, dashing to the edge of the tabletop, her eyes wide. A moment ago, she'd been pouting because when she'd shaken off her sugar coma, I'd nixed another spoonful of honey. Now she was all about the sword whisperer.

Dan shook his head. "Of course not, but I can sooth the metals, quiet them. They're drawn to you, young lady," he used the tip of the blade to point to me, "and they don't like being kept away."

"I think there's a spell, actually. One that made Excalibur seek me out." Aengus jolted, looking up at me from his seat, and I realized I'd neglected to tell him about Sissy's vision.

Dan nodded. "Yes, definitely." He twisted the sword from one flat side to the other. "The sword seems overly agitated."

I winced. "I might have driven it into a stone floor and left it for a few months."

"Ah." Dan laid the sword on the table and Nibs patted the blade affectionately, leaving spots of sticky honey on the metal.

Aengus stood, his chair loudly scraping against the wood floor. All eyes turned his way as he spoke. I could hear the forced calm he used to hide the edge from earlier. "Can you break this spell, convince the metals to want me?"

Dan shrugged. "It might be done."

Aengus smiled in relief, and his whole body relaxed. "Brilliant."

"But not by me."

"What?" Aengus growled through clenched teeth, low and menacing. He slapped his palms against the tabletop, rattling the sword and coffee mugs. Nibs squeaked and glared at him and the room seemed to hold a collective breath. "You must. You will."

I'd never heard Aengus so desperate.

Slowly, purposefully, Cathal stood, his gaze firmly locked on Dan like a parent poised to sweep in and carry their child away from a dangerous situation. Nibs rushed to me, and I helped her up to my shoulder, so she could perch, holding my ear for balance. Eugene hovering near the kitchen entrance, seemed eager to disappear back down the hall. Tension electrified the air. I almost grabbed Excalibur up from the table, but who would I point it at?

Dan paid no attention to anyone else, just continued to look at Aengus. "I'm sorry you feel that way, brother."

Aengus leaned his weight onto the tabletop, the wood creaking, his lips pulling back almost in a snarl. "You have no understanding of the calamity that will befall this realm if I do not return to my slumber."

"Enough," Cathal commanded Aengus.

When Aengus narrowed his eyes, Cathal held up a pacifying hand and cocked his head at Dan. "The boy deserves a reason."

The druid huffed and turned away, stomping into the kitchen. "Excalibur won't let me; the girl's got to do it." He grabbed up the kettle, banging it against the side of the sink to fill it. Then set it on the stove to boil.

"Me?" I squeaked.

Dan didn't elaborate.

The druid rummaged through cupboards, opening canisters and sniffing their contents. Some canisters he placed on the counter, others he returned to their place. At one point, Cathal tried to speak up again, but Dan raised a finger and the fae didn't continue. From one cupboard, Dan pulled out a chicken shaped porcelain teapot, and a mug covered in hummingbirds. Then he reached into each of the canisters, pulling out a pinch of dried herbs and dropping them into the open back of the chicken. I couldn't read all the labels, but I saw yarrow and mugwort. What the heck was mugwort?

Everyone remained quiet as he worked, even Aengus. All except Nibs, who sang her favorite pop song off key in my ear. When the kettle screamed on the stove, he lifted it and poured a steaming stream into the teapot, sending a bouquet of scents into the air. My mind reeled, picking out notes of cinnamon and cloves among the less familiar smells.

Dan gave the tea in the pot a stir, letting it steep for a few more moments. Then Dan poured some into the mug, through a tiny metal strainer, and walked straight to me, holding it out for me to take.

I shook my head. "No, that's okay. I'm good."

"Imogen," Aengus barked, his voice harsh and almost reminiscent of his tone deep in the catacombs when he'd turned.

"You can't make me drink that," I snapped back.

Aengus closed his eyes and took a deep breath. When he opened them again, he seemed more himself. "My apologies. It is your choice, I only wish to succeed in this quest."

My gaze jumped from Dan to Aengus and back again.

Dan held out the mug again. "You've yet to fully bond with the sword. We can't break any spells until you do."

Cathal cocked his head, his brow pinched. "But that tea isn't for bonding."

Dan threw back his shoulders and glared at Cathal. "Of course it is. Are you insinuating I don't know how to brew the correct tea?"

Cathal let out a deep hum and moved in close to me, whispering out of the side of his mouth. "The tea won't harm you, but something is being set in motion and I think we should see it through."

Resigned to my guinea pig fate, I reached for the mug and wrapped my fingers around the heated ceramic. Nibs leaned over, holding her nose. "It smells awful," she whined.

I agreed but didn't say it in case Dan would take offense. Hesitantly, I brought the warm liquid to my mouth, blowing across the surface. Before I could take a sip, Cathal placed a hand on my arm and I paused.

"Just to be safe. You're not pregnant, correct?"

"What?" I sputtered, dropping the mug away from my lips and splashing hot tea over my hands. "Damn," I hissed, rubbing away the liquid from my fingers on the side of my pants. I flashed Aengus an embarrassed glance, as a flush rose up from my neck. "No, I'm not." I managed to answer.

Cathal smiled widely. "Good. Good." He gestured for me to continue.

What was in the tea? I took a moment and studied everyone's face. Even Eugene appeared curious. No one seemed overly concerned that what I was about to drink was apparently unsafe for pregnant women. With a fortifying breath, I brought the mug back to my mouth and took a sip.

Dry bitterness hit my tongue, followed closely by the aftertaste of dirt.

Desperate not to gag, I focused on Dan through the steam and gasped. The mug dropped from my grip as my fingers lost their strength. The sound of shattering pottery like a cymbal crash proceeded the splash of hot tea in every direction.

Chapter Sixteen

ot tea soaked my shirt front and pant legs, yet only a vague awareness of heat reached me. Distant and muffled, Nibs and Aengus called my name. But I couldn't speak to assure them. All my attention remained locked on Dan and what my sip of tea revealed.

He still stood before me with his gray hair, stubbled chin, and well-worn clothes, but that image appeared to be attached with hooks of sharp shadows to another form underneath. The longer I stared, the more "Dan" ripped away inch by inch, revealing a figure whose features balanced between feminine and masculine, creating a beauty both ephemeral and devastating. They were almost too much to look at.

Possibly a reaction to the tea, my magic reached out instinctively, searching for a life thread and found not one but two. One appeared normal, but one glowed blindingly bright, a strip of unadulterated sunlight. Instead of having to fight the desire to devour, my hunger sank into the shadows, hiding, unwilling to engage.

My knees wobbled. I fell against the wall, barely missing the wood stove, and slid down to the floor, Nibs hanging off my ear like a dangling earring. I could feel her trying to scramble back onto my shoulder but couldn't find the energy to lift my arm and help her. She patted my cheek and when I didn't respond, she cried, "What did you do?"

Movement drew my blurry vision upward as four forms rushed to stand over me. My eyes landed on Eugene first. A blue-ish glow outlined him and obscured his features. I blinked and rubbed at my eyes.

"Imogen?" Aengus dropped to his knees beside me and I rolled my head to look at him. I smothered a squeak. Were his eyes completely black? And his teeth had never been that pointed, I'd have noticed, right? I rubbed my eyes again and Aengus was himself again.

Nibs patted my cheek again. "Genny?"

"I'm okay, I think." I said, as I tried to stand back up. Seriously, what was in that tea? Aengus reached around my waist and helped me up the rest of the way. Nibs's sharp fingers dug into my earlobe. The room tilted and I leaned into Aengus, shutting my eyes until my equilibrium settled.

Who wanted a drink that gave you all of the worst parts of drinking and none of the fun? When Cathal had said the tea wouldn't harm me, I certainly hadn't expected to have such a reaction. Truthfully, I still wasn't convinced I hadn't been harmed.

Dan, no longer two people but firmly himself, wrung his hands. His eyes darting from me to the broken mug on the floor in anxious confusion. "It shouldn't have done that."

Cathal patted Dan's arm as he pointed toward me with the other. "No harm done. Honest mistake."

Nibs growled in my ear. Aengus, his arm still around me, tensed and I felt his grip curl tightly into my side.

Dan again scratched absently at his patchy scruff as he shuffled into the kitchen, picking up each canister to check the contents. He even lifted off the teapot lid and took a deep sniff. "But this isn't right," he mumbled to himself.

Cathal clapped his hands together, drawing all our attention. "It's been a real pleasure. Sadly, I'm sure you'd all like to head back before the sun sets and the roads freeze."

"But Excalibur," Aengus roared. Although he'd brushed off my concern this morning, I was now certain if he didn't get back to the Seelie Court soon, things were going to get bad really quick.

I reached for Excalibur still resting on the table, wrapping my fingers around the hilt. Did the tea even work? Nothing felt different.

Dan stopped shuffling around in the kitchen and spoke up. "Bonding tea! I need to make bonding tea!" He started up the whole tea making process again.

Cathal held his arms out wide, wanting to herd us out of the kitchen. Aengus refused to be led away, and I stayed, wanting answers, too. The fae huffed in frustration. "Look, the tea isn't necessary. It just encourages a connection. You can do that with some meditation. But whatever happened here, it will be some time before —" Cathal seemed to choke back the next words he wanted to say. "We cannot help you," he finally got out.

Eugene dragged his hands back over his gray hair and nodded. "We've taken up enough of your time and we've enjoyed your hospitality," he said, his words markedly free of a blatant expression of thanks. I guess the rule—never thank a fae—still held even if he was your great, great, great, great, great, grandfather. "It's good to see you, as always." Eugene's lips pinched and twisted as he scanned the room.

"Ah, to be human and lie," Cathal said wistfully and Eugene looked guilty. Cathal's held out his hand for Eugene to shake. "May your next visit be less interesting."

Eugene dipped his head in a nod and shook the fae's hand then turned to us. "I'm going to warm the truck. Meet me out there?" He left the kitchen without waiting for an answer.

Cathal held out his hand toward Aengus to shake. He grasped the fae's forearm and yanked him in close. "You will not help save this world?" Aengus asked, each word bursting with indignation and suppressed violence.

"Aengus?" I hissed and in my ear, I heard Nibs let out a long "oooooooo," insinuating he was in trouble. I hushed her.

Cathal didn't look concerned and didn't try to pull free. "We cannot."

Aengus let out a frustrated growl and threw Cathal's arm away from him, then stormed out of the kitchen.

"I'm sorry," I apologized. "I think he's honestly just hangry." The comment was flippant, but deep down I was really worried.

Cathal lifted a questioning eyebrow.

"You know, angry because you're hungry, anyway, doesn't matter. I just wish you both could've helped, but I get it." I didn't actually understand, but I also knew we had no choice but to accept it. But maybe Cathal could help in a different way. "Do you think you could offer Aengus," I tilted my head and pointed to my neck. "You know."

Cathal chuckled. "I can offer."

We made our way to the hall tree. Aengus and his coat were already gone. I set Nibs on the floor and grabbed my coat, switching the sword between my hands to get my arms in.

"Imogen," Cathal started, then paused. He seemed to open his mouth to say something only to shut it. Finally, he spoke. "The tea," was all he said.

The tea? His eyes pulled at me with a wanting I didn't understand. Did he want me to tell him what I saw? Telling him seemed okay. I couldn't think of a reason he shouldn't know. "There was something else—someone else—there with Dan. Like one painting over another. Both with their own life threads. And Aengus, even Eugene, appeared different. I don't know what it all means." Cathal's eyes brightened. I wanted him to explain, but he didn't. He just stood there. "Why aren't you saying anything?" I asked.

Nibs piped up from her pocket. "He's got a geas."

I pulled out the side to see her. "A guest?"

"A geas. A spell." Nibs pulled herself up and turned to Cathal who gave a slow nod. "Stops people from talking," she explained to me.

The barest quirk of a smile spread across Cathal's mouth.

"A geas," I repeated.

Cathal smiled wider, finally speaking. "Dan is very good with herbs. He never makes mistakes."

I let those words sink in before I responded. "Which means unconsciously, he wanted me to see. But what did I see?"

Cathal reached toward me and hugged me hard. Confirmation without words that what I said was true. "I'm pleased to know you, Granddaughter. Dan and I will be here. We're always here. Visit soon." Cathal gave my arm a light squeeze.

We stepped back out into the cold toward the rumbling truck. Aengus stood by the truck, drooping against the side, the afternoon sunlight bouncing off the snow from every direction. Cathal left me to go to him. At least if Aengus fed, it was one less thing to worry about.

Aengus wrenched open the truck door and yelled, "I want nothing from you. I'm fine!" He jumped in the truck, slamming the door behind him.

Or not.

Chapter Seventeen

The last streaks of sunlight had long disappeared behind the mountains and dusk had given way to night. Only a sliver of moon hung ineffectually in the sky.

We'd left Eugene's house late. The ride there had been mostly silent and when we'd reached the house, Aengus had refused to go inside, which seemed to please Eugene. Eugene didn't seem angry, but he immediately disappeared into his bedroom, refusing to speak about what happened. Diana had begged me to tell her everything and I couldn't say no. Not after feeling bad about not telling them about Aengus. By the time I'd pulled Nibs away from the puppies and the three of us had gotten into Theo's truck, the sun was dipping low.

Then Aengus wouldn't be swayed from stopping by Pyramid to encourage Amicus to move to a lake situated closer to Carson. By then the dark had settled in and the temperature had started its inevitable plummet. Snowmelt on the road crunched beneath the wheels. The monstrosity of Theo's vehicle was a bitch to handle in the best of circumstances. I gripped the wheel so tightly, my knuckles were trying to burst out from under my skin.

At least, Aengus seemed calmer now that we were on the road. He'd curled up on the backseat, his coat pulled over his head.

Nibs had resumed her favorite place on the dashboard. Part of me wanted to tell her to get down just in case we hit a patch of ice and spun, but the other part valued her ability to point out the wildlife. In the low light, I worried a wild animal might step out into the road before I noticed.

"The puppies wanted to come home with me," Nibs said nonchalantly, her chin sitting in one of her palms.

"They did, huh? What did you tell them?" I smirked, playing along.

"That they were way too young, but they could when they were older."

"Nibs you know we can't have seven dogs, right?"

Nibs jerked her head toward me, her face a sea of confusion. "But I promised!"

"How about we help Diana and Eugene find good homes for them and then you can visit."

She plopped her chin back onto her palm and grunted—possibly in agreement.

We roared down the road in silence as the first sign for USA Parkway rushed past. Tall, shadowed hills rose up nearly vertical on the right. Down the snow-covered embankment on the left, the lights of east bound traffic passed us like a carnival ride. And farther down into the valley, I could just make out the oily, dark expanse of the Truckee River and the broccoli shaped trees along the edge.

Aengus shifted and leaned over the seat. "I wish to apologize."

"Okay," I said, not able to take my eyes from the road to look back at him.

"My behavior toward Cathal and the druid...my anger...I may not be as well as I would like," he admitted.

This time, I chanced a glance over my shoulder. "We'll be back home soon."

He nodded with a wan smile.

Nibs cried out from the dashboard.

I jerked my gaze forward in time to see a herd of mustangs leap over the guardrail into the road; the whites of their eyes visibly flashing in the headlight, their ears flung back, panic coursing over them like a sheet of electricity.

I slammed my foot on the brake, which immediately locked, and the truck pulled hard to the left, toward the embankment leading down into eastbound traffic.

With a sound like I imagined ringing the world's large gong might make, we hit the guardrail, snow spraying like surf, and bounced over it like a monster truck. My ears ringing.

Airborne, Nibs screeched, and I snatched her from the dashboard with one hand as the other gripped the useless steering wheel. Out of the corner of my eye, I saw Aengus with his arms up, holding himself away from the ceiling. Oh god, he wasn't wearing a seatbelt.

The road seemed to rise to meet us. The squeal of the metal grill buckling as we slammed into the graveled shoulder made my teeth hurt. My seatbelt and gravity slammed me back down into my seat and Aengus flew forward, tumbling into the front seat next to me, his head connecting with the glove box.

I pumped the brake against the floorboard.

Nothing.

The truck didn't stop.

Nibs trembled harder in my hand, her fists grabbing my skin through my shirt.

We careened across the two-lane highway, a miraculous lull in traffic letting us pass unimpeded. Only to barrel into the guardrail on the opposite side.

Almost in slow motion, the entire truck flipped, the world spinning upside down. The inertia ripped Nibs from my grip. I heard a scream and realized it was mine when I tasted blood in my throat. Aengus called my name, but it sounded distant and unreal.

The truck came down. I squeezed my eyes shut against the squeal of metal and the burst of glass like a rain shower. Something hard and cold punched into my temple.

I didn't want this to be the end.

My head throbbed. A metronome of pain.

Slowly, I blinked my eyes open.

Light seared through my brain like an ice pick, and I yelped, closing them again.

Was I lying on a pillow? I jerked my eyes open despite the pain.

A lace canopy swooped overhead.

We'd been tumbling toward the river. This was not the riverbank. This was not the remnants of Theo's truck.

Nibs! Aengus! Where were they? What was going on?

With a heave, I tried to sit up. Darkness tinged the edges of my vision and I clenched the heavily stuffed comforter on either side of my legs, managing to stay upright. Certain that my head had doubled in size, I laid a hand against the side of my face. A fist-sized knot burned like fire beneath my fingers and I pulled away with a sharp intake of breath. Only to notice a face staring at me from the end of the bed. Shallow cuts speckled across her and a large wine stain bruise covered half her face. One of her eyes gleamed red from a ruptured blood vessel. Oh, my god! It was me. Gently touching my features, I tried to reconcile the "me" in the mirror.

I found it easier to just look around at my surroundings instead.

A sea of pastels and lace swam before my eyes. In a white wicker chair in the corner, Aengus sat hunched, fingers laced behind his head, elbows on his knees.

"Aengus?" I tried to say, but my voice scraped along my throat and came out hoarse and barely audible.

He visibly flinched and pulled himself tighter, his fingers digging deeper into his disheveled curls. Dried blood cracked along the back of his hands and his hair looked dark and matted. Was it his blood or someone else's? I looked at my own hands. They were completely clean. A few minor cuts stood out pink against my pale skin.

I couldn't say the same about my clothes.

"Aengus?" I tried again.

I scooted gently toward the side of the bed, the silky comforter hissing beneath my jeans. The throbbing in my head intensified despite my careful movements. Someone had removed my shoes, so I set my bare feet down on the plush, mauve carpet. My left ankle barely held my weight as deep shooting pains raced up toward my hip. I held in a moan and stayed leaning against the mattress, holding the bed post tightly.

Aengus unlaced his fingers and looked up. For an instant, the bestial face from my memory flickered in his features. "Don't," he said low and quiet.

This was very bad. I eyed the door, would it be unlocked? Because I knew where I was. The décor alone gave it away.

The Unseelie Court.

"Aengus," I said softly for a third time.

He looked down at the floor, his fists clenched on his knees, letting out a groan that was almost a growl.

Part of me trusted Aengus, but the other, logical side, knew that he'd been made into a weapon and might not have a choice. "Is the door locked?" I asked. He gave one quick nod of his head. I'd figured as much. And Aengus's strength was useless against a fae made door.

This was ridiculous.

What would be the point of pulling us from the wreckage only to have Aengus—

I refused to think about it

Maybe the queen hadn't known how bad off Aengus was. Which meant we could be left here until it was too late.

Think! There had to be something we could do. Aengus needed Honeythorn blood.

Aurnia's, or Theo's or...Cathal. He was Honeythorn too, and my ancestor!

His blood ran in my veins. I wasn't full fae and I had the mix of witch blood, but would it be enough to sate Aengus's bloodlust? I tried to suppress the shudder that coursed down my back and soured my stomach. We wouldn't know unless we tried. And it wasn't as if we had any other options.

Like my shoes, my winter coat was gone. I rolled a shirt sleeve, baring my wrist, and stumbled forward, catching myself against the side table. I held out my arm toward Aengus. Please universe, let this work. "I think you should..." was all I could manage to say through my fear.

Aengus jerked his head up and his gaze jumped from my wrist to my face, my own fear mirrored back at me. "Get back," he said turning away from me.

"But Cathal's my ancestor, maybe it will be enough," I pleaded.

"Or maybe I will kill you." He lurched to his feet and stumbled to the other side of the room. I made a move to follow but teetered having to re-grab the side table. "You can barely stand, Imogen. Lie down."

"No." I said as I straightened. "We don't know how long they'll keep us here. The longer you wait, the worse it will be, right?" Aengus winced as he reluctantly nodded. "So you could kill me then or you can take a chance now." I could feel him wavering. "Just a little, and we'll see."

Aengus let his gaze drop to my offered wrist, his eyes intense. Finally, he sighed like a man accepting a gallow's fate. "Stay very still."

"Okay," I whispered. A chill slid over me, and I trembled. What if I was wrong? What if he couldn't just take a little? What if he took it all?

Aengus inched forward, shoulders hunched, head almost bowed. I stayed as still as I could, barely breathing. He reached out and cradled my offered hand. I couldn't stop another shudder from coursing over me.

He looked into my eyes. "I am without a knife. I will have to use my teeth and it will hurt."

I tried to give a reassuring smile, but his expression told me I'd failed. All I could do was squeeze my eyes shut and nod before I lost all my resolve. His breath raced over my wrist and my whole body tensed as a point of pressure pushed down against my skin. Pain followed and I locked my lips, trying to smother my cry.

The rasp of his tongue burned over my skin and my eyes sprung open.

This was a very bad idea.

Chapter Eighteen

He lapped at the welling blood, vibrant red against my pale skin.

And every cell in my body screeched with the desire to rip his life thread from his body.

I froze, my muscles tensing, causing me to shift slightly, and Aengus growled, pulling my arm closer. His mouth latched harder onto my wrist; the pain worsening.

Nothing about this was sexy or sensual.

My brain screamed for me to pull my arm away and my magic threatened murder. I should have expected both parts to instinctively protect me, but I hadn't. Now I fought them, to hang on a little longer.

"I think you should—" I started to say and Aengus snarled, ripping his mouth away.

His hazy and unseeing gaze stole the rest of my words, as he gripped my arms and slammed me down onto the mattress. Mouth wide, he leaned in toward my neck. A low, animalistic rumble uttered from deep within him. It was easy to believe this wasn't Aengus, nothing about him was familiar.

"No, stop!" I cried, thrashing beneath him, unable to pull free. I didn't want to die. I didn't want to kill Aengus, either. His hot breath seared my neck. "Aengus, don't!" I screamed, twisting under his hold.

Teeth scraped against my neck.

My magic broke free and struck rattlesnake fast.

His life energy poured into me and for a moment, the desire to keep pulling nearly took over before I struggled to shut it down.

Aengus paused, teeth resting against my skin.

Slowly, he sat up, blinking rapidly, and released me.

"Aengus?" I cautiously asked, worried my lapse in holding my magic might have made this whole dangerous experience moot.

With a jerk, he fell to the bed beside me, his breath coming in large heaving gulps, his hands pressed against his face and eyes. My own heart thundered loudly in my chest and I felt lightheaded. He didn't drop his hands when he spoke, and his voice was muffled against them.

"Are you okay?"

I raised my wrist so I could see the mark. Blood welled and dripped from the small angry rip in my skin. "I think so," I answered. I put pressure on the wound and let out a hiss of breath, then looked at him. "Are you?"

"What?" he asked, incredulous, as he scrambled off the bed. "I almost...You could have..."

I levered myself up, still trying to staunch the bleeding. "Did it work?" Had he taken enough? Had I taken too much? I needed to know.

Irritation pulling his lips tight, he dropped his gaze to the floor and seemed to search inward. "The blood was diluted," he murmured. He found my eyes. "But it is enough for now."

I sighed and smiled.

"No," he said, coming back to the edge of the bed, fear brightening his eyes into golden orbs. "Do not smile. I could have killed you."

I sat up straight, lifting my eyebrows and cocking my head to the side. "I could have killed you."

Aengus looked away, sighing deeply. "We cannot chance it again."

"Agreed. Not unless it's absolutely necessary."

He let out a defeated huff, and I scooted to the edge, letting my head fall into his chest. He wrapped his arms around me and I melted fully against him.

"It worked," I whispered against his chest.

"Yes," Aengus agreed softly as his lips brushed the top of my head.

For a moment, I just allowed myself to be held, then I pulled back. "We need to find Nibs." One crisis averted and onto the next one.

From the front of the room, the handle jiggled, and the door creaked open. A very large bald figure stood in the doorway dressed in a robin's egg blue track suit, its features hidden under folds of drooping skin. "The queen wishes to speak with ya," it said through a flap lower on its face. "You'll come with me."

I slid down to the floor and Aengus gripped my elbow to keep me steady. I held out my hand toward the fae. "Lead the way. I want to talk with her, too."

The overwhelming smell of potpourri made my eyes water and Aengus sneeze as floppy skin guy led us into a sitting room decked out like the 80's version of a Victorian parlor and not the large receiving hall I'd been dragged to last time I'd "visited."

The Unseelie were displaying a very worrisome habit of kidnapping.

Queen Saoirse lounged on a pink settee in a white peignoir hemmed with white feathers along the edges. Even her heeled slippers, tucked up beside her, had tiny feather poufs. Beneath a large pastel purple turban, her face was done up in her signature loud and vibrant makeup. She smiled as she watched us walk in, her smile screaming predator.

"Where is Nibbleink?" I demanded. Maybe it wasn't the smartest play to anger the Unseelie queen, but my head hurt, I'd been kidnapped again, and I'd just had to let the guy I loved drink my blood. My day was shit already, and I wanted my Brownie.

Saoirse tittered. "I knew taking her would get your attention."

"Because, what, kidnapping wasn't flashy enough?" I snapped and Aengus's grip on my elbow tightened. I forced myself to back down. Pain and fighting my magic earlier had put me on edge.

Saoirse leaned forward and narrowed her eyes. "A certain Brownie may have told me you still have my Green Knight?" The last word lifted in a question, but I refused to answer.

"Where. Is. Nibs?" I repeated.

She flitted her hand as if my anger was trivial. "The Brownie is with the others of her kind, and she'll stay there until you've returned my knight, and I'm brought Excalibur."

Aengus jolted. "What?"

Suddenly, I was back in the truck as it tumbled down the ravine. I touched my fingers to the goose egg lump. Excalibur had been in the truck. That's what probably hit my head. Confused, I looked at the queen, "You didn't find it?"

"I was told the sword was not there. Not in the vehicle nor the area around it." Saoirse said. With a flourish she gained her feet. She gestured to a tall narrow side table with a sweating glass filled with what looked like lemonade and ice. "Drink that, you'll feel better."

There are only a couple of hard and fast rules when dealing with the fae. One is never thank them and the second is never eat or drink while in their company. "I feel fine," I lied.

Saoirse rolled her eyes. "I can't have you limping around when I need things to get done." She put a hand on what might have been her heart. She was fae so who really knew where or if she actually had one. "I swear the drink will only heal you and nothing more."

I glanced at Aengus, and he gave a subtle nod. I limped to the table and raised the glass to my lips. The cool liquid coated the inside of my mouth like a sugar glaze. I nearly gagged on the sweetness even as I gulped it down. In moments, the glass was empty. I ran my tongue over my lips wishing there was more even as my stomach threatened to heave. Stories of people lost to their desire to consume, eating and drinking until they died, raced through my mind and I almost accused Saoirse of lying even though I knew the fae could not.

Like a tidal wave, my entire body flushed, and heat suffused every inch of me. Just as the intensity teetered on the precipice of pain, the heat vanished. The temperature whiplash made me stumble. Only Aengus's continued grip on my arm kept me from falling on my face.

Saoirse smiled knowingly. "How do you feel?"

I opened my mouth to tell her to go to hell, angry that she'd tricked me into drinking something that was obviously harmful but stopped. Aside from a slight achiness all over, I felt good. I reached up to touch my temple and found the skin cool and painless. My ankle held my weight and even the bite mark on my wrist was gone.

"I'm healed," I stammered.

"Just as I said you would be." Saoirse clapped her hand together and said, "Peakie, I want to get dressed."

A fae resembling a walking mushroom rushed to her side and followed the Unseelie Queen behind a tall four paneled screen. The dressing gown flew up and draped over the top like a deflated doll. "Now when can I expect my knight and Excalibur?" Saoirse asked from behind it.

Excalibur not being found where we crashed didn't make sense, but what had Jane said when Excalibur first found me—with that much magic the sword could go wherever it wanted. Had it not wanted to be found? That would make finding it a little more difficult. "Why do you want it now? It's been months," I asked, stalling.

"I was content to let the sword stay where it was, unable to be drawn by anyone but you, but once it left the stone, its part in this drama resumed."

The mushroom skittered into view and pulled a bundle of neon fabric from out of a cedar chest in the corner. The wood smell blessedly overrode the intense floral scent, but sadly faded quickly.

"You want to keep the sword from being used to close the veil?" I asked.

"Bright child. Yes."

Aengus took a step toward the panel, raising his voice. "The Unseelie are just as vulnerable to the wild fae. The longer the veil is open the more they will come through."

Saoirse stepped out from behind the screen, dressed in pink neon leggings with yellow tiger stripes and a long, bright blue shirt hanging seductively off one shoulder, belted at the waist. She glared at Aengus as she made her way to the vanity. She settled on the seat and slowly unrolled her turban. "Did you know once Oberon made that ridiculous decree about the human realm, the Seelie tricked many of my people into being trapped here? We did the best to adapt, but we have the right to choose to go home again."

"Is that why you're working with Leannan?" I asked.

Saoirse snorted. She picked up a comb and a blow dryer. For the next few moments, Aengus and I were forced to stand there as the roar of air filled the room and the queen teased her hair into a halo of riotous curls. She could have easily glamoured herself to look anyway she wished. The fact that she was manually doing her hair probably had more to do with her wanting us to have to wait. Honestly, I was still very curious about what Saoirse really looked like. Being as old as she was, her glamour was strong enough to actually alter her appearance instead of just cover it. Finally, she shut off the appliance and set it down.

She swiveled on the seat to face us again and crossed her legs.

"We Unseelie are only working for ourselves. At the moment, Leannan's goals and mine align, but she is consumed with vengeance as much as Aurnia is attached to her power. Neither care what happens to my people in the process."

"Your people? You mean people like Dennriall?" I accused without thinking. Dennriall had been Saoirse's seneschal. I still wasn't clear on what that meant, but it seemed like an important job and yet The Leannan Sidhe might have killed him or at the least had him trapped. Wasn't Saoirse mad about that?

She laughed. "I might have negotiated for his return if the form of his betrayal hadn't knocked on my palace door."

Return? Then he was alive. Relief fluttered through me. Aside from Nibs, Dennriall was the only other fae I almost trusted, and half way liked.

"A human! Can you believe it?" the queen continued. "He came demanding to know where my seneschal was, claiming he was his husband and deserved to know. To think that Dennriall had kept this dalliance from me. I mean a fling here or there with a human is to be expected, but to shack up with one. To bind oneself to such a lowly being. Unacceptable. I've chosen to leave Dennriall where he is for the time being."

Dennriall was married? To a human?

I'd known the fae looked down on fae/human relationships, but the way Saoirse spoke made me suddenly worried. "What happened to the human?" I asked, remembering all the stories of what happened to those who wandered into the fae realm. None of them were happy stories.

"I had a trell throw him out. The amount of potpourri I had to use to cover the smell of human was astronomical." The mushroom attendant brought over a pair of high-top sneakers. They held them out one at a time as the queen kicked off each heel and delicately dipped her feet into them like sliding on glass slippers. She patted the fae on its rounded head and stood up. "Now I need you to go and bring me back what I've asked for."

Aengus opened his mouth, but I cut him off.

"Not without seeing Nibbleink," I demanded.

Saoirse's lip twitched in irritation.

"Proof of life," I said, staring at the queen with what I hoped looked like strength and determination. Two things I definitely wasn't feeling. Demands made to a fae monarch could easily turn deadly, and again I was stuck with great power and no way to use it safely.

A long moment passed before Saoirse snorted and shrugged a shoulder. "Fine, I'll have her brought to you, but we will walk out now. I don't have time to waste on sentimentality."

"Walk? Don't you have one of those portal doors like last time?" I asked. The Nugget still wasn't my favorite place, but it sure beat trying to get down the mountain and back into town by foot.

She smirked. "Portals are for winners, sweetie. No knight or sword? You walk."

At the junction where the hidden Unseelie tunnel met the main mine, a trell caught up with us with a furious Nibs clutched in their hand, screaming every swear word she knew. I gave the queen an exasperated look. "Did you really have to take her clothes, again?"

"I had no part in divesting your pet from her clothes. That is pure Brownie business."

I reached out my hand asking for Nibs, but Saoirse shook her head and the trell took a step back. Fine.

"Nibs, are you alright?" I asked as I pulled out one of my fingerless gloves from my coat pocket. Saoirse had returned my shoes and our coats now that we were leaving. Nibs stopped the endless string of profanities and nodded, rubbing her arm under her sniffly nose. I ripped into the seam of the glove, creating a matching hole in the other side. I held it out toward the trell. They looked at the queen for confirmation and she rolled her eyes but nodded. The trell dropped Nibs into their open palm and she immediately reached for the glove, quickly pulling it over her head and sticking her arms through the holes. Instant slip dress.

"I want to go home," she whined, hugging the dress around her middle.

I clenched my fists. Aengus reached around my shoulder and hugged me to his side. "I know." I tried not to cry. "We'll be back as soon as we can. You'll be safe until we do." I glared at Saoirse, fighting my tears with anger.

She smirked. "Bring me what I've asked for and no harm will come to the Brownie." She made a motion toward the trell and they curled their hand around Nibs again and stomped back down the mine shaft, disappearing into the darkness before I could even call out her name. "Come along," Saoirse directed, taking a step.

I didn't move. "How do I know you won't hurt her?"

The queen's eyes narrowed, and she twisted her lips in irritation. "This is ridiculous!" With a huff, she swirled her hand, creating a very tiny portal. She reached through and pulled out a hand mirror. "Here," she said angrily, shoving it at me. I fumbled a little as I grabbed it but managed not to drop it. "This mirror will show you Nibs whenever you wish. Is that sufficient?" I nodded in amazement. "Wonderful, can we walk now?"

Soon daylight started to overtake the electric light around us. I turned to Saoirse, suddenly curious. "How did you even know the sword had been pulled from the stone?"

Saoirse paused, hands on her hips. "Aurnia thinks her tight hold keeps everyone in line, but it only causes more to slip through her fingers. I have my spies. They keep me informed." She took a step toward me, her big hair looming like a lion's mane. "What they couldn't tell me is how you managed to destroy the spell on my knight."

I decided not to tell her my father would soon be consumed by it once more. I shrugged my shoulders. I could tell she wanted to push for a better answer but said nothing and moved on.

We stepped out under the mine shaft opening, my eyes tearing and blinking in the bright sunlight. Aengus stopped at the edge of the shadowed entrance. I glared at Saoirse. "You know he won't be able to walk anywhere until the sun goes down."

The queen pointed out toward the parking lot. "Your friends have come to claim you anyway."

The Wylde House Retirement Home van skidded into view, spraying gravel behind it, Everett's massive form behind the wheel. Mr. Friedman hung his head out the passenger side window and waved. "We've come to save you!"

Chapter Nineteen

I was hiding, and I knew it.

But I needed a moment.

Everything was spinning out of control.

From having to leave Nibs behind, to the ride home peppered with questions, to the *ossorians* bombarding me with their emotions upon our return, to my father awake and slowly being subsumed. What had happened with Aengus in the trailer...and at the Unseelie Court...

I took in the barren room around me as I sat on the floor, my back against the door. No personal items, no sheets on the mattress, everything boxed up and stored away so that nothing was left of my grandparents, except for memories. And yet the room still fed me comfort.

In the corner, there had been a cot with a sleeping bag where I'd spent many nights, refusing to sleep downstairs by myself. As a child, my nightmares had bordered on night terrors. I eventually grew out of them, but even as I got older, I sometimes wished I could grab my pillow and camp out in their room, listening to them both lightly snore.

What I would give to be able to ask them for advice. Even as an adult, there'd been a safety in having someone to go to for answers. I didn't have to make the decisions. Not when ultimately there was someone else in charge. Now that someone was me. I had all the questions and yet I was expected to find the answers, too.

I couldn't get a full breath under the weight pressing down on my shoulders and the tight ball in my chest. Everyone—they expected too much. My head thunked against the solid door. The sound of bone hitting wood echoed in my head. Too exhausted to hold back the tears any longer, I just let them slide free.

My meltdown only lasted for a few minutes at most, before I took a deep breath and rubbed my cheeks dry.

A soft knock vibrated the door.

"Imogen?" Aengus asked.

Someone must have told him where to look. I scrubbed at my cheeks again and stood up. When I opened the door, Aengus looked stricken, no doubt noticing my red and puffy face. "I'm fine. It's just been a really rough couple of days," I said, stepping to the side to let him in.

Aengus entered, his gaze scanning the room. "Agreed."

I closed the door and leaned against it. "How are you?"

He kept his distance. "I came to tell you I am returning to the Seelie Court."

My first instinct was to tell him I didn't want him to go. The reaction was partly attachment, he'd been at my side for the last two days, and I'd gotten used to it. But I also had to admit I didn't want to be alone to figure out what to do next. "I thought you said my blood worked?" I said, trying not to think about how passive aggressive my words were.

"For now. The dilution worries me." Aengus said, and I could hear the guilt in his tone.

I wasn't being fair, and I knew it. "I'm sorry. Of course you should go if you think it's important."

Aengus took a step closer. "It has been pleasant, staying so close."

"It has been," I agreed, and my stomach did a little swoop.

A delicate flutter of a knock broke the moment, and I turned around to open the door.

Sissy stood in the hall, her eyes wide and fearful. It had been Sissy who'd seen us stranded in Virginia City and sent Everett and Mr. Friedman. She'd never had so many in a row, Mrs. O'Cleary told me. As if I needed more proof things were going south and quickly.

"Is everything okay?" I asked her.

"The veil," she whispered.

Aengus came up behind me and I flashed him an uncertain look. I prompted Sissy for more detail, "Did you see something?"

Sissy nodded as her whole body shuddered. "Someone plans to destroy it."

"Destroy the veil?" Aengus repeated in disbelief.

Shutters closed over Sissy's expression. She calmly pushed her glasses back up onto her nose and shuffled away without another word.

My mind buzzed with a million thoughts all at once.

What would that even mean? No veil. Would Innisfail then exist in the same reality as the human realm. Would everything living there, suddenly exist here?

"We must close it immediately," Aengus stated.

Immediately? "What do you mean?"

Aengus stepped out into the hallway, his gaze following Sissy. "Tomorrow might even be too late."

Tomorrow? There was no way we could find Excalibur and cast the spells by then. But there was no arguing that our timeline, which up to this point had been hazy, had now snapped into clarity. We needed to close the veil as soon as possible. But that would mean I'd lose Aengus. I'd lose Excalibur. Without the sword, I couldn't save Nibs or the *ossorians*. I wouldn't be able to control my magic. And without control I'd be unable to save my father.

It was at that point, I let myself contemplate Aengus lying in his tomb—in limbo between life and death—forever.

I wanted to scream as frustration squeezed me from the inside.

There had to be better options. I needed someone to tell me how to fix everything. Where was an adultier adult when I needed one?

What's that snarky saying, "be careful what you wish for"? I hadn't wanted Aengus to leave me today, and now with the veil in peril, we needed to stay together until Aengus could ultimately leave me for good. If I could give the middle finger to the person who started that saying I would.

Aengus still planned to return to the Seelie Court, but he insisted we search for Excalibur first. When I grumbled about the long drive to where we'd crashed, he'd told me we'd check a closer place first.

In the retirement home van once again, I backed out of the driveway. It had taken a few minutes extra for me to convince the *ossorians* I wasn't abandoning them, that our constant leaving had everything to do with trying to save them.

But was that even true, now? Because it was beginning to look like saving the human realm meant I had to give up saving everyone else.

As we drove, Aengus seemed to tick off a list, mostly to himself. My curiosity piqued when he said, "I will need to purchase a plane ticket."

I threw a quick glance his way. "Wait, how did you even get a plane ticket to come to the U.S. in the first place?"

Aengus peered over at me, confused.

The reasons he couldn't have gotten a ticket seemed pretty obvious to me. "Because you don't have a passport. Because you're over a thousand years old."

"But I do."

"You do what?"

"Have a passport." Aengus opened his coat and pulled out a slim blue book with a golden crest on the front.

I let go of the wheel with one hand and plucked it from his grip. Holding it awkwardly, I twisted my thumb beneath the cover to open it. There was Aengus, looking very uncomfortable with the name Angus Scott, no middle name. I handed it back to him. "How did you get this?"

He slipped it back into a hidden pocket of his trench coat. "A fae in Glasgow agreed to trade my armor for papers and new clothes. Said he "could make a killing", by which I assume he meant a lot of money." I nodded yes. "He even wanted my small clothes." Aengus' expression seemed puzzled.

I snorted, figuring "small clothes" meant an old form of underwear and shrugged. "Yeah, people are weird. I bet there's some person out there whose entire collection is ancient undies."

The van lost some power as we started up the hill out of Carson. I put a bit more pressure on the gas. The engine revved but didn't go much faster. "Why do you think Excalibur will be at the lake?" I asked, changing the subject back to what was really on our minds.

"It is merely a guess," Aengus admitted.

I couldn't help the sigh that escaped my lips. "Well, if it's there, how are we going to do all the things? I can't leave Nibs with the Unseelie."

Aengus reached across the middle console, and I put my hand in his. "We will find a way."

I really wanted to believe him.

Maybe if I could possibly see a way through, I would have.

Big Washoe, and its companion Little Washoe, were shallow lakes nestled at the bottom of Slide Mountain and the Virginia Foothills, with communities on either side. I have fond memories of Grandpa and the lake. Every time he watched "The Shootist" with John Wayne, he'd pause and say proudly, "That's right here. Right in our backyard."

I turned off the exit for Old Washoe City, but instead of heading into the old money neighborhood, I pulled into the rest stop and picnic area to the right. The bright sun had melted most of the snow in all but the shadowed areas, and a light breeze had the water lapping gently through the marsh grass. I turned off the van, leaving the keys in the ignition.

For a moment, we both sat in silence. Neither moving to get out. I spoke first. "Is it bad that part of me really hopes we don't find it? I mean, then at least we'd have more time." I turned to him. "And I don't mean just for us. More time to fix everything."

It was Aengus's turn to sigh. "If the veil is destroyed, it would mean chaos."

"I know," I groaned, slapping the steering wheel. My head fell back against the headrest. "I have to save them all." My voice broke around the lump sitting in my throat.

"You will, but we must save this realm first," Aengus said as he gently turned my face toward him. "But I admit, given a choice, I would never wish to leave you." The air between us seemed to magnetize, pulling us closer. The desire to squirm across the seat and into his lap overwhelmed me. If Aengus hadn't pulled away and opened his door. I'm pretty sure I would have.

I followed him, pointing toward the lake a few hundred yards from the end of the pavement. "Why are we here?"

He glanced over his shoulder, grinning like a small boy. He raised his fingers to his mouth and whistled shrilly through them. Water bubbled and frothed near the edge of the lake. Then impossibly Amicus popped his head out of what was surely only a barely a foot of water. The kelpie leaped completely clear of the water, landing on the marshy ground, and thundered toward Aengus, his wet mane and tail sending banners of water behind him.

The kelpie skid to a prancing stop and Aengus ran his hand down Amicus' slick neck. His nostrils flared with a snort and he shook his head sending water in every direction, causing Aengus to laugh and wipe the drips from his face.

"How was that even possible?" I asked, taking a step closer. Amicus dipped his head and reached for my hand, his lips moving like appendages. I scratched his muzzle.

"Water is a separate magic. An older magic. It is part of this world and yet it is also connected to Innisfail. The same water that runs there, runs here."

Wait, what? I set my hands on my hips. "Are you saying we could get to Innisfail through water? Then what's the point of the veil?"

"Someone *could* travel to Innisfail through water, but that would require permission from the Lady of the Lake and she is not inclined to give it. She would much rather pull you down and keep you in her watery mausoleum. And Amicus and other watery creatures like him would just eat you. Amicus here had a penchant for young vulnerable women once, didn't you?" He said playfully, patting the kelpie on the neck again. Amicus snorted and seemed to nod in agreement.

I took a step back. "That's horrible."

Amicus squealed and threw his head in the air, ears pinned. "Hush," Aengus soothed. "It is only your nature, and no judgement is given."

"I don't know. I'm a little judgy about murder," I grumbled.

Aengus ignored me. He placed his hands on either side of Amicus' long face and stared into his eyes. "I need you to tell the Lady we are here for the sword. Will you do that, my friend?" The kelpie bobbed his head, before affectionately slamming his nose deep into Aengus's stomach, causing Aengus to huff out a burst of air. "Go on." Aengus gave the kelpie a shove with mock annoyance. Amicus trotted away, disappearing beneath the surface with a leap.

"How long will this take?" I asked.

Aengus continued to stare out across the water. "Time moves differently in Uisce. We shall not wait long."

Before I could even ask what the heck was "ish-cah", tentacles burst from the water, curling and pulling against the shore to lift what vaguely looked like a human torso onto the ground. The sound of a popping water bubble echoed loudly across the valley and the octopus-like creature disappeared, replaced with a stunningly beautiful curvy woman draped in a shining silver gown.

"Ah, almost like old times, Anguselus," the octopus/lady purred, stepping toward Aengus, the silver of her dress gliding around her rounded curves like rivulets of a waterfall. "You haven't aged a day. You must tell me your secret." She held out the back of her hand and Aengus reached for it, bringing the honeyed skin to his lips. Her coal rimmed eyes fluttered closed at the touch.

He smirked as he let it go of her hand and stepped back. "I believe the Lady has no such need."

"Always the charmer," The Lady of the Lake said with a soft smile, tossing her dark hair over her shoulder.

They spoke to each other as if they were two old friends meeting up for a drink. And as much as I logically knew not being noticed by a woman that could turn into a large tentacled creature was probably safer, I was starting to get a little irritated they were acting as if I wasn't there.

The Lady of the Lake reached up and twirled one of Aengus's golden curls around her finger before letting it bounce back onto his forehead. "Am I to guess you're here for Excalibur? Not very knightly of you to lose your sword," she teased.

Aengus didn't react to her comment. "I assume you called the sword to you when we landed near the river."

"Well, I wasn't about to let a bunch of disgusting Unseelie minions take her." Her tone went from coy to cutting in an instant and although I didn't see the tentacles, I had a feeling they were still there, thrashing.

"Excalibur must be returned to me. There are those who plan to destroy the very structure of our worlds."

"But Excalibur is no longer yours." The Lady's eyes darted in my direction, finally acknowledging my existence. I instantly wanted to go back to being ignored. Hadn't Aengus said she had a mausoleum of dead people? "She calls to this twig of a girl."

Aengus moved to stand near me and his tension flooded my senses. As much as he spoke and acted as if the two of them were friends, I knew the truth. We were not safe. Not by a long shot. "My apologies for not introducing her sooner. My lady, this is Imogen Wylde."

I gave what I hoped was a decent curtsy. The Lady of the Lake glided toward me, her whole body swaying as if buoyed by water. She stared deep into my eyes.

"Do you want the sword for the same reason as my handsome Anguselus?"

"Yes," I answered weakly.

"Water knows all secrets. Do you speak truly?"

"Yes," I repeated, but found myself adding, "but not the only reason."

"That's what I thought." The Lady laughed loudly and her body swelled, rising and forming until she was once again the large octopus-like creature. Her vaguely human face split in a wide grin. From beside me I heard Aengus cry out, but before I could respond, a tentacle rose up around me and twisted me in its grip. With a surge, both the Lady of the Lake and I were diving beneath the surface of the lake into an impossibly deep darkness.

Chapter Twenty

I held my breath as we dived, but the squeeze of the tentacle around my middle threatened to force out the last of my air. I pinched my lips tight against the ache in my lungs. Vaguely, I was aware I should try to stop our descent, but my mind could only focus on not having air and despite plummeting deeper into the dark, lights flashed before my eyes as my body begged for the last bits of oxygen.

When there was nothing left, my body did the only thing it could. I opened my mouth in a heaving gulp.

Nothing happened.

Well, not nothing—breathing happened.

Impossibly, I took another deep and effective breath and laughed out of sheer confusion. "I'm not drowning," I said in disbelief.

The Lady of the Lake paused and swirled around to float her body in front of me. A slim light from an unknown direction hit across her face and illuminated only the high points, giving her a skull-like appearance, and the tentacle tightened around me as she stared. "And why would you?" she asked. "This is Uisca."

As if that explained anything. "I'm not a fish. That's why," I snapped. My hair floated like seaweed around my head and I angrily pushed it away from my face. Wait. What if I'd magically been given gills or something? I frantically patted at my neck, and breathed deeply in relief when I didn't find any.

"It's odd that the sword picked someone so vastly ignorant," The Lady said with a huff. "But if you can fix this mess, who am to argue?" Without waiting for a response, she dived again, pulling me downward in her wake.

Now that I was no longer focused on breathing, I quickly realized what rushed past and over my skin wasn't quite water. My clothes weren't saturated, just damp. It reminded me of a trip I'd taken to Florida once, where the air felt thick and heavy, like walking in a warm cloud of water vapor. And the unmistakable scent of a building rainstorm filled my nose.

The light that had illuminated the Lady of the Lake's features earlier intensified as we continued deeper. Rocky spires rose around us, but soon they gave way to clearly chiseled and sculpted columns that shimmered like the inside of clam shells. Shiny with a hint of rainbows.

White tiles materialized on the surface below us and just as we reached them, the Lady released her tentacle holding me and I dropped, butt first, with a bounce upon them. I scowled up at her, but the Lady ignored me as she shrank once again into a human form and alighted on the tiles with a gentle hop.

"Follow me," The Lady of the Lake called, her gown and tresses swirling as she walked towards arches of white stone carved with reeds and fluted flowers, almost Egyptian in style.

I thought about what Aengus had said earlier, about how the Lady of the Lake pulled people down into her mausoleum and couldn't find the courage to take a step further. "My lady," I started weakly, hoping it was the right honorific to say. "I just need Excalibur."

She swung around, placing a hand on her rounded hip. "Nimue," she said.

My face must have telegraphed my confusion.

"My name is Nimue," she explained, as she walked back to me, strutting as if the tile path were a catwalk.

"Oh okay, Nimue, ummm...could I just have the sword? We're in a bit of rush."

Nimue blinked slowly, and her lips twitched in an unsettling smile.

"Please?" I added.

She took a slow step closer. "You're in a rush?"

If I could have slapped the back of my own head, I would have. Pissing off a powerful sea witch was definitely on the list of "don'ts." Would she turn squid and squeeze me until I popped? A touch of panic sped up my heart. I reached for my magic in panic and gasped.

Instead of finding golden life strands or even a river of magic like Underhill, what I found were millions of bits of dandelion fluff saturating the air, shifting back and forth as if caught in an ocean eddy. I was literally surrounded by magic. My panic melted into wonder. "What is this place?"

"This is Uisca," Nimue said.

I frowned. "You've said that before. It doesn't explain anything."

"Fine." Before I knew what she was doing, she'd wrapped her arm through mine and pulled me toward the arches, my feet barely brushing the tiles as she marched. "Shall I explain it as if you were a toadstool? Uisca is the beginning. She is all magic."

The path led into a vaulted corridor; the walls stretching toward the ceiling, pearlescent with carved reliefs of water plants twining upwards.

"Are you saying that all magic comes from Uisca?" I asked. Could that really be what she was saying?

"What is land without water? What is the body without blood?" Nimue's words were enigmatic, but they also made a kind of sense. A witch pulled their magic from the earth, and the fae pulled their magic from their blood. But water was a commonality of both.

Nimue pulled me along, down hallways and corridors. It felt like a labyrinth. Wasn't there a myth about a man-eating Minotaur in a labyrinth? Maybe that's how Nimue killed her captives. Being eaten by cow was definitely not how I wanted to go. Before I could find a way to get free of Nimue's arm, we stopped at the opening of a cavernous circular room. It took a moment to comprehend what I saw.

Then I wished I hadn't.

Within alcoves that spanned the radius of the room hung white robed people—women—suspended above the floor by no visible means, they floated, arms and legs swaying like seaweed in a gentle current. And in the middle of the room, within a circle of tall uncarved stones, floated two men and a woman.

My heart pounded so hard it roared in my ears. I tried to yank my arm free of Nimue. A scream ripped from me when she only held on tighter. I reached for my magic again, and despite being literally surrounded by it, nothing obeyed me.

"What an odd reaction," Nimue said, her grip unrelenting.

"Odd? You want to put me in some kind of serial killer display case and I'm what, supposed to be happy about that?"

She laughed and patted my arm. "They sleep."

I struggled as she dragged me closer to the stones. "That doesn't make it better!"

She pointed up at one of the men. "Look," she commanded and jostled me until I lifted my gaze. Gray streaked his shoulder length dark hair, but his beard was pure white and trimmed to a stiff point. He wore leather armor, water dark, and across his chest stretched a strip of stark white cloth held with an intricate silver pin at his shoulder. He hung, chin to chest, like a fallen warrior, but although his skin looked sallow, and his eyes sunken, he truly appeared as if sleeping. "Of the three, Merlin came to me first."

I went still. "Merlin?"

"Yes. His last spells took almost everything from him. I hold what remains." Nimue let go of me now as if realizing the information she just shared had paralyzed me. She pointed up toward the other man. In the blueish light, his hair and beard appeared almost purple, likely red in the light of day, and he wore only a simple tunic with leather leggings beneath. Nothing about him proclaimed who he was, yet I felt that he was someone important.

Nimue raised her hand as if to touch him, but merely held it near. "Arthur followed soon after."

"*The* King Arthur?" I exclaimed in disbelief, even as I knew it to be true. I pointed to the woman floating near him dressed surprisingly in armor much like Merlin's, but without the sash, her long dark braid swishing like a tail down her back. "And Gwynevere?"

Nimue nodded. The first touch of sadness in her eyes. "She would not be parted from Arthur. Her words, 'Beside you in battle, beside you in death.'"

"And the other women?" I asked, gesturing to the outside circle.

Nimue's eyes shone with unshed tears, and she placed a hand on her chest. "My acolytes. I couldn't stop the destruction of Avalon, but I could spare them the horrors that would have befallen them."

I shuddered, turning away from the doomed women and back toward Arthur. "The legends are true, then? Arthur sleeps until he's needed?"

Nimue shrugged, all emotions from earlier gone as if it had never been there. "Who's to say? Arthur may wake or he may not. But this isn't why I've brought you here." She walked around the floating legends and I hurried to follow.

In a smaller alcove hidden from direct view, Excalibur floated. Without thinking, I reached for the sword, but Nimue stopped me, not aggressively, but firmly. "Only if you agree to one condition."

It seemed dangerous to agree to something I hadn't heard yet, but we needed the sword, so I nodded.

"You are not to let Anguselus return to his tomb."

I stared at her blankly. The shock of what she said stealing my words. "What? But the veil?" I managed to get out.

She released my arm. "If you wish to regain the sword that is what you must do."

"I don't understand. The veil being open is a bad thing."

"Is it?" Nimue asked, a slight raise to one of her eyebrows.

"That's what everyone keeps saying," I huffed in frustration. "And we've been told someone is trying to destroy the veil completely."

Nimue smirked. She reached into the alcove and grasped Excalibur's hilt. She pulled it easily to her. With a swish of her hips, she sashayed back toward the arch leading out of the mausoleum, Excalibur in hand. I jogged after her. "You can't want the veil to be destroyed?"

"Of course not," Nimue snapped, shooting me an irritated expression over her shoulder.

I halted, my hands resting on my hips, seething with frustration. "If you don't want the veil destroyed, but you also don't want Aengus to recast the spell and close the veil, what do you want?"

Nimue stopped and slowly turned around. She glided back and loomed toward me, her smile wide. "Finally, a clever question."

She held out the sword, pushing the hilt into my hands. Comforting heat coursed up my arm and swelled in my chest as if the sword wished to express happiness at being back in my grip.

Nimue took a step back. "I want the lie revealed, and the hidden druid to stop hiding."

I nearly rolled my eyes. Couldn't the fae, or whatever she was, just come out and say what they wanted instead of riddles? "That's not clear, at all—" I started, but from down at the end of the hall the clatter of hooves drew both of our attention. Aengus astride Amicus galloped over the tile. Amicus slid to a stop directly beside me, haunches brushing the floor.

Aengus stared down at me from the kelpie's back, hand pointed toward me like an arrow. His hazel eyes almost glowed with intensity. "Grab hold!"

Chapter Twenty-One

Nimue laughed. "Anguselus, how dramatic."

Aengus ignored her and further thrust his hand toward me. "Imogen, we must go now."

He'd come to save me, no doubt believing the Lady of the Lake would place me in her mausoleum. The memory of the hanging bodies made me shudder. As much as I didn't think she actually meant me harm, I wasn't naïve to think she couldn't change her mind. Excalibur bit into my shoulder where I had it resting. We had what we needed. There was no reason for me to stay. But I glanced from Aengus to Nimue anyway, hoping for some indication I could leave without truly pissing her off.

Nimue just dipped her head once and said, "remember your promise."

I nodded in return.

Slapping my hand against Aengus's forearm, he pulled me up behind him. Holding Excalibur across my lap, I threw my free arm around his waist. Amicus gave a slight buck and shuffle, his hooves scraping the tile. Had anyone asked the kelpie if he wanted another rider? But Aengus pressed his legs into the kelpie's sides and Amicus jumped forward, nearly landing on top of Nimue before he skidded into a turn and galloped back down the corridor.

The hollow echo of Amicus's hooves followed us until we reached the last arches. With a leap, we ascended into the unusual waters of Uisca. Amicus moved as if galloping, pulling us upward with every stride. Impulsively, I let go of Aengus to let my hand slice through the heavy air, like I used to do out the car window as a child. A sheen of damp coated my skin.

Under my sleeve, a sharp sting made me yelp, and I pulled my arm back in. My bracelet slid down to my wrist and the stinging followed its movement. What the hell? I rubbed the bracelet against my jeans trying to get it off, but I couldn't get the right angle one handed.

"Are you well?" Aengus asked over his shoulder.

I glanced up to answer and froze. A figure hovered in the distance, incorporeal and almost too small to recognize. But I'd have known who it was, even if the bracelet hadn't screamed at her appearance.

My mother.

"Stop!" I cried out.

Violently, Aengus pulled back on the knotted tresses of mane in his hand. Amicus paused mid-leap, a carousel horse with his legs folded under him, his ears flat against his head and his mouth open with teeth large and bitey. "What?" Aengus asked, swiveling his head in all directions.

I pointed. "It's my mom."

He followed the line of my finger and shook his head. "There is nothing."

"She's there," I pleaded.

Aengus didn't argue. He leaned forward, urging Amicus in the direction I'd indicated. The kelpie flung his head up and leaped forward with an irritated snort.

My mother's eyes widened as we approached.

"Genny. What are you doing here?" she exclaimed.

I could see straight through her, but she didn't move or sway. Her feet seemed planted somewhere firm and elsewhere. For the briefest moment, I'd allowed myself to believe that I'd finally get my mother back, and now I knew she was still missing. I might be able to see her, speak with her, but she wasn't actually there. I opened my mouth to answer her, different words tumbled out instead. "I searched for you. I called for you. You never answered."

Her expression fell. "Oh baby, I wanted to see you again. I tried." My mother held out her arms as if in supplication, and I thought I could see thin red tubing running from the inside of both.

"Where are you? How can we get to you?" I asked.

My mother jerked her head as if listening to an unheard sound. Her face going from worried to frightened. She turned to me. "You must go. I don't know how aware Leannan is of that bracelet. I don't want her to find a way to break our connection."

Leannan? The Leannan Sidhe had my mother? "Mom?" My voice warbled with uncertainty.

"Go," she encouraged.

I gripped Aengus's arm. "We have to go, now." I urged.

Aengus leaned over Amicus's neck, wrapping his fingers into his mane. I followed him, throwing my free arm around his middle. "Fly, my friend," he said, and Amicus leaped upward once more, cutting through what began to feel more and more like water until we burst from the surface and landed in the shallows of Washoe Lake once more.

After Amicus splashed back beneath the surface, Aengus and I started walking across the marshy scrub grass to return to the van.

Aengus climbed in as I slid the side door open and set Excalibur on the floor before the first row of seats, then I took the driver's seat. Leaping in and out of Uisca had only left us damp, but the heater seemed to take forever to warm. My teeth chattered as I shifted into reverse.

We both remained quiet as the van chugged back up the hill and out of the valley. Aengus lay against the window, his trench coat once again used as a blanket against the sunlight. Holding the wheel like an anchor in the middle of a whirlpool, my mind spun with everything that had happened with the Lady of the Lake and my encounter with my mother. Hypothetically, how many more things could I add to my list before I was crushed under the weight?

Aengus shifted and I glanced over to find him staring at me. First things first, I needed to tell him what Nimue had made me promise.

"I have to tell you something," I said, gripping the wheel tighter and trying not to sound as uncomfortable as I was. Aengus quirked an eyebrow. "The only way Nimue would give me Excalibur is if I promised not to let you go back to your tomb."

Aengus sat up, his trench coat falling to his shoulders. "You agreed to this?"

I didn't like what he was implying. I threw a hand up in the air; the van weaving a bit within my lane. "Of course I did! I have to save Nibs, and my dad, and my mom, the *ossorians*." My voiced had reached peak screech. "We needed Excalibur. I would have promised part of my liver for it. So yeah, I promised."

"If we fail to close the veil—" Aengus started, but I cut him off.

"What? What will really happen?" The words left me before I registered what I'd said. But the more I thought about it, the more I wanted to follow it to some kind of conclusion. "The veil has been open for what—a year—more than? Shouldn't we be overrun with dangerous creatures by now? Isn't that what everyone keeps saying?"

"The scolex," Aengus offered, but I could tell he wasn't disregarding what I said.

"Right, but that was months ago. Nimue said she wants 'the lie revealed, and the hidden druid to stop hiding.' I think there's something else going on and I need you to help me figure out what it is."

"My duty is to—"

"You're a fucking human being, Aengus, not a tool. I know you promised Arthur and Gwynevere, but you're here and they're floating in a fish tank. You get to make your own decisions." Aengus looked stricken at my words. I instantly wanted to take them back. Instead, I gently lifted my foot off the accelerator, halting the mad dash we were making coming into Carson Valley.

"What do you mean, 'floating in a fish tank?'" Aengus asked.

I bit my lip, definitely not wanting to be the person to tell him.

"Imogen?"

"The Lady of the Lake showed me her mausoleum. Only the people inside aren't dead, they're sleeping. And that's when she showed me Merlin, and Arthur, and..."

"Gwynevere," he finished. I nodded. He sucked in a sharp breath. He was silent all the way down the hill until we hit the first traffic light. When we stopped at the red light, he looked over, "Did they look old?"

I knew what he was asking. How long after he'd been entombed had they lived? "They looked older than you, but no, they didn't look old."

Aengus made a sound as if stabbed in the back and turned away to stare out the window.

"I'm sorry," I said, knowing those words were useless. He nodded in response, but didn't look at me.

I focused instead on obeying the traffic laws.

The silence in the van sat heavy and oppressive. Finally, he spoke again. "My duty," he started and lifted a hand to keep me from interrupting, "is to protect the human realm above all else. I believe closing the veil will do this, but I will not discount what you have said."

"So, you'll help me figure out what Nimue wanted?"

He nodded. "But we must work quickly. We cannot allow the veil to fall completely."

"Agreed." The complete destruction of reality didn't sound like a fun time.

"But in regard to those you must save," Aengus said and I spared a quick glance at him. He looked resigned. "You are *custos*."

I couldn't hold back the scoff. "How does that help?"

"You are *custos*," Aengus repeated. "Which means you are not alone. You have reminded me that my first oath was to my family, my fellow *custos*. I cannot forsake my duty to close the veil, but I must not fail to help you. Your father and the *ossorians* are with us now. Let us focus on them first."

"Do you really think we can help them?" I asked, turning down the road to home.

"It is my hope that with your magic and the assistance of the coven, we will."

We neared the driveway and Aengus pointed toward the front yard. "Is that your father?"

I looked and groaned. Yep, there on the front lawn stood my father in a pair of tighty whiteys, feet bare in the snow, arms raised toward the winter sun. The cops were definitely going to be called this time.

Chapter Twenty-Two

As a child, I loved the few nights a year a fire was lit. I loved how the antique wood of the mantle, salvaged from the original house, looked nearly as warm as the flames recessed within. How the flickering candles covering every surface sent up small puffs of white smoke. How dozens of small pots that Sissy had tended in the west-facing windows all January would be bursting with delicate snowbells. And how the smell of the pine boughs weaved in and around it all spiced the air with their sharp scent. It felt like Christmas, but smaller, more intimate. A holiday only for our unique household.

Now I'd learned what had seemed like a grand excuse to light a fire and decorate the house, had in fact been a tradition both ancient and important. And with everything that had happened, I hadn't even realized it was tonight.

"And you think this'll work?" I asked for likely the tenth time since Mrs. O'Cleary suggested it.

"No, I think it's worth a try," she clarified, lighting another candle. Each time she did, she closed her eyes and whispered words too low to hear. She looked my way again. "You have the sword and Imbolc is the festival of purification. We won't get a better chance."

That was the consensus the coven had reached when Aengus and I had discussed my father and the *ossorians*.

Aengus came into the room from the hallway. He'd refused to return to the Seelie Court until I'd attempted the spells. While his clothes and mine ran through the wash, he'd borrowed some clean clothes from Mr. Perez, a pair of comfortable looking linen pants and button-down shirt in a crazy, colorful pattern. He looked ready to board a cruise, which was likely what Mr. Perez had last used it for. I tried to stifle a giggle, but Aengus noticed. "My choices were limited," he defended.

"You look very handsome," Mrs. O'Cleary said, her words directed at Aengus, but her eyes on me as she winked.

I ignored her. "How's Geoffrey?" I asked him, grateful that he had taken charge of my father, while I'd explained to the pair of understanding police officers that he was ill, and it wouldn't happen again.

Aengus moved to the fireside and leaned against the mantle. "He is calm. It seems Sissy's idea to soak him in a salt bath has slowed the spell. I left him resting, but he asks for you."

"I'll see him later," I said as I shrugged my shoulder and unnecessarily adjusted a pot of snowbells. Mrs. O'Cleary let out a judgmental, "hmmm."

"Of course," Aengus said without argument, and I could have kissed him.

I ignored the guilt that niggled at me, telling me I should go see Geoffrey if only to tell him I'd seen Mom, but I couldn't make myself. Too many uncertainties weighed heavily on me.

It was the same reason I'd set the mirror Saoirse had given me to keep in contact with Nibs on my desk facedown and hadn't tried to use it. I couldn't bear seeing her sad little face begging for me to take her home when I had no idea how I'd accomplish it.

I was beginning to think I should hand back my *custos* club card.

Me, a guardian? A protector? More like coward. The truth was, I didn't even feel confident about my role in the evening's plan. My record for magical success remained low. And the hunger that always followed my magic use filled me with a fear that I'd end up hurting people I cared about.

"Do you need me?" Mrs. O'Cleary asked, lighting the last candle. I shook my head. She extinguished the match and laid it in the dish with the other spent sticks. "Then I'll leave you to reset the wards."

Aengus gave a brief bow as the old woman started up the main staircase and she smiled, her back straightening under his gaze. Aengus kept an eye on her as she took the stairs slowly, seeming to keep her steady with his eyes. I watched his concern and felt a warmth rush down through me. He truly was a white knight. And how did he look attractive, even in ridiculous, borrowed clothes?

Excalibur glinted from the corner where it rested and I walked to it, wrapping my fingers around the hilt. Maybe I'd feel more confident after I reset the wards. The twentieth time had to be the charm, right?

When my fingers touched the door while holding Excalibur, I immediately felt the difference. I dipped forward into my magic and easily pushed all the tempting strands of life energy behind an imagined barrier. I almost laughed with joy at how easy I found it, like shutting a window.

Surrounding the house, the remnants of the ward spell hung like an afterimage—a gossamer web of weaves. I started small, weaving new pieces like quilt squares, following the previous spell as closely as I could, then I let the pieces multiply like dominoes over the entire house. When the last parts attached, a jolt of static snapped through the air.

Aengus sprang upright from his lean with a surprised "oh!"

I smiled over my shoulder at him. "Pretty neat, huh?"

The sound of Mrs. Liu's cane smacking down the upstairs hallway carried until it reached the top of the stairs. "Too much spillover. Use less power next time."

"Of course, Mrs. Liu," I called up as my shoulders jumped with contained humor.

She humphed and clacked back to her room.

It was only then that I realized the hunger wasn't there, even after using my magic. That wasn't quite right. The hunger existed. I could feel it like a predator pacing along an outside wall, but Excalibur kept it from entering. Maybe I really could successfully cast the spells I needed to tonight.

A howl pierced the air outside the door.

I winced, looking over at Aengus. "I might have restored the wards and left the *ossorians* outside."

He actually laughed!

"It's not funny," I groaned as I opened the door. The smaller *ossorian* sat on its haunches while the larger one lay prone behind, hackles raised, ears back. "Magic?" The small one practically barked the word.

"The wards," I said, making a gesture over my head. "Sorry, I'll take it down and let you in."

"Break?" it asked.

"Are you asking if I'm going to break your spell?" It nodded. "The answer is I'm going to try." Both *ossorians* growled low, the larger one lifting a lip. The distrust I felt from them made me take a step back just as Aengus moved to my side. He placed a steady hand on my back. "I told you I can't guarantee I can break it, but I think we have a chance." I tried to sound like I believed it. And the truth was, I desperately wanted it to be true. Just like Aengus they deserved better.

efore Everett left for the evening, he helped push all the furniture to one side of the room to make space for a circle. No nurses would be on call tonight. There never was on Imbolc night, but each year since coming to the retirement home, Everett had insisted he be called if anything went wrong. I knew he was talking about the health of the residents, but tonight I'd teased and asked if he wanted me to call if I screwed up and turned my dad into a toadstool. Everett had emphatically said no.

The coven filtered into the front room one by one, their private ceremonies finished. When I'd asked if I needed to perform a purification, too, Mrs. O'Cleary patted my shoulder and told me Brighid would understand that there wasn't time to teach me both rituals.

The *ossorians,* able to step through the ward if my hand was on them—Mrs. Liu's magic knowledge to the rescue—and my father, now out of his salt bath and dressed, stood off to the side with the rest of the furniture.

I had set Excalibur against the wall, but now I grabbed it again. For a moment, I couldn't make my body move. How was I possibly going to do this? I wasn't a trained witch. People were counting on me and I had no way to guarantee I'd actually be able to help them.

Why had I agreed to this?

A gentle hand guided a lock of my hair behind my ear and startled me out of my thoughts. I gazed up at Aengus's concerned face. "What if I fail?" I asked faintly, looking past Aengus to my father as he chatted with Sissy. Or, more accurately, chatted at her as she nodded along at his words with a subtle smile. If I failed, the green lines that were twining visibly over his skin, even upon his cheeks, would eventually engulf him completely.

"Then we will try again," Aengus said, turning my face back toward him. "And once more, if need be."

I let out a breath, realizing I'd been holding it, and nodded.

Aengus brushed a hand down my arm as he stepped away to find a spot outside the coven's circle drawn with chalk and misted with salt water. I tried to ignore the lingering heat on my skin where he'd touched it.

Five minutes to midnight, we turned off all the electric lights and now the only glow emanated from the fireplace and candles. Geoffrey assured me that a lot of spell work was instinctual. I needed to follow what felt natural and pivot when it didn't. No one could answer how I was supposed to know what was "natural" and what wasn't. Everything I did felt like I was winging it—that's probably because I was.

Mr. Perez, the last to arrive, came from the kitchen with a bowl of water. When he neared the *ossorians,* they growled low. "It's for the ritual," he said kindly, and after a moment, the smaller one backed up, pushing the larger one back with him. Mr. Perez stepped into the spell circle, placing the bowl at my feet. Then he took his place between Sissy and Mrs. Liu.

"Everything is ready," Mrs. Liu said, and the room silenced immediately, all eyes on me.

I swallowed hard. "Here we go," I whispered to myself as I stepped up to the bowl on the floor as Geoffrey moved to the middle with me.

I dipped the blade tip of Excalibur into the bowl at my feet and held it there as Mrs. O'Cleary reached out and handed my father a goblet full of water. He drank it down.

After I'd spoken about Uisca and how both magics, blood and earth, were connected, she felt confident she'd cracked some kind of code and water was the answer. Honestly, I'd have sat in a bath, drinking pond water, and dumping ice over my head if she thought it would help. Thankfully, that wasn't necessary. With Excalibur placed in the bowl and the recently swallowed water in my father, I was to follow that connection and find the origin of Geoffrey's spell. Whether I could do anything about it once found was an unknown we were all worried about.

The coven held hands, calling to the four corners of the earth and requesting her mercy and assistance. Then they went silent and a hum like electricity vibrated the air.

I closed my eyes and almost instantly I sensed the water in Geoffrey. It almost seemed to have exploded through him like a firework, reaching all corners, and exposing what looked like a green almond resting in his abdomen, thin tendrils of green reaching out in all directions. Instinctively, I knew that the spell originated there, in that seed. I could pull it out, I was certain. I just needed to isolate it.

With mental fingers, I quickly ripped free the tiny vines, which withered and disappeared once separated from the seed. Then I pulled all the water my father had drank together and surrounded the seed. My mental fingers wrapped around the spell and yanked.

Geoffrey grunted as if punched.

My eyes flew open. Oh no! I knew I'd end up messing it up. But Mrs. O'Cleary rolled her hand, urging me to continue. My father bit his bottom lip against the pain and nodded.

This time I watched, ready to stop the minute I thought I was hurting him too much. I gave the seed another pull. My father groaned as I dragged the spell up through him. He cried out and panicked I let go of my magic and the spell. Geoffrey dropped to all fours and violently retched. Water gushed from his open mouth and with it a green, wiggling seed.

I dropped to the floor beside him, Excalibur falling with me, splashing the bowl of water everywhere. "Are you okay?" I asked him.

He looked up and gave me a weak, tight-lipped smile.

"Get a container," Mr. Freidman said urgently.

Aengus came forward already holding a canning jar and lid and a pair of tongs. "I had a feeling." He reached down with the tongs, grasping the seed. He dropped it into the jar and screwed the lid on tight.

Geoffrey sat back on his knees. He gazed around the room. All the green veins now vanished. A weak smile spread across his face. "My daughter is brilliant."

The coven released each other's hands and clapped

enthusiastically. Sissy affectionately patted Geoffrey's head like a puppy. But when the *ossorians* stood up on their back legs and howled, the room went silent. "Now uth," the large one snapped through its teeth.

Reaching over, I grabbed Excalibur and stood up. For the first time, I felt powerful. I'd fixed my father. Maybe the sword really had chosen me for a reason. A tiny thought formed, the hope so fragile I barely breathed. If I fixed *ossorians* and broke their spell, wouldn't that mean I could do the same for Aengus?

The veil needed to be closed, but after promising Nimue to keep Aengus out of his tomb, I was beginning to think there had to be another way. If I could make Aengus human again, what would that mean for him? For us?

Chapter Twenty-Three

I ignored the soft knock on my bedroom door but found it harder to ignore Aengus saying my name in a quiet, pleading voice for the third time. "Imogen?"

With a groan, I rolled off the bed and shuffled to the door, cracking it open. "I don't want to talk about it."

"As you wish," Aengus said in a tone used for convincing stray animals of safety. He touched his fingers to mine as they rested on the inner door handle, his warmth comforting and distracting all at once. "May I enter?"

"Fine," I said, stepping away from his touch and pulling the door open all the way. Beyond him, the rest of the house had finally quieted, and all the candles had been extinguished. I suspected everyone had found a room or space to sleep what little was left of the night. "But I don't want to talk about it."

"I know," he answered, stepping in.

The bed squeaked under me as I crumpled onto it, my head in my hands. "I can't believe I failed."

Aengus settled next to me, the mattress dipping and sending me into his side. Instinctively, his arm wrapped around me. "That was not the way of it."

I turned toward him to better glare. "I couldn't break the spell."

"No," he agreed. "Nor, from what you have told me, could anyone."

"But I promised I would free them, and I didn't."

"Those two men lying in the other room would disagree."

Aengus's argument felt like semantics. Yes, I was able to alter the spell, so instead of having one form, the *ossorians* now had two—human and wolf. Aodh and Fintan, brothers, had been changed so fundamentally, down to the very DNA, that destroying the spell would have destroyed them as well. Luckily, I had realized this before going further. Again, the witches had been right. My instincts had steered me and helped me pivot. It still felt like failure. "I just really wanted to fix them." I whispered.

Aengus placed his palm on my cheek. "There is something more to it?"

I nodded against his hand.

"You wanted to fix me," he guessed.

And I nodded again, tears prickling my eyes. Aengus looked down and let out a deep sigh. When he looked up, his pupils had widened until only the barest ring of gold could be seen. I blinked, sending the unshed tears over my cheeks. He brushed them away with his thumbs, then trailed his hands down over my shoulders until he reached my wrists. He raised the one with the faint white scar where he'd fed and touched it hesitantly.

"Do you need more?" I asked, and I tried to hide the tremor in my voice.

"No." He didn't lookup, instead he brought my wrist to his lips. "And never again." His breath hot against my skin.

"I don't think we have much of an alternative." Which only served as a reminder that I could never change Aengus back. He'd never be human again.

Aengus met my eyes. "I will never again put you in that danger."

"I don't want to argue about this again," I cut him off, placing a hand against his chest, my fingers curling into the fabric.

He let out an amused huff as his head dropped. He stared for a long time at my hand clutching his shirt. Finally, he lifted his gaze, regret shadowing his expression. He was pulling away, protecting us both from the grief of loss, because he didn't believe I'd find a way to keep him from the tomb. And after tonight, I wasn't sure I believed either.

When he stood, I did too, my arms falling to my sides. He'd leave the room if I didn't stop him. I had two options: let him go, avoid the hard feelings like I had with Nibs and my father earlier, or I could actually behave like the badass witch fae I was. Before I lost my nerve, I chose. "Would you stay? I want us to finish what we started in the trailer."

Aengus froze as if my words had physically grabbed him. "*Cor meum,*" he said, sadness heavy in his words, then shifted as if to step back.

I stopped him with a touch on his arm. "You've said that before. In the catacombs. What does it mean?"

His lips lifted in a soft smile. "My heart."

"Your heart?"

Aengus nodded.

His words burrowed into my chest, warm as embers. "Will you stay?" I repeated, resting my hands against his chest.

"Will you hold me here if I say no?" he asked, one eyebrow raised higher than the other playfully.

My fingers slowly worked the buttons on his shirt free. "Never," I whispered. I slipped my hands into the open shirt and ran my hands back down his muscled chest. "But I will try to convince you."

"Hmmm." Aengus made a noise in the back of his throat as he closed his eyes under my touch.

"Are you convinced?" I repeated as I rolled the shirt off his shoulders to the floor, the crazy pattern looking much better as a floor covering than as a shirt. His whole body quivered as my hands trailed down over his abs to the waistband of the linen pants and my fingers gripped it. His eyes flew open, hungry. "Yes," he practically growled, and his lips were on mine in an instant.

I let go and threw my arms around him as we fell to the tiny twin bed. The springs screamed under our sudden weight, and I giggled. Aengus pulled back, running a hand through my hair. "It's a full house," I said, feeling suddenly shy. "We're going to need to be quiet."

"I make no promises," Aengus said as he leaned in to kiss at the juncture where my neck met my shoulder. His breath, like fingers against my skin, made me stifle a low moan. "Just be glad for a door. A luxury I often did without," he said between delicate kisses up the side of my neck.

"What do you mean?" My curiosity fighting my desire to use my lips for things other than questions.

Aengus found the hem of my shirt and pulled it over my head, but paused with my head free, but my arms trapped. He held me there with one hand while the other pulled my thigh up against him, heat spreading between us hot enough to melt iron. "Private rooms are for nobility. Everyone else shares."

He dropped his lips to mine, his body sinking heavier against me, as his tongue dove deeply until we were kissing as if we each wished to consume each other. I shifted to get my arms free and Aengus pulled back, releasing the shirt. My arms fell around his head and I slid my fingers into his curls.

"You're right," I agreed. "I'm very glad there's a door." My lips reached for his again, but he moved back. His gaze focused on the strap of my bra as he drew a finger along it, following it down and over the cup. My body shivered beneath his touch. The desire to have him, all of him, rose up, carving out my middle and leaving behind a hunger. A hunger not unlike when I let my powers loose.

"Aengus?" I said my voice hoarse with need.

Finally, he looked up into my eyes. "The thought of leaving you pains me." His words were so laden with emotion that they seemed to land on my heart and crush it.

No, I wouldn't let that happen. Maybe I couldn't completely fix the *ossorians,* but that didn't mean I couldn't find a way to change Aengus's fate. There had to be a way. There had to. But until then, forever or for one night, I would take Aengus anyway I could have him. I let my hands follow the lines of his face, my thumbs tracing the curve of his lips. I pulled myself up and let my teeth give a light pull against his bottom lip. "You're here now."

Flames ignited within his eyes, and his hand tightened against my side, possessive. "Yes, I am," he said, his tone low enough to rumble through me, and then his lips found mine once more.

Pants shimmied down legs until lips, limbs, and torsos melded together, whispering promises to never separate. In a way, love was its own kind of spell. Irrevocably altering those it touched. I knew that even if Aengus left me to close the veil, there was nothing I could do to remove him from my soul.

Chapter Twenty-Four

Aengus lay curled around me on the narrow twin bed, his back pressed up against the wall, with one arm thrown over me and the other lying across my pillow above my head. He breathed, but the pause between each breath was long and I found myself trying and failing to sync my own with his. From my little window, morning purpled the night sky with new and fragile light, just like what had happened last night.

I brushed the tips of my fingers down the arm that lay across me. Part of me marveled over the fact that the legendary Lancelot lay next to me in bed. That there was a man in my bed at all. The other part reveled in how perfect it felt.

I shifted, pressing my back more firmly against Aengus's chest, and he nuzzled into my neck with a sigh. I'd never shared my bed with anyone. My only boyfriend in college had always claimed he was too much of a light sleeper to have me stay over the few times we'd made love. I probably wouldn't have stayed even if he'd wanted me to. He'd never truly put me at ease. I think I'd always known what we had wasn't lasting.

So different from what I'd felt with Aengus.

Was still feeling!

And yet I wasn't certain what I had with Aengus was any more lasting.

Avoiding where that thought led, I pondered who'd be stuck with telling Nibs she'd now have to share the bed.

Nibs. Guilt flooded me. I'd avoided contacting her, and last night I hadn't thought of her once. I was a horrible friend. Wriggling out from under Aengus's arm, I slid off the edge of the bed and plopped to the floor with a soft thwump.

Cold air instantly attacked my arms and legs. I'd pulled on a large t-shirt and underwear before we'd fallen asleep knowing, door or not, I'd never feel comfortable enough to sleep nude with all the people in the house. A pair of sweatpants rested on a pile of dirty clothes at the end of my bed and one of my hoodies draped over the desk chair. I reached for them both, pulling them on as I shivered.

On the seat of the chair, the hand mirror glinted. I lifted it and ran my hand down the side of the mirror, whispering Nib's name like Saoirse had instructed. It was early. Nibs might be sleeping, but I needed to apologize and make sure she was okay.

The reflection wavered, my face dissolving and replaced with a dimly lit earthen den.

"Nibs," I whispered. I waited a moment and then whispered again, "Nibs."

Something rustled and then Nib's face poked in from the side. "What?" she asked, her tone whiney and irritated.

"Sorry, I know it's early," I said with a smile, keeping my voice low.

Nibs furrowed her brow and shifted fully into frame. "Why so quiet?"

"Because it's early."

"And she was trying to let me sleep," Aengus said over my shoulder, causing me to yelp and startle.

I looked up and all I could see was bare chest, chiseled jaw, and tousled blonde curls. "Put on a shirt," I said, batting him back with one hand as I tried to keep him away from the mirror with the other.

Nibs giggled. "Oh, I see."

I glared down at the mirror. "No, you don't."

Aengus leaned down, the bed creaking, and kissed my cheek. "Yes, she does," he said, chuckling. Before I could bat him away again, he rolled out of sight.

No way to put the cat back in the bag. I switched topics. "Are you doing okay?" I asked, really looking at Nibs. She still wore the fingerless glove shift, but it had started to fray and looked grimy. I wished I could get her another outfit, but even if I found a way to get it to her, I doubted the other Brownies would allow her to wear it.

Nibs let out an extremely dejected sigh. "Want to go home."

"I know," I tried to give a smile, "But isn't it nice seeing your family?" Nibs rolled her eyes. "Alright, I get it. I'm going to try and get you home soon."

"How soon?"

The talk was quickly adding more guilt instead of eliminating it. "Soon," I repeated.

The sadness in Nibs's, "Okay," hit against my chest hard and heavy. If I could stop failing people, that would be great.

CRASH!

Something large and solid slammed up against the bedroom door. "What the hell," I squeaked, nearly dropping the mirror.

Aengus leaped from the bed. "Stay here, Imogen. I shall see what has happened." One hand grasped for a non-existent weapon on his bare thigh as the other reached for the doorknob.

"Wait," I called out. From the mirror in my hand, Nibs laughed hysterically.

Aengus paused, then slowly looked down at himself, before slowly looking over his shoulder at me. "Possibly attire first."

"Possibly," I said, stifling my own giggle.

An enormous wolf stood atop the kitchen island, ears back and teeth bared. An even larger wolf paced back and forth across the floor, its shoulder nearly reaching the countertop. At the entrance of the hallway, Mr. Perez stood, arms and legs spread as a barrier. The shuffle of feet and the hum of whispers from the rest of the coven filtered down the hall from behind him. The determined set of his mouth beneath his mustache almost masked his fear.

Last night, the coven and I had only split the spell that had created the *ossorians*, separating the human from the beast. None of us had known what that would mean for the two men in the future. Now it was clear, instead of them resembling werewolves, we'd actually made it even more true. And silly me, when their minds had disappeared from mine last night, I'd assumed I'd be free of their emotions, but there they were now, filling my head with anger and confusion.

I leaned into his shoulder. "Aodh and Fintan." At least we had names instead of calling them the "large one" and the "small one." Aengus dipped his head in a nod of agreement.

A banging on the backdoor window drew all of our attention. Both wolves snarled.

Everett stood outside in the growing morning light. "We got wolves now?" he yelled through the door.

I shrugged and winced. "Maybe try going around front."

"I already did that," he countered. "I'll be in my car. Let me know when y'all figure out what to do with the zoo." Everett turned and disappeared from view.

The wolf on the island perked his ears forward and leaped down, sending a basket of fruit to the floor. Apples and oranges rolled in every direction. Both wolves threw their whole bodies against the

188

back door, making the same sound from earlier that Aengus and I had heard from the room, as they stood on their back legs, looking out and growling low.

"Fintan? Aodh?" I asked hesitantly. Neither wolf acknowledged me.

I took one step and the larger wolf, likely Aodh, swung his head in my direction, his eyes locked on me, his body rigid. "It's me, Genny. Remember?" Aodh sniffed the air and snarled. Fintan dropped down from the door and snarled along with his brother.

Aengus eyed the wolves with mistrust. "You should grab Excalibur."

"No," I said firmly. "I don't want to hurt them. This is my fault, and I'll figure it out."

"Do you have any other weapons in this house?"

Mr. Friedman called from down the hall, "Nothing that isn't an antique."

Aengus let out an irritated hum.

"I'm going to try reaching them mentally," I told Aengus and went to take a step closer.

He swung his arm up, blocking me. "Best try from here," he said as Aodh crouched, lip curling.

Having their emotions in my head was bad enough, but when I reached out to try and interact with them, the emotions hit me like an avalanche. Fear, confusion, and anger were in the forefront, flooding my mind and surely theirs as well.

I gritted my teeth and let go of Aodh's mind, unable to hold both at the same time. I placed all my focus on Fintan, who seemed the slightly calmer of the two.

Memories flashed by in a hazy flurry and grabbing hold of a single thought seemed impossible. Until I noticed a memory repeating every few moments. I pushed toward it until it solidified. A tree by a flowing stream and Fintan, human, curled up against the trunk, his chin held up by his knees, eyes closed with a gentle smile on his lips.

"Fintan," I called out. His head jerked upward. "You need to wake up, Fintan. I need help with your brother." I repeated his name, hoping it would trigger awareness.

Memory Fintan stood up. "Aodh?" he asked.

"Yes."

I felt when Fintan's mind ordered and his consciousness regained control. I stepped free of it, opening my eyes to see a very human Fintan on all fours where a wolf had been. And the moment Fintan called his brother's name, Aodh immediately turned as well.

Apparently, "naked men" was this morning's theme.

Mr. Perez abandoned his guarding to run back down the hall to grab up the sweatpants the brothers' had worn when they'd gone to sleep, but that had obviously slipped off when their form had changed. He returned from the front room and handed the men each a pair as they apologized profusely.

"This isn't your fault," I said firmly. The fault rested heavily on me. Not only had I not fixed them, but I'd created new issues. My best guess, when the men fell asleep, their subconscious took over, causing them to revert to what was left of the spell, and becoming wolves.

"Can I watch *NCIS* now?" Mr. Friedman called down the hall.

"Crisis averted," Mr. Perez answered. The tromp of feet followed his response. "I should go tell Everett it is safe to come in."

I thanked him and he made his way back down the hallway. I turned to the now half-clothed brothers. "We'll need to figure out an easier way to keep your conscious minds awake. Waking up as angry wolves is going to get real dangerous real quick."

"This will happen every time?" Aodh asked.

"Yes, I think so," I admitted.

Mrs. O'Cleary, wrapped in a terry-cloth robe, stepped into the kitchen. "A talisman may work. I've seen them used to stabilize a spell. It may allow their consciousness to stay available even when they turn, allowing them to switch back and avoiding mauling their friends."

"Preferable," Fintan agreed. Aodh scowled but nodded.

Mrs. O'Cleary looked to me. "Your father might have more knowledge with his study in witch artifacts."

"Perfect," I said.

"Not sure where he is, however," Mrs. O'Cleary said her shoulder lifting in a shrug.

"What do you mean? Where did he go?" I asked her, then looked around the room.

They all looked at me with expressions that were about as useful as the fake toothpick on the back of a flosser.

Chapter Twenty-Five

"You can't just run off like that!" I yelled at Geoffrey, who was still a few yards away. The sun had barely risen and frost still coated the grass along the sidewalk. My father was barely dressed for a chilly spring day in lounge pants, sandals and a t-shirt, much less a cold winter morning. He'd gained a few pounds in only a matter of days, but his bones still protruded aggressively.

"I needed a stroll," he finally answered when we were closer.

"You could have at least put on a coat," I said, gesturing to his complete lack of warm apparel.

Geoffrey rubbed his arms and nodded. "You might be correct."

We headed back toward the house, shoulder to shoulder. Despite the current cold, there were no clouds in the sky and the rising sun felt warm on my face. "Why did you need a walk?" I finally asked.

"It's odd, really. I can't help feeling something is missing or has been taken. An organ, or a limb. As if my body remembers having more connected to it and now it's gone." While he spoke, he ran a hand over his face and over his arms, flexing his fingers into fists and releasing them.

The little Green Knight spell seed remained safely contained in the glass jar with Mrs. O'Cleary. I never once considered he miss it. "I'm sorry."

"Don't be. This feeling is only discomfort, but I'm glad to be me, again." He glanced over at me and smiled.

I returned it. "I'm glad you're *you*, too."

"We have much catching up to do."

Speaking of catching up, a pang of guilt reminded me I still hadn't talked with him about seeing my mother while in Uisca. Now that I'd waited so long, I felt awkward and changed the subject quickly. I needed to tell him. I knew I did. Maybe when we got back to the house. "Our cobbled spell from last night for the *ossorians* has hit a bit of snag." I said instead.

"Oh?" Geoffrey paused and I stopped, too.

"They revert to full wolf when they sleep and don't remember themselves."

He jerked his head in the direction of the house. "Cripes. They're not still wolves, are they?"

I waved my hands in the air. "No. They're human now, but what I did isn't a permanent solution. Mrs. O'Cleary thinks a talisman would work. She thought you might have some ideas."

Geoffrey visibly relaxed and his expression switched from alarmed to purely academic in a blink. "She's right, a talisman might be able to harness their consciousness. Of course, we'd need a druid to forge it. I'm not sure if there are any left."

"Funny enough, I know a guy."

Goeffrey chuckled. "You are definitely my daughter."

Daughter. The acknowledgment in the word overwhelmed me and I stopped walking, stunned. I had a father, a dad, and he was here. Not just a biological fact, not a living statue of plants, but a human breathing parent walking beside me. Half of what had created me came from him, but I didn't even know his middle name. Did he even have a middle name? And would knowing the answers to my questions change anything?

Maybe not but keeping secrets certainly would. I needed to tell him about what happened in Uisca.

Geoffrey stumbled to a stop when he realized I wasn't next to him. He looked back at me as I stood frozen on the sidewalk.

"I saw Mom—Mira."

I heard his intake of breath from where I stood. "Mira? You saw Mira? Was she well?" His tone deepened when he said her name.

"I think so." I thought about the weird red tubes. "I hope so. The Leannan Sidhe has her."

He asked when I'd seen her, as his entire body trembled in the cold. I promised to tell him if we kept walking.

Even knowing mine and Aengus's visit to Uisca was real, saying it aloud felt unreal, and I even began to doubt what I'd seen. I wondered if Geoffrey would even believe it.

"I must admit, I'm jealous. I have only read of such places," Geoffrey said without any doubt.

"Believe me, it wasn't as fun as it sounds."

"As you say," he said, but I clearly hadn't convinced him. He ran a hand roughly through his rumpled hair. "I feel we are missing something. Leannan has Mira, but for what reason? It can't be only because she is part fae."

I raised my hand and splayed my fingers. "We know that there's a connection between Leannan and Danu," I said, ticking down a finger. "We know she has killed Cailleach fae for power before, which is why she is after me." Geoffrey nodded, following along. "And Mira is my mother." I paused, searching for the through line.

"That does not imbue her with any additional power," Geoffrey reasoned, and I agreed.

What else was my mother? She was Grandpa's daughter...the red tubing..."The blood! Leannan is taking her blood," I nearly yelled.

Geoffrey startled and paled. "For what reason?"

There was certainly more about this whole thing that I hadn't figured out yet, but I suddenly knew exactly why mother was being held. "Leannan is using Mira's blood to feed the missing *fola tráil*. The Wylde's have fae blood, royal blood," I explained.

Geoffrey furrowed his brow. "How do you know that?"

"I kind of met my great, great, great, grandfather and Lady Aurnia's first-born son. He's lives with the druid."

"I guess, contrary to what my parents thought, I married above my station." Geoffrey said, his eyes wide in disbelief.

I hadn't even thought about that. I had a whole family whose names I didn't even know. Did I have aunts and uncles? Cousins? But if they didn't like my mother, they probably wouldn't think much of being related to me, either. Lovely, not only did I have to contend with small town judgmental neighbors, but I apparently now had snobby relatives.

"They didn't like Mira?" I asked.

"Less about who she was and more about who she wasn't." Geoffrey sounded guilty. "I was supposed to marry the daughter of one of our coven members. Keep the magic in the family. Not marry a poor American from a tiny town in the wild west. God forbid if they'd known she was *custos* and that we'd had a child, a..." he paused.

"An abomination," I filled in.

Geoffrey grabbed my arm firmly and stopped us. Wylde House stood visibly a few yards ahead. "You aren't an abomination. You are just too powerful to be controlled, and neither side—the fae nor the witches—accept that. They believe power should always be under someone's rule. But they're wrong. Never apologize for not being what others expect."

The cold air hadn't disappeared, yet I suddenly felt warm and tears sprang up in my eyes. I guess I'd never grown out of wanting validation, even from a parent I'd only just met. "Thanks," I whispered.

We started walking again.

Geoffrey cleared his throat. "Aengus, he seems like a nice enough bloke."

"Oh no, we are not having this conversation," I said, slashing my hand in the air as if to cut out any further words. Of all the topics I wanted to have with my new-to-me father, my love life was not anywhere near the top. In fact, I'd completely left it off the list.

"You know, Imbolc has always had a fertility element. It's nothing to be embarrassed about."

"Oh, my god!"

Geoffrey and I barely had room to step inside the front room. The television was not on and all the furniture remained pushed up against the far wall from last night. But now colorful foam mats filled the space, the chalk circle from last night still visible beneath them in places, and all the residents balanced on one foot, arms raised to the ceiling. Everett towered over everyone, his raised hands nearly touching the light fixture. Even the *ossorians* and Aengus had joined in. They stood out, three well-muscled bare-chested men in a sea of gray hair and track suits.

Near the door, Mr. Friedman wobbled and dropped his raised foot to the floor, giving me a resigned smile. "Forgot today was Yoga Monday," he grumbled.

My days were so jumbled, I hadn't even remembered what day it was either.

From the front of the group, Mrs. O'Cleary encouraged everyone to breathe as she gracefully moved to the next pose.

I gave Mr. Friedman an encouraging smile. "The beauty of streaming. NCIS will be there when you're done." He harrumphed in answer as he wobbled into the next pose.

Geoffrey and I scooted around everyone and headed back toward the kitchen. I caught Aengus's gaze as I looked over my shoulder and he winked. I felt the blush bloom over my cheeks and I smiled back before ducking my head and making my way down the hall.

"Coffee?" I asked.

"I suppose it's the better option than the ancient Lipton tea bags I found in the cupboard," he said, taking a seat at the island.

I laughed as I pulled the carafe off the hot plate and filled two mugs. The creamer from the fridge turned mine into a very nice tan, but Geoffrey waved his hand no when I asked with a gesture if he wanted any in his.

"Those brothers seem to be doing well. You say they were wolves this morning?"

"Yeah," I answered as I handed him his coffee and took a sip from mine.

"Brilliant work, truly."

There was that word again. Brilliant. I hid my smile behind another sip of coffee. I didn't think I'd ever tire of hearing the pride in his voice.

Geoffrey took a sip from his mug and grimaced. I pushed the creamer toward him and he took it, dumping in a generous amount.

"You really think a talisman will work?" I asked, setting down my mug.

Geoffrey took a moment, looking over his shoulder toward the hallway, then turned back to me. "I believe so, yes."

"How does that even work?"

"In theory, if we link their consciousness to the metal of a talisman, then it would never be completely suppressed. They would be able to access their consciousness no matter which form they inhabit."

Access their consciousness. Those words reminded me of how my mother reached me through the bracelet. I lifted my arm, and the bangle glinted. "Is that what you did with this?"

Geoffrey stood up abruptly, swaying on weak legs, and pulled my arm toward him. I didn't resist. "Your mother's bracelet," he said softly and his fingers reached out with a tremble. He pulled his hand back without touching it.

"I found it at the Seelie Court. It's linked to Mom."

He nodded, still staring at the metal around my wrist. "I bought it when I went back to England for business. From a magic dealer for an exorbitant price." He let out a self-depreciating laugh. "I had it engraved, and then your mother and I performed a bonding ritual over it." Geoffrey fell back down on the stool, exhausted.

The engraving. A bonding ceremony. I remembered wondering, probably like every orphan ever, if my parents had wanted me. If they'd loved each other. And knowing the answer was yes to both reassured the inner child still lingering within me. "But how did it get to me?"

"Anything druid forged has a bit of sentience. Not enough to communicate, but enough to know where it's needed."

I thought about how I found Excalibur on my bed that first time, and how Jane said that the sword went where it wanted. Sentient swords and bracelets? Sure, why not.

Aengus flushed, a smile stretching across his face, came into the kitchen, followed by Aodh and Fintan. "Mrs. O'Cleary has defeated us," he said and the three men laughed.

I pulled three glasses from the cupboard, filled them from the sink, and set them on the island. Fintan watched me with complete fascination. I couldn't blame him. Running water was pretty helpful. I couldn't wait until he realized it would also come out hot. Aengus still delighted in that one. The men sucked down the liquid in seconds. I refilled them and they downed them again. I tried not to let my gaze linger on the sheen of Aengus's chest or the flex of his bicep as he raised his glass to his lips. Flashes from last night flickered through my mind, and my heart thumped excitedly. I forced myself to turn away.

"Geoffrey and I think we know how to solve the waking-up-as-a-wolf problem." I said when the second glasses were set down empty.

"We'll need to work out the details, but we'll try to do it as quickly as possible."

Aodh grunted with a nod then lumbered out the back door, letting it slam shut behind him.

Fintan looked awkward. "My brother is grateful. As am I. You have given us back our lives."

Guilt flooded me. "I wish I could've done more." Out of the corner of my eye, I saw Aengus frown.

Fintan shook his head. "We chose this. Maybe we lacked a true understanding of what we were agreeing to, but we were ready to chain ourselves to Morgana for the power she offered. Whatever amount of life has been returned is more than we could ask for. Or deserve."

"Morgana?" I recognized the name, but they couldn't possibly mean...

"Yes. Morgana of the fae, The Leannan Sidhe, you must know of whom I speak?"

"Of course," I choked out.

Fintan bent at the waist in a short bow. "I must see to my brother. Thank you again." He left, closing the door softly behind him.

Geoffrey stood up, his eyes glassy and lids drooping. I could clearly see the walk had taken a lot out of him. "I think I'll go have a lie down. Just for a moment," he said, and I just nodded, unable to form words at the moment. He shuffled toward the infirmary, leaving Aengus and me alone in the kitchen.

"This feels like information I should have had sooner," I finally said. "Is there anyone else from legend you'd like to spring on me?"

Aengus stepped close and rubbed his hands up and down my arms. "I did not realize you were unaware. Forgive me."

I sighed and gave him a resigned smile. "It's fine, but why doesn't anyone call her by that name? No one. They always call her Leannan or The Leannan Sidhe."

Aengus let his hands slide down my arms until he found my palms and held them. "Leannan means lover. When it was discovered that Morgana was the consort of Danu, those jealous of her connection called her The Leannan Sidhe, "the fae lover", but what they really meant was whore. Morgana heard and demanded after everyone call her Leannan."

"She took away their power."

Aengus nodded.

Somehow, knowing we were fighting *the* Morgana le fey, the one who defeated Merlin and brought the downfall of Camelot, seemed much more insurmountable than it had before. I felt suddenly very sick.

Chapter Twenty-Six

The coven napped. All the furniture had finally returned to their original places and all the yoga mats were rolled up and put away. *NCIS* had played until early afternoon, but now the only sounds were the ticking of the mantle clock and the white noise hum of Mrs. Liu's fan from upstairs. Even Everett lounged in his desk chair. His breaths deep and relaxed and a book cracked open on his chest.

I couldn't help but be unsettled by the quiet. The retirement home was never this sedate. Not since I'd brought home chaos in the form of a Brownie. I missed Nibs. Chaos that she was. I needed to use the mirror again to check up on her.

The damp ends of my hair tickled my neck, and I ran my hand through the tresses, giving them a shake, hoping to dry it faster so I could put it up in a ponytail again. Bending my elbow, irritated where the needle had poked in earlier, causing it to burn and itch. But only a little. Everett was good at his job. He'd made drawing my blood quick and mostly painless.

I wasn't even sure I could get Aengus to drink them. If I couldn't, I'd need to get the vials out of my back pocket and into the fridge.

Should they go in the medicine fridge or the food fridge? Why was I now a person who had to ask that question?

From what was becoming its place beside the hearth, Excalibur gleamed, a glint of light sliding over the blade, seemingly with no source. I stepped around a wingback chair and stared down at it. Another play of light danced like a falling star, gliding from the guard to the tip. I reached out and wrapped my hand around the hilt.

The screen door squeaked, followed by the creak of the front door. I looked up as Aengus stepped inside alone. He'd showered earlier and replaced his borrowed linen pants with the familiar black-on-black outfit. His black duster swished around his feet like a cape, but his head was bare, no beanie. Clean and glossy golden curls bounced around his forehead, but their vibrancy couldn't belie the dark circles around Aengus's sunken eyes and sallow skin. When had he last gotten enough sleep?

"Will the garage work?" I asked, still holding the sword at my side.

Aengus brushed an errant curl off his forehead. "In the event, we are unable to create talismans, I believe your vehicle stable will hold the brothers while in wolf form. The stones are exceptionally smooth and without apparent weakness."

I looked toward the door. "Where are they?"

"Going through the boxes of clothes you suggested."

Grandpa and Grandma's clothes. I'd boxed it all up and hadn't gotten up the courage to donate any of it. They remained stacked in the garage. I hoped there was something in there that worked.

Aengus placed a hand on the back of the chair. He seemed to wobble slightly. I remembered the vials in my back pocket and pulled them out. He looked at the glass tubes in my hand without recognition. I opened my fingers, so they rested on my palm. "I had Everett draw them."

Surprise widened Aengus's eyes. I stepped closer so he could reach them easier. He clenched the back of the chair until his knuckles whitened. "I cannot."

"Why? What you took from me before wasn't enough. You're feeling it now. I can see it in your face. Drink it." I reached out farther.

Aengus pulled back and sighed. "We need to recast Merlin's spell. I have no wish to take from you again."

My fingers snapped closed around the vials and I pulled them to my chest. "What?"

"The spell that connects me to the earth."

"I know what spell you mean," I said sharply. "But why? If I recast it, you—we—what we have—" My eyes darted toward the hallway and the bedroom. How easy it was last night to pretend I was okay with Aengus leaving. Now a mention of the first step and I couldn't breathe through the panic.

Aengus was suddenly by my side, his hands running up and down my arms, before coming to rest around my fists.

"We must prepare," Aengus said, his words low and gentle.

I looked up into his golden eyes. "We have time. There's no reason to rush."

"Your blood is not an option, even this way." He held up my hand holding the vials. "As the days lengthen, I only grow weaker. I am no use to you. With Merlin's spell connecting me to the earth, I will be able to protect you. And I may serve my purpose and close the veil."

"What about Nibs? My mother? I promised a large tentacled goddess I wouldn't let you go back into your tomb. How am I supposed to do that?" I argued.

"If I'm stronger, I am better able to help them. And Nimue will not blame you. She will know you tried."

I pushed the vials toward Aengus's chest and he instinctively grabbed at them before they fell and broke on the floor. "You should still drink these. I'm not saying I won't do the spell, but we don't know how long it will take me to cast it. I'm not Merlin."

Aengus pulled the rubber stopper off one of the vials. His nostrils widened, and he looked away, pained.

I held up my wrist. "It's either those or this."

Aengus narrowed his eyes, but I could see he lacked an argument. He brought the vial to his lips and drank it quickly like a shot of tequila, but instead of a full body shudder, he seemed to relax with pleasure. In quick order, he down the other three. For a moment, he eyed my wrist but forced himself to look back into my eyes. "Pleased?" he growled.

"Immensely," I answered with a large triumphant smile, but my lips quickly fell under the weight of knowing soon the end would begin.

Seeing me frown, Aengus dropped the stoppered vials on the seat of the chair, the glass tinkling like chimes, and reached out to me, laying a hand against my cheek. I leaned into it. He rubbed a thumb along my cheekbone. His other arm pulled me closer. He looked down into my eyes. "Your love gives me the strength to do what I must do."

"Well then, I don't love you and now you have no strength and have to stay," I mumbled.

Aengus chuckled as he bent down, running his nose along my jawline. I met him in the middle, our lips coming together. What might have started as a gentle, soft kiss quickly intensified as a frenetic energy took hold. His lips and tongue tasted of salty iron, which might have bothered me if I'd taken a moment to think about it, but the only thing I could concentrate on was getting closer.

Holding a sword made throwing my arms around Aengus impossible. His hands were already in my hair and splayed against my back. I lifted Excalibur to toss it in the chair, not caring if it damaged the fabric. Just as I went to let go, it felt as if someone punched me in the gut, sending me backwards. Aengus's arms tightened around me. An unknown weight crushed my chest and a searing whine roared in my ears. Lack of air caused tiny lights to burst before my eyes. And just when I thought I would pass out, everything popped back into existence. I could hear and breathe once again.

What the hell just happened?

For a moment, I thought it was too dark to see until I realized I was still burrowed into Aengus's chest, behind the flaps of his duster. I shifted, but Aengus held me tighter and whispered, "Shhhh," against my ear.

An echoing voice called out. "Have you brought the sacrifice?"

A very familiar voice.

The Leannan Sidhe.

Morgana le Fey.

Chapter Twenty-Seven

The Leannan Sidhe? How had she gotten through the wards? And sacrifice? What the hell was going on?

I pulled free of Aengus's arms, my head spinning in all directions, and sucked in a sharp breath, when Aengus yanked me back. I'd nearly collided with a protruding rock a few inches from my nose. Where was the retirement home? Where were we? In one direction, obscured daylight filtered in under a low opening, bouncing off the jagged edges of the stone that surrounded us from floor to ceiling. In the other, light gave way to deep darkness.

A cave.

"How?" I demanded in a whisper as I slipped out of Aengus's grip once more and flung my hands wide.

"Excalibur," he answered, and didn't seem surprised.

"The sword?" I said a little too loudly. Aengus gave me a look, and I dropped my voice, "brought us here?" I gestured around us. "Where even are we?"

"The air is without water and smells similar. We are no doubt still on the far side of this country."

Why was he so chill about this? "Did you know it could do that?" I hissed.

"It has happened before."

"And you didn't think it was important to tell me?"

Aengus opened his mouth to either apologize or defend himself but was cut off from either by a shrill squawking, not unlike an angry flamingo. It echoed from deeper within the cave and we both jerked our head toward the sound, staring into the dark.

"Stay here," Aengus ordered as he took a step into the shadows.

"I'm the only one with magic *and* a sword," I reminded him, lifting Excalibur and pointing at it.

He let out a thwarted chivalry sigh, but didn't argue. The legends had obviously done him a disservice. "Lancelot" was strong, but he was also smart.

The shadows weren't nearly as complete once our eyes adjusted and soon a soft wavering glow reached out from around a corner as we neared. Aengus held up a hand, signaling that he was stopping. We paused and he leaned around it.

"What do you see?" I asked.

He pulled back and briefly gazed at Excalibur with longing. I knew he hated being without a weapon. And to be perfectly honest, I wished he had one too. "There is a portal open up ahead," he answered. "And Leannan."

"A portal?" I repeated in surprise.

Suddenly, Aengus jerked and lifted his nose to the air. "I smell *fola*." His top lip curled up in a snarl and I caught a glimpse of fang.

"We were right. Leannan is using them."

He nodded.

I pressed close to Aengus, trying to see around the corner. I wished I had one of those cool "across the back sheaths" that look badass or even one that hung from a belt. Instead, I had to hold Excalibur towards the floor and try not to stab Aengus in the ass.

Further into the cave, Leannan stood dressed in her white gown. The one I'd first met her in. In her hand she held the spear Birga. A familiar portal swirled on her right. A vortex of prisms, I'd seen her use before. But on her left..."What is that?" I whispered against his shoulder, unable to reach his ear.

The only way I could describe it was it appeared to be a softened spot in the fabric of the world. A fuzziness stretched across the rock and although the cave wall could be seen through the haze, it was as if a curtain of water obscured it.

"The veil," Aengus answered.

"You mean beyond that is—"

"Innisfail."

I thought I'd understood the concept of the veil, but now, faced with the very doorway into a fantasy kingdom, it felt too unreal to comprehend.

Ripples undulated across the surface of the veil, as two dots appeared near the top. Quickly the two dots grew in length and began to curl upward, widening in girth until horns appeared, followed by a complete figure. A mostly human shape stepped out of the watery entrance with goat-like legs. Bright orange eyes blinked, pupils horizontal and wide.

"We almost left you behind," Leannan said, but there was no threat in her voice.

The horned fae smirked, tilting his head and horns to the side. "You would never leave without me."

"Don't try me, Janquil."

Aengus tensed.

I leaned in again. "Someone you know?"

He dipped his head once. "We have never met, I know him only through rumors. I believe he leads the Wild Fae for the Horned King."

"The Wild Fae?"

"Those who refuse to join either court. They loosely follow the Horned King and only because he asks nothing of them. Janquil is his seneschal."

"Like Dennriall?"

Aengus nodded.

Janquil strode toward Leannan and stared down at her. She raised her hand to lay it lovingly on his cheek. "Did you bring one?" she asked.

Janquil leaned, reaching toward her, his arm circling her waist and pulling her up hard against him. The giggle Leannan let out was high and girlish. Janquil buried his face against her neck and she sighed. "Yes," he rumbled.

I'd never seen Leannan make the expressions she did at that moment. She looked young and light. All the bitterness was either hidden or tempered.

Leannan smacked Janquil's shoulder playfully and he set her down. Leannan gripped Birga in both hands as Janquil reached back through the veil. Slowly, he pulled his hand back, leading another fae through.

The unknown fae had variegated skin resembling bark and, where hair might grow, twigs covered in delicate leaves sprouted. The fae closed her dark eyes and dipped into a low curtsy in front of Leannan.

I had a bad feeling.

"Do you give yourself willingly?" Leannan asked, and the fae stood up straight as they answered yes.

A really bad feeling. "You don't think..." I started to whisper to Aengus when Leannan pulled back her arms and slammed the spear through the fae. My hand flew to my mouth, catching my scream.

The fae crumpled around the spear. "We thank you for your sacrifice," Leannan said and then yanked the spear free. The fae fell to the floor, still, as blood pooled around them.

That's how Leannan was so powerful. It made a horrible amount of sense. How many fae had she stolen magic from?

Leannan moved toward the portal, the spear dripping red down her arm. "Was she the last?"

Janquil bent and grabbed a leg of the dead fae. "Those that have stayed behind won't be swayed. What we have must be enough," he answered.

Have enough of what? I thought about how Aengus and Aurnia had claimed having the veil open would leave the human world vulnerable to dangerous fae, but aside from a few incidents, there hadn't been any real change. I pulled on Aengus's sleeve. "What if there have been no fae attacks because Leannan is taking them? She's taken the *fola*, why not the wild fae, too?"

"She could possess an army," Aengus growled, darting his gaze back to Leannan and Janquil. "We must find out."

Leannan and stepped through her portal and Janquil dragging the fae followed her. Before I could register what Aengus was doing, he was already halfway across the cave, running toward the shrinking portal. I dashed after him. Without hesitation, Aengus leaped and disappeared through the portal.

I skidded to a stop, my brain screaming that leaping into portals created by villains was a terrible idea.

I leaped in after him.

Chapter Twenty-Eight

I hit the floor in a heap, bright sharp pain radiating from my hip and elbow and the hilt of Excalibur digging into my abdomen. Ignoring the pain, I scrambled to my feet and weakly raised Excalibur up in defense. "Aengus?" I called as I turned in a circle.

The room, floor to ceiling in wood and no bigger than a closet, seemed empty. There also didn't seem to be an exit. Even the portal had vanished behind me. The only furniture in the room resembled a roman settee heaped with fabric and pillows. Everything looked rimed in blue. It reminded me of Uisce, but different. Here the blue was cold, sharp ice.

Where was Aengus? Where was I?

What I had dismissed as merely fabric, shifted and sat upright. The face covered in hair and shadow. "Genny?" The disheveled figure asked as they pushed strands out of the way.

I recognized the voice even before I could fully see her features. "Mom?"

My mother stumbled from the lounging chair and moved toward me, her movements jerky and uncoordinated. She no longer had tubes running from her arms, but bandages marked her elbows where I'd seen them. "Genny, what are you doing here?"

"I...I..." I started unable to find the right words. "Mom," I said again in an exhale.

She reached for my face, her hands and gaze rushing over me. "You shouldn't be here," she said and I could tell she was trying to sound upset, but she only came off as exhausted.

So many important things I wanted to tell her, but they warred in my brain until I couldn't land on one to start with. She pulled me against her, and I let my sword arm fall to my side. I felt her warm tears against my hair. So many years had passed. So much anger I'd felt over what I'd thought was her leaving me behind. Now the anger sat in a corner without a motive, but unable to fully dissipate. I squeezed my eyes shut and just let myself be hugged. It didn't feel like home, but maybe someday it would.

When she pulled back, I finally knew what to say. They were the words I'd want to hear if Aengus had gone missing. "I found Dad."

Mom blinked, her eyes disbelieving. "Geoffrey?" she murmured.

I nodded.

She let out an almost hysterical laugh, as if her mind was unable to process what response was correct. "He's alive?"

I nodded again. She reached out and laid a hand on my cheek. "I didn't want to leave you." Her eyes were glassy, and she tried to smile, but it looked more like a grimace as she tried not to let her tears fall again.

"We can talk about it later," I assured her. I stepped away and circled the room. Maybe there was a door I missed. "We need to find a way out."

My mother shuffled to the settee and crumpled down upon it. "There's no way. I've looked."

"Yeah, but have you looked with magic?" I asked, unable to keep the satisfied smile off my face. I lifted Excalibur before me. "Mom, meet Excalibur my cynosure. Excalibur, meet Mom."

"Do I dare ask how that happened?"

216

"I'm counting on it and the minute we're safe I'm going to tell you the whole story, whether you like it or not!"

She smirked and motioned her hand for me to proceed.

Tipping over the edge of the cliff and into my magic, I looked for evidence of a spell, just as I had for the wards. One group of paneling looked odd. I stepped closer to get a better look. "I think there's a door here," I called over my shoulder.

I touched the wall with my free hand and the glamour hiding the door melted away. Now the metal hinges and an ornately curled handle of iron were visible. I gave it a yank, and it opened freely.

With a turn and a hand flourish, I gestured toward the open doorway. "Come on, Mom. I'm busting you out of this joint." I looked out into a shadowed hall. No guards. That was good. I pulled my head back in and shut the door. I turned to my mother. "Do you know which way is out?"

"I've never left this room." She gave a self-deprecating laugh.

I glanced over my shoulder and really looked at her. Honestly, she seemed no older than she had in the pictures I'd found in Grandpa's closet. Some people naturally stayed looking young, but this was more than an illusion of youth. "Did it feel like years in here?" I asked.

Her expression dropped, and she rubbed at an arm. "Part of me knew that years were passing, but nothing changed in this prison. I couldn't even mark the days on the wall. The mark would disappear the next day. Each day was the same until the day you appeared here. I'd dropped my bracelet and when I looked up, you were standing in this room. Not like you are now, but more like a ghost. I didn't recognize you at first and I begged you to help me. It was only later, when Leannan mentioned you, that I realized you were my Genny, all grown up. Somehow, you wearing the bracelet allowed me to see you—to speak to you. But after I helped you save that young man, Leannan must have suspected something. I couldn't reach you anymore."

I blinked. Her monologue was too much to take in all at once.

Mom twisted her lips in a half-smile, raising her hands in surrender. "Sorry, I've been so alone. It feels good to speak. But to answer your question simply: No, it didn't feel like twenty years for me."

There was a fragility to her, and it made me want to take away her worry. I smiled. "It's okay, Dad will just have a trophy wife now."

The snort that exploded from my mother made us both laugh out loud and then we shushed each other.

I slowly reopened the wooden door. The wood planked hallway remained empty, but the eerie silence made my skin crawl. I lifted Excalibur in front of me like I knew what I was doing and took a step out of the room.

The further we walked, the more the air smelled of brine and damp wood, and the walls creaked and moaned. Were we on a ship? Despite the smell and the sound, the floor seemed solidly stable. We followed the hallway to the end, where it turned left or right. Mom looked pale and shaky, and when we paused, she seemed to relish the chance to be held up by the wall.

I'd watched enough action movies to know how to look around a corner. My back pressed against the wall, I leaned slowly around the edge only to get a face full of warm fabric. Arms grabbed me and yanked me close. Before I could cry out, Aengus gasped my name. "Imogen." With another jerking motion, he pushed me out to the ends of his arms and I could finally see his face. He looked panicked. "I turned around, and you were gone."

"Excalibur strikes again," I said, lifting the sword. "I think it brought me to my mom." I glanced over my shoulder and Aengus followed my line of sight. "Mom, this is Aengus. Aengus, this is my mother Mira."

Aengus finally let me go and bowed. When he moved, I caught sight of someone standing behind him. "Dennriall! You're alive!" The fae stood in human form, his sleek black hair falling around his sharp-featured face, red eyes glowing faintly. I reached out to hug him.

He put up a hand to stop me. "That is not necessary."

I smirked and wondered if he let his husband hug him. His husband. Dennriall didn't know what had happened after he went missing.

He must have seen the concern on my face. "What is it?" he asked.

"The Unseelie Queen knows about your husband."

Dennriall went from aloof to raving in seconds, reaching toward me. "Nicholas? What has she done to him?"

Aengus moved quickly between us. "Peace. We were told your husband showed up at court demanding he be told where you are. The queen claimed she tossed him out of court. That is all we know."

Dennriall ran a violent hand through his hair, before dropping it down over his features, ripping away his human glamour. Behind me, my mom pulled in a frightened breath. Dennriall now stood a good foot taller on eight legs. Instead of two human looking eyes, three glowing orbs sat within his round face and when he opened his slit-like mouth, angry pincers clicked. He loomed over both Aengus and me, but his stare was hyper focused on me. "I call on the debt that is owed. You will free me from this prison or die trying."

Aengus stiffened. "No one is dying."

"Of course not," I said, giving Dennriall an exasperated look. "Saving you has always been part of plan." I looked down the hallway. "But where are we?"

Dennriall squeezed the line of his mouth tight with disdain. "From what I've seen, I believe Leannan has created a hidden space using Uisce and the veil. Like a bubble resting between."

That must have been why I could see my mother when we were traveling through Uisce. Behind me, I heard a whimper. I looked back just as my mother slid down the wall to sprawl along the floor. "Mom!" I dropped to my knees beside her.

She weakly waved her hand. "I'm just tired."

Aengus crouched down on her other side. "May I lift you?"

Mom's eyes widened, and she looked at me for guidance. "He's really strong, Mom. You should let him. We need to hurry." She turned to Aengus and nodded.

Aengus gently slid his arms underneath her and pulled her up. One of her arms dropped limply, and Dennriall skittered forward. He looked from the angry bruises on her arms to her face. "They have been draining you?"

She nodded.

"Leannan stole Aurnia's *fola triáll*. She needs Honeythorn blood," I explained.

Dennriall canted his head. "So you now know whose blood flows through your veins."

"Yes," I answered. "I've even met him."

With the speed of a spider trapping a fly, he grabbed my arm and yanked me close. What was it with all the yanking today? I was not a fan.

"What do you mean, you've met him?" Dennriall's eyes flared, the brightest I'd ever seen them, and his pincers clicked viciously.

"Unhand her," Aengus snapped, but couldn't do anything with my mother in his arms.

Dennriall didn't let me go and only tightened his grip. "What do you mean you've met him?" he repeated, his tone cold.

I knew Dennriall was old, like over millennia if not older, but this was the first time I felt the power in his age. I trembled and stuttered, "C-C-Cathal. He lives here, well not *here* here, but you know, in Nevada."

"Impossible," Dennriall hissed.

"I'm not lying." It felt as if my wrist bones creaked beneath his grip. That's when I realized I still held a sword. I lifted the tip until it touched where presumably his human torso met his thorax. "Let me go. I'm not lying."

With a huff, Dennriall released me, folding his four arms against his chest. I rubbed where he'd held it, trying to get the feeling back.

"Are you all right," Aengus asked.

I scowled at Dennriall but nodded. Continuing to point my sword, I asked. "Why is it impossible?"

Dennriall clicked his pincers and frowned before he answered. "You could not have met the Honeythorn heir, because he's been dead for centuries."

"Then he looked pretty good for a corpse," I quipped in irritation. "I did meet Cathal. He claimed his family sent him to watch over a druid."

"A druid?" Dennriall repeated, no longer giving off murder vibes. I nodded, finally letting the sword tip drop to the ground.

Aengus shifted to get past us with Mira in his arms. "We should speak of this later. Do you know of a way out?" This last question he directed at Dennriall.

"I have not left the room you found me in since I was first brought here." There was a slight droop to Dennriall's shoulders. All his bluster left him and his voice was weak when he asked, "How long has it been?"

"Three months," I answered. This seemed to be better news than he was expecting. I thought of how young my mother looked and she claimed it hadn't felt like twenty years had passed and understood his fear.

Aengus paused. "You said this place is connected to Uisce. Did you see water anywhere before they locked you in that room? If she created this space using Uisce's power, there must be a water source."

"No, but Leannan spoke of a lake within my hearing once."

"Then that is where we shall go. We find this lake, we find our way out." Aengus said confidently.

Sure, no problem. It wasn't as if we were locked in a time-altering prison with free roaming vampires, werewolves, and violent wild fae. I frowned. Although, why hadn't we seen any of them?

Right on cue, a low, menacing growl echoed down the corridor.

Chapter Twenty-Nine

Three *ossorians* stepped into view, the wood floor creaked beneath their claws and their snarls vibrated the air. The moment they saw us, they picked up speed, heaving their bodies forward.

Aengus set down my mother as quickly as haste allowed, then rushed past me to stand next to Dennriall. They stood, arms and legs braced for a fight. Through the space between them, I watched the *ossorians* charge. Who were they behind the spell? Aodh and Fintan's kin? Their soldiers?

Desperate to release them from Leannan's hold before they hurt anyone, I practically threw my mind into my magic. Reaching without hesitation, I grabbed a hold of the black threads binding them to Leannan. It seemed the spell already knew what to do and the threads snapped free, slithering in the air, before snaking immediately toward me, sinking deep beneath my skin.

Emotions, raw and vicious, ripped across my brain. I couldn't clearly make out who they were beneath the spell, but three distinct voices combined into a solid chorus of pain. Excalibur clattered to the floor, and I grabbed my ears. A cry filled the tunnel, the wail probably alerting everyone to our presence.

"Imogen?" Aengus spun toward me, pulling my hands away from my head. Air burned where my nails had dug into my scalp. I snapped my mouth shut, realizing the sound came from my own throat.

The tsunami of emotions still pressed down on my mind, but I heaved a shuddering breath and straightened my shoulders. Incrementally, the emotions dimmed until they were just a low hum in the back of my mind.

Aengus squeezed my hand, pulling it closer.

"I'm okay," I said, looking up at him with what I hoped was a smile. He didn't look as if he believed me. "Their emotions were just very intense." He brought my fingers to his lips.

Dennriall leaned close. "Should I assume you control the beasts now?"

The *ossorians* sat on their haunches, their lips still raised to show off their dagger-like teeth, but they didn't move closer. I shook my head. "I don't control them, but neither does Leannan." Technically, I could try to control them, but unless absolutely necessary, I didn't want to. They had been used enough for too long.

"But you could ask them to lead us to the lake?" Dennriall prompted.

"Yes," I answered with a real smile.

The *ossorians* led us straight to the lake. I had wanted to ask where the wild fae and the *fola* might be, but it seemed too complicated a question and I worried they'd misunderstand and take us to them instead.

We stood on black sand, having exited from what now looked like a beached shipwreck covered by a sand dune. A cavern stretched deep before us. So deep the walls on the other side remained shadowed and unseen. A wall might not even exist at all if Dennriall was right, and the lake was the representation of where this bubble connected to Uisce. Stalactites hung like claws over the inky water as black droplets dripped from them, breaking the surface tension with rings in every direction.

Aengus gently set my mother on the sand.

"What do we do now?" I asked, staring out across the water.

Aengus moved right to the edge, tiny waves rolling up gently upon the shore, and looked out. A moment passed in silence, then he glanced over at Dennriall. "This place is connected to Uisce. And Excalibur is also connected to Uisce."

Dennriall scuttled forward and clicked his pincers. "Of course, with Excalibur we can—"

The *ossorians* snarled and we all spun around to find Janquil holding my mother up by the back of the neck, a dagger to her throat. Leannan stood near the top of a large sand dune, surrounded below by a literal army of *fola* and wild fae.

"Mom," I cried, taking an unconscious step forward.

"Stay where you are, or your mother dies," Leannan warned.

I halted, planting my feet, but I didn't take my eyes off my mother. The universe wouldn't be shitty enough to take my mom now that I'd found her, right? Yeah, I was pretty sure I knew the answer to that question.

Aengus leaned in and whispered. "When I command, throw Excalibur into the lake."

"What?" I asked, barely remembering to keep my voice low. "No. They have my mom. I'm not giving up my magic."

The *ossorians* grumbled beside me, feeling my distress. Janquil dragged my mother to Leannan's side and I gritted my teeth against the anger.

Aengus furrowed his brow. "What would you do?"

"I don't know. Maybe I could pull their life force." I still whispered, but even I could hear to the sharp edge in my voice.

"From all of them?" Aengus looked warily up at the stalactites. "And when you release that energy? Trust me, throw Excalibur into the lake. It is our only way out."

I wanted to argue more, but Leannan's voice boomed through the cavern. "Bring me the girl. Kill the others."

A tingle raced up my arms, lifting the hairs like static. I peered around Aengus. Leannan stood with her hands in the air. Magic singed the air, the taste at the back of my throat, as a gossamer web fell in a dome around us. Despite feeling her magic surrounding us, it felt weaker than when she'd appeared on the front porch of the retirement. Whatever she'd gained from the fae earlier must not have replenished the spear.

Either way, we were hemmed in. Aengus braced; his fists raised. He glanced back at me. "Stay behind me. She must not know what we plan." Dennriall skittered to obscure me more. The *ossorians* leaned forward, bodies tense, their paws sinking deep in the sand.

The *fola* and wild fae charged.

"Throw it now!" Aengus urged as four of the *fola* broke ahead of the horde. They descended upon Aengus.

I froze.

Moving faster than I'd ever seen him, Aengus's fists connected with faces and torsos, but the *fola* did not retreat. A punch landed solidly in Aengus's gut, and he let out a deep wheeze and curled his body inward. The rest leaped on him and Aengus disappeared from view.

"Aengus!" I cried, raising my sword to attack. What I wouldn't have given for the ability to throw a fireball, or pull down some lightning, anything. Wasn't being magical supposed to come with battle spells?

The rest of the advancing horde reached us and Dennriall and the *ossorians* waded into the fray, hands, feet, and teeth connecting with whatever came near.

Aengus burst from the middle of the pile. "Throw it!" he yelled.

Panic had my thoughts swirling. My mother was in danger, Aengus, too. Dennriall. The *ossorians*. Why would I throw away the only weapon I had? It made no sense. Out of the frazzled thoughts one appeared of a hand rising from a lake, grasping Excalibur. Bedivere. Bedivere had thrown Excalibur in the lake when Arthur died and the Lady of the Lake had reached out and grabbed it. The lake was connected to Uisce—and Nimue!

I turned and heaved Excalibur as far as I could out into the Lake.

Nothing fucking happened.

Chapter Thirty

Two *ossorians* lay still and unmoving in the sand, blood adding a sheen to the blackness. Only the lone *ossorian* fought on. Aengus, blood dripping down the left side of his face, swiped a hand across his eyes, trying to keep them clear as two more *fola* joined the first four. Dennriall stumbled as two wild fae leaped onto his back. One threw an arm around his neck and another yanked on his arm until I heard it snap and Dennriall cried out.

And I stood by the shore unable to help because I'd stupidly thrown my only weapon into the lake.

Screw it.

Unpredictable without Excalibur or not, I still had magic. I glanced up just for a moment at the hanging daggers of stone and hoped Aengus's fear wouldn't prove correct, that releasing my magic would cause a cave in.

Dipping forward over the cliff into my magic felt much less steady without my cynosure and the moment I reached out to the surrounding life threads, the hunger made me gasp. How quickly I'd forgotten how intense it could be.

Just as I focused, ready to grab hold of them, Leannan called out over the battle from her dune, "The Cailleach Fae surrenders now, and I will allow the rest of you to live."

The fighting halted, leaving a void of sound now filled with ragged breathing.

Aengus. Where was Aengus? I'd heard what Leannan had said, but the hunger inside me would not calm until I knew he was okay. I found him and Dennriall both alive, but swaying, barely standing. They wouldn't last much longer, not against so many.

My mother whimpered as Janquil pressed his dagger deeper into her throat. A small stream of blood dripped down the blade.

"No," I yelped, reaching toward her despite the distance. Every part of me wanted to yank Janquil's energy and watch him drop. But even if I removed one threat to my mother, there were so many fae between her and safety.

I let my magic go and walked forward, my arms held out in surrender. What choice did we have?

"No!" my mother screamed, drawing Aengus and Dennriall's attention to me. They shifted, reaching out to stop me.

"They'll kill my mom," I pleaded trying to push past them.

In the hushed cavern, all sides froze at the sound of bubbling. We turned to see the lake roiling, Right where the sword had disappeared beneath the surface, Excalibur rose from the water, followed by a hand gripping the hilt. The hand gave way to an arm until finally a head broke above the water and Nimue appeared.

Beside Leannan, Janquil dropped the arm holding the dagger and my mother sank to her knees. The *fola* and wild fae stumbled back away from the water, clearly aware of the Lady of the Lake's power. And Aengus fell to one knee, exhausted. I dropped down close to him.

He and I watched as Nimue, in human form, sashayed across the water's surface. She stepped onto the beach and drove the sword into the sand, then glared at Leannan. "Morgana," she sighed in disgust.

"I don't go by that name anymore," Leannan said, showing her teeth in a smile that looked more like a snarl.

"As you wish." Nimue shrugged. "I'll use whatever name you choose, but I will not allow you to harm my acolytes." She gestured toward Aengus and me and then pointed to Dennriall, who held his mangled arm close. Near him, the lone *ossorian* was helping one of its downed kin to stagger to its feet. "Or the Unseelie seneschal."

"Your acolytes?" Leannan asked, unbelieving.

Nimue looked down at me with a pointed stare. "Did you not make a promise to me?" I nodded. "And does this knight aid you in that promise?"

The Lady of the Lake was definitely stretching the truth with that bit of semantics, but I nodded completely fine with agreeing if it meant we would live.

"Why do you stop me when you should be joining me?" Leannan marched down the sand and the fae split to let her pass. She was taller than Nimue, but it was clear the Lady of the Lake held all the power. What was she? A very old fae? A goddess?

"Join you?" Nimue scoffed.

"Do the fae even give you reverence anymore? Do they even know your name?"

"I have no need of sycophants."

"What about the humans? They use us for their own gains and then dismiss us? Like Merlin. He left you, too."

"Yes, I remember—for you, wasn't it?" Leannan seemed to startle at Nimue's accusation. "Your bitterness only poisons you. I have no quarrel with human or fae."

Nimue pointed out toward the middle of the lake and curled her finger as if urging someone closer. The water swirled and bubbled again and Amicus leaped free, landing in the shallows and spraying dark water in all directions. What looked like a long, jeweled sword blade without a hilt hung around his neck with a leather strap. Nimue pulled it up and over the kelpie's head.

Amicus snorted and shook his mane.

"You'll allow my acolytes to leave and the seneschal as well," Nimue ordered.

"But my mom—" I cried out, looking in her direction. My mother shook her head and tried to smile, but I knew it was forced. Confusion flared from the *ossorians*, I only felt the two now. I couldn't leave them either.

"I have no claim to her," Nimue said softly. "Take Aengus and the seneschal and go. Don't forget your promise to me." She held out what I now recognized as a scabbard.

Dennriall reached down with his good arm and helped Aengus to his feet. I pulled Excalibur from the sand. My magic settled just as the sword settled snuggly within the jeweled casing. Ducking my head and pulling my arm through, it thumped against my back. I'd wished for the very thing only a little bit ago, but now any joy felt hollow.

I placed my hands on Amicus's back to pull myself astride, but stopped when Leannan snarled, "I will take the Cailleach Fae's magic and I will tear it all down." I glanced at her. Magic swelled around her, whipping her shock-white hair about her face.

"You, child!" Nimue snapped. "If the veil falls, the magic of Innisfail will flood this realm and destroy it."

Leannan smirked.

That was her goal? To tear the veil down completely?

Nimue's body leaned back and shimmered. Her legs gave way to curling tentacles. "You plan to destroy both realms over the fickleness of men?"

"No, I want to topple their institutions, their courts, their judgement." Without warning, Leannan flicked her hand and sent a surge of lightning in our direction. The sand burst in a spray, solidifying into glass as it heated. The shards rained down on us. Aengus, unable to move fast enough, raised his arm just in time to keep a sizable chunk of glass from taking out an eye. As it was, the glass stuck into his forearm like a blade.

He yanked it out with a cry, causing blood to flow freely down his arm.

I stepped away from the kelpie, looking out at Leannan and her army. Anger tinged my sight in rabid gold and everyone's life thread sparkled alluringly. But with Excalibur returned to me, my focus had returned. I reached out with my magic. Frustratingly, Leannan's life force was blocked, so I zeroed in on the next most important person, Janquil.

"Run, Mom!" I cried as I took hold of his thread and yanked hard. Janquil crumpled with a groan, but I watched in horror as he fell to the left, knocking my mother to the ground and landing heavily on top of her. "No!" I screamed.

"Janquil," Leannan screamed at the same time.

Beside me, Nimue grabbed hold of my waist and threw me up onto Amicus. "You must go."

"My mom, I have to save her," I said, pointing back to where she struggled under the goat-legged fae. The two surviving *ossorians* whimpered. "And what about them? We can't leave them."

Nimue pushed Dennriall and Aengus closer to the kelpie. "I will do what I can, but you must go now."

Dennraill helped Aengus mount behind me before he dropped a hand over his features and shifted into his human form. Holding his injured arm tightly to his chest, he grabbed Aengus's offered arm and pulled himself astride. Amicus's back seemed to grow as needed to allow three grown people to ride without issue. I wanted to dismount and run to my mother, but Aengus wrapped an arm around me, holding me tight. "Where do we go," I asked weakly.

Dennriall lowered his hand against the kelpie's flank. "I know where."

Nimue raised her arms and bellowed, "You will no longer take the power of Uisce! It is closed to you!" The sound of the ocean roared and over my shoulder the dark water of the lake rose in a tsunami sized wave.

Amicus turned and galloped after the receding water as behind us Nimue quipped, "I suggest you find a new place to hide."

As the wave descended, we dived straight into it.

Chapter Thirty-One

Amicus burst from the deep end of a jellybean shaped pool and skittered across the concrete pad, halting inches from two striped loungers, his sides heaving. Dennriall leaped down, even before the kelpie had fully stopped, and raced toward a pair of french doors leading into a two-story house.

I opened my mouth to ask where we were, but his cries of "Nicholas?", answered my questions. When he tried one of the handles and found it locked, he kicked out at a potted plant and a light glinted off a hidden key. Dennriall snatched it up with his uninjured hand and frantically unlocked the door. With another cry of "Nicholas?" he disappeared inside.

Over the roof of the house, the last light of the early winter sunset highlighted the shadowed presence of mountains. The sun had been poised to set when Excalibur had sent us traveling. How could we have only been gone an hour? Both Slide Mountain, its familiar finger-like striations splayed and reaching toward the valley, and off to the far right, the rising cradle of Mount Rose, oriented me to where we were. Still, I felt unmoored. I glanced toward the pool, wishing I could look back through the water to Leannan's realm and make sure my mother was okay.

The *ossorians*, too. Would Leannan kill them as she threatened earlier?

Aengus shifted behind me and slid down to the ground, his knees buckling, forcing him to grab my leg to stay upright. He paused, then reached toward the kelpie's chest and pulled himself close to his neck. Amicus dropped his head and nosed at Aengus's side. The kelpie let out a squeal and snort when he found blood. "Shh shh," Aengus whispered in a low, soft voice, giving him an affectionate scratch. "I am well, old friend."

I snorted. Aengus's lips twitched in an almost smile. "Alive then, if not well."

I leaned across Amicus's neck and swung my leg over, dismounting next to Aengus. Excalibur, secure in its scabbard, clunked against my back. Grabbing Aengus's closest hand, I gently led him to a lounger. He dropped to the striped cushion with little grace.

With a cursory look, I took in the oozing bite marks marring Aengus's neck and the gleam of shiny blood covering his shirt beneath his duster. I also didn't miss the red tingeing the whites of his eyes or the way his lips drew back in a frown, revealing his sharp incisors. The blood loss had been significant. Whatever those four vials of blood had provided was gone. Aengus would need to feed, and soon.

Amicus snorted, tossing his head and pawing at the concrete with hollow thunks of his hoof.

Aengus gestured toward the pool. "Go, we are safe." Amicus hesitated, flicking his ears forward and back. "I will call you if I have need, now go." With a rear, the kelpie turned on his back legs and dived into the depths of the pool, disappearing instantly beneath the surface.

I settled on the cushion next to Aengus and thrust my wrist

directly under his nose. He violently leaned away and growled out a "No."

"We've had this discussion before," I said forcefully. "I'd rather not wait until you lose control."

He pushed my arm down into his lap and held it there. His usual warm palms clammy and cold. "I did lose control. I nearly killed you."

"Nearly," I pointed out.

From the open french doors, a completely un-Dennriall-like voice carried across the yard. We both turned.

Dennriall stood just within view with his broken arm wrapped in gauze and supported by a sling of fabric around his neck, but the other held a landline portable phone. I hadn't realized they still made them. "I know, baby. I'm an asshole for making you worry. I'll make it up to you." He chuckled low. "Yes, in all the ways...I love you, too...I'm not going anywhere until you get here." There was a long pause, and Dennriall squeezed his eyes shut. "Please, don't cry again, baby, I'm safe...Promise...See you soon." Dennriall pulled the phone away from his ear and fumbled to press the disconnect button with the same hand.

Dennriall looked our way and noticed us staring. He coughed, seeming to realize just how much we'd seen of his private life. He tossed the phone onto a plush chair and walked outside.

"Nicholas?" I asked, knowing the answer.

"Yes," he said, a bit strangled. "He was in LA for work. He's taking the next flight possible. I'm going to catch hell for not telling him about this." He gingerly lifted his arm.

I nodded, wondering how long it took a fae to heal a compound fracture. I pulled my hand from Aengus's grip. "Aengus needs to feed. He's worried he'll hurt me. Would you be able to hold him?"

Dennriall touched his bandaged arm. "I'm not certain."

Aengus stood up, swaying and Dennriall and I both reached out to keep him steady. "We cast Merlin's spell now," he demanded.

I sprang to my feet. "What? No!"

"Instead of threatening your safety, I would already be healed."

"I promised a goddess, or nearly one, that I wouldn't let you return to your tomb. I'm not recasting Merlin's spell. Not unless I have no other choice."

Dennriall set a hand on Aengus's shoulder. "If you refuse to feed from Genny, then you must return to the Seelie Court."

"No way!" I chopped a hand down between them. The fear that had seized me at the thought of Aengus returning to the court was illogical, I knew it.

"I don't see any other choices," Dennriall said with a sigh.

We needed another option.

I smiled widely. "Cathal. He's Honeythorn, he's full fae, and he's strong enough to keep you in check," I said to Aengus. "I mean, we'd have to get Eugene to tell us the location since we didn't drive there last time, bu—"

"Enough!" Dennriall roared. I stumbled back from his ferocity and Aengus weakly put up a hand as if to calm him, but Dennriall ignored are reactions. "Before the veil closed, the Seelie King announced the death of his oldest son, Cathal. He was distraught. I have no doubt you met a fae, but it couldn't have been the Seelie heir."

I set my hands on my hips. "You're wrong. I'm telling you, if he wasn't under a geas he would have told me everything."

Finally Dennriall seemed to regard my words. "A geas?"

"Nibs figured it out and Cathal confirmed it—sort of."

Aengus fell back to the lounger, face pale and almost bloodless. "The fae was old, Denn. Older than you or I."

Dennriall's shoulders drooped and he rubbed a hand roughly over his features. "It makes no sense. Why would Oberon lie? And why in all the realms would the Seelie Heir have been sent to watch over a druid?"

Not that much of the fae world made sense, but I had to admit this situation made even less sense than usual. "If it makes any difference, I really don't think Dan is a regular druid. Not that I've met one or anything. There just seems to be something else going on with him."

"Hmmm," Dennriall mused. "It might make all the difference."

The french doors slammed against the side of the house, shattering the glass, and both Dennriall and I spun toward the house. Three trell stomped into the backyard. "Saoirse has been waiting," the trell in front said.

At that exact moment, the blood loss finally got to Aengus. With a howl, he turned feral.

Chapter Thirty-Two

"Are you sure he'll be okay in the trunk?" I asked Dennriall for the fourth time—maybe the fifth. The curvy road had me sliding in my seat. The seatbelt flopped uselessly off my shoulder and over my hips, long ago giving up any hope of holding anyone.

Just as useless as my ability to help Aengus. Ugh! Why had he argued? If he'd just taken some blood, he wouldn't be in this mess.

"He's fine," Dennriall said, still in his human-esque form and still holding his severely injured arm. For being the Unseelie seneschal, the soldiers hadn't treated him with much consideration aside from not injuring him worse.

Apparently, after Nicholas had arrived at court searching for his husband, Saoirse had staked out their house. When we had shown up, we alerted whatever was watching, and immediately, the trell had arrived. Aengus going feral had complicated their plans. It was decided by others—who were not me—that the trunk was the safest place to stuff him.

From behind our seat, Aengus snarled and pounded on the metal. I glanced out the back window and by the moonlight saw

dents in the trunk lid. "I don't think it's going to hold him for long."
Aengus pounded again, and another dent appeared. "He can breathe,
right?"

"Genny!" Dennriall snapped, and I jerked my head to look at
him. He took a deep breath before continuing. "Aengus will be fine.
It's everyone else in this vehicle who's in danger."

I'd only ever seen him confident or slightly annoyed, but now his
expression held anxiety mingled with pain.

"I'm glad Nicholas wasn't home," I said, guessing at his biggest
concern.

Dennriall nodded stiffly. "As am I."

"Do you think the note you left will keep him from following?"

Dennriall sighed once more. "Not at all."

I'd managed to nap a few minutes, despite Aengus howling
behind us. When we arrived, the trell reluctantly let me carry
Excalibur into the Unseelie Court when neither of them could
lift it.

This time there was no canopied bed or private dressing room
discussion. The trell dragged us all forward, straight into the great
hall where I'd first had my introduction to the fae what felt like a
lifetime ago. Unlike the first time, the full Unseelie Court was not
present, giving an unhindered view of the floral couches and pastel
colored walls. Saoirse sat on her wicker fan throne as we shuffled
across the burgundy carpet. A broad rock-like being stood behind her,
replacing the role my father has served as the Green Knight.

It took all three trell to hold Aengus. His howls of rage scraped
over my nerves like sandpaper. I cringed. How long in this state could
he hold on to his humanity? If the guards lost control of him, they'd
have a bloodbath. I had no delusions that if he bit me now, he'd kill

me. Only a full fae would survive. Ugh, I actually wished for Theo. Had hell frozen over?

"Dennriall," the Unseelie Queen sang out, in mock surprise. Instead of neon pink makeup, today her pallet gave off cherry blossom vibes, probably to match the horribly appropriated Asian style gown with a slit almost up to her waist.

"My lady," he acknowledged.

"We were so worried," she continued, saccharine sweet.

"Apologies, The Leannan Sidhe held me hostage," Dennriall droned calmly, bowing low.

His deference pissed me off. The queen totally knew where he was. She'd admitted it to Aengus and me. I bit my lip trying to keep quiet.

"Yes," the queen's voice dipped low and dangerous. "Your human was very distraught over your absence."

Dennriall straightened stiffly, wincing as his broken arm shifted. "My husband, my lady," he corrected.

Saoirse sprang from her chair and flew down the carpet to point her finger into Dennriall's chest. "I gave no permission to marry," she threatened.

I reached up behind me, fumbling for Excalibur's hilt. Dennriall threw me a quelling look. I dropped my hand to my side reluctantly, frowning. He mouthed the words, "Trust me."

Dennriall dipped his head, his throat bobbing as he swallowed, but his voice was firm when he responded, "I married in the custom of a human, not a fae. I needed no permission."

A snarl of fury ripped through the queen. "I should kill you where you stand!"

"As my lady wishes, but may I say I was only disloyal in love."

Saoirse rolled her eyes and flung an arm in the air. "Fine, keep your human filth." She turned her gaze to me. "You can heal him now. I appreciate you waiting until I meted out judgement."

I blinked in confusion. "I can't heal him. His bone is sticking out of his arm. That's way beyond what I know how to fix."

"The scabbard," she drawled, clearly annoyed. I must have given another confused look. "Excalibur's scabbard, on your back," she pointed, "it has the power to heal."

I yanked up on the leather strap and pulled the sword and sheath off to scrutinize it. "Wait? Really?" I asked.

"For someone who claims they're *custos* you are still woefully ignorant."

Aengus howled again, and I jumped forward, looking behind to make sure he was still well in hand. His pupils were so wide and dark, the whites of his eyes were barely visible. More shark-like than human. Could the scabbard help him too?

I turned to Dennriall first. "Do I just touch you with it?" I whispered. He lifted the uninjured shoulder in a shrug. "Okay, here goes," I said, reaching the end of the sheath toward Dennriall's arm. When it touched, he yelped in either surprise or pain. I didn't know which. Before I could ask, a blue glow encapsulated his arm and in moments, a smile reached across his face. When the glow dissipated, I pulled the scabbard away. Dennriall removed the bloodied bandages to reveal a completely healed arm. "Wow," I let out in a long breath.

Eagerly, I turned toward the three guards holding Aengus.

"Don't bother," Saoirse said, as if reading my thoughts. "The only thing that will fix him is the executioner's ax."

"What?" My brain took a moment to fully understand what the queen had said. "No, he needs my blood, that's all."

"That *thing* is a danger to everyone here." The queen paused. "And if he dies today, Aurnia will have to find a new knight to serve her purpose." She smiled darkly down at me. "Really, it's a win-win."

"Wait!" I screamed. "I have news of Leannan's plans. I need him, we need him, if we wish to stop her. Let me try."

Dennriall pulled me toward him, his grip tight and his tone fearful. "Genny, you can't. He will kill you."

I twisted free. "He won't." I almost believed it myself.

Saoirse settled back against her throne. "What news?"

"I'll tell you after you let me help him."

The queen let out an exaggerated hum. "Well, if he kills you, Leannan won't have her Cailleach Fae magic she so desperately wants either." She waved her hand in encouragement. "Go ahead."

She was right. Without me, Leannan would have to find another Cailleach Fae if she wished to complete her plan of destroying the veil. I guess that was my consolation prize if Aengus killed me.

Dennriall swiped away his glamour, his carapace clicking as he skittered close to the three trell and Aengus.

I threw Dennriall a weak smile. "Take care of Nibs if—"

"Enough," he said, snapping his mandibles. His four hands reached toward Aengus and the nearest trell released his hold to him. Dennriall looked at me. "Let's get this over with."

I took slow, steady steps towards Aengus. There was no recognition in his eyes. He was mindless with hunger and if the guards and Dennriall let him go, he'd attack and kill everyone he could in an effort to find the blood he needed. I pulled Excalibur free and dropped the scabbard to the floor. The sword was too heavy for me to just run it across my skin without slicing off my hand. Instead, I hitched it under my arm and held it still while I pressed the flesh of my palm against the blade. With a sharp burn, the skin parted, and I dropped the sword to my feet, holding my wrist against the pain.

Blood pooled in my palm. Aengus's nose flared, and he roared.

"Hold him, tightly," Dennriall demanded of the two trell. They didn't respond, but their fingers whitened as their grip tightened.

I stepped close. Aengus's wet and feral breathing twisted my stomach into a giant knot, but I held out my hand to his lips. Like a snake, he latched onto it biting down as if to rip my thumb from the rest of my hand. I held in a scream. "Please, Aengus, please, Aengus," I whispered, unsure if I was asking him to come back to me or to stop.

His eyes flickered. I almost missed it. When they flickered again, I sucked in a sharp breath. "Aengus," I cried.

He snarled against my hand. Then with a bellow, he ripped his fangs from my skin. His head dropped, his chin hitting his heaving chest. Dennriall didn't let go and neither did the other two trell. Pressing my wounded hand to my chest with the other, I whispered his name. A shudder raced over his entire body. I whispered it again. Finally, he brought up his head and I saw recognition in his eyes. I reached toward him and Aengus flung his head back, his eyes wide.

"I'm sorry," I said, quickly taking my hand away. "Was it enough?"

"No," he growled. "This won't last the day." His eyes dropped to my bloody hand and his eyes grew flinty. "I told you not to try it."

I glared. "The queen was going to take your head. You're welcome." I reached down and grabbed the scabbard from the floor. Irritated, I dropped it into my hand harder than I should have and drew in a sharp breath, but the pain disappeared as my skin stretched and knitted back together. I wouldn't say it hurt, but the feeling wasn't pleasant.

"Are you well?" Dennriall asked me and I nodded. He looked at Aengus. "Are you?"

Aengus dipped his head toward Dennriall, then turned to Saoirse on her throne. "I am myself again. You may release me."

For a moment, I worried Saoirse would change her mind and call for his head anyway. But even though she frowned, she flicked her fingers, indicating the trell and Dennriall could move away. Hesitantly, they released their hold. Aengus stayed still.

Saoirse stood. "Now, what is this news you claim to have?"

Excalibur clinked against the sheath as I settled the leather strap over my neck and shoulder. I knew I'd already bargained for Aengus, but there was one other thing I needed to do. "First, I want to see Nibs."

Chapter Thirty-Three

Nibs nestled in my arms. She seemed well, but the fingerless glove "dress" she still wore had unraveled along the edges. Nibs had tied a colorful scrap of cloth around the middle like a belt and a smaller piece around her neck, trying to make it look better, but it only made her appear more pitiable. When we got home, I'd let her purchase whatever she wanted. Credit score be damned.

Saoirse, silent with her mouth held in a hard, pinched line, let me recount everything we'd seen. When I reached our escape, she halted me with a raised hand. "You're sure you heard the name Janquil?" I nodded. "And you saw this army of wild fae and *fola?*"

Aengus growled low and yanked the neckline of his shirt down to show the bites that had only closed enough to look red and angry. "She plans to destroy the courts and the veil. We all heard her."

Dennriall, and I nodded in solidarity.

Saoirse narrowed her eyes. "Are we to assume Nimue destroyed Leannan's hidden realm?"

I shrugged. "It seemed that way."

Saoirse tapped a finger against her lips. "Hmmm. Leannan is trapped here, then."

"Or Innisfail," I added.

The queen laughed. "Leannan would die before she returned there."

"But she's fae?"

"Only in body, not her soul. She's what her enemies and her lovers have created—an outcast, but none more so than in Innisfail."

Aengus clenched his fists. "Created or not, she cannot be allowed to destroy the veil."

"No," Saoirse agreed. Slowly, she stood from her throne. She wiggled, adjusting her tight dress and the buttons and slit shifted back into alignment.

Dennriall skittered forward and bowed his torso. "My lady, there is something you should know." Saoirse inclined her head for him to continue. "I believe the Honeythorn heir is alive."

Saoirse stepped down onto the first dais step and leaned toward Dennriall. "How is this possible?"

Dennriall seemed to twitch with agitation as he pointed back at Aengus and me. "They claim to have met him."

The Unseelie Queen, pushing past her seneschal, stomped down the last two steps to loom inches from us on her stiletto heels. "Is this true?"

Her proximity had my sense of danger going off like a klaxon and I fought the urge to grab at Excalibur from my scabbard. This was the second time someone had reacted completely unhinged at the possibility of the Seelie heir being alive. Why was it such a big deal? "I met a fae. I was told he was my ancestor and that his name was Cathal."

Saoirse ran her gaze over Aengus and then down at my hand, clearly analyzing the fact that my blood had restored him. With a jerk, she turned toward Dennriall. "And yet you didn't tell me she had royal blood when you tasted it."

He didn't even flinch. "As a Cailleach Fae, I was uncertain of what I was tasting. I said only what I knew for certain."

I knew it was a lie, but Dennriall said it with such conviction I almost believed it myself.

Saoirse huffed. "What the hell is the Honeythorn heir doing here after all this time?"

"Apparently, he's watching over a druid," Dennriall answered.

"A druid?" Saoirse repeated, looking at me for confirmation. When I nodded, she spun on Dennriall a wicked smile on her face. "I think we need to find out who this druid really is."

Dennriall grinned back at her. "Agreed."

Dennriall's four articulated arms circled in the air, encouraging the swirling portal wider, until the whirlpool of rainbow colors blotted out the dais and Saoirse's throne behind it. The queen stood off to the side with her arms crossed. There'd been a heated discussion before opening the portal and although we had all agreed on the next step, she wasn't particularly happy about it.

Both Saoirse and Dennriall grilled us for information about Dan. When they realized we didn't know much, we agreed the geas on Cathal would need to be broken. For that, I'd need the coven's help. No way Aengus and I could get to the retirement home and then up to the ranch where Cathal and Dan lived in any good amount of time without magical help.

Apparently, only certain fae had an affinity for making portals. Dennriall and Saoirse being two of them. Aengus and I needed to almost be in two places at once, and Saoirse desired to speak with Lady Aurnia about Leannan's plan to destroy the veil and about

Cathal. As much as the queen clearly didn't like the idea, we needed to split up.

Dennriall let his arms drop. "It's ready."

Saoirse regarded us with an imperious gaze, as if debating internally whether to let us go at all. Finally, she gestured toward the swirl of colors. "Go but keep me informed. Use the mirror."

Nibs opened her mouth to say something to the queen, but I covered her head with my hand, blocking what was certainly a string of profanities. "We're going home." I reminded the Brownie. "Where your clothes are." Nibs stilled, and I removed my hand slowly. The smile Nibs had across her face proclaimed her anger gone and her desire for what really mattered had taken over—fashion.

Aengus took a step back from the portal and I reached for him, grabbing his sleeve. "Aengus?"

He stopped, staring at my fingers twisted in the fabric of his shirt with a pained expression. Finally, he looked up. "I will go with Saoirse to the Seelie Court."

"What? No!" I argued. Logic agreed with Aengus. Of course, he should go where he was guaranteed to feed. Who knew how long it would take to get the coven together and then to portal to Cathal. But was it truly a guarantee? Aurnia had never instilled me with trust and Theo—forget it.

Aengus gently pried my grip from his arm. "My hold is tenuous. I am a danger to you and all those you care about."

"*You are* one of those I care about." I cringed at the whine in my voice. He had to go. I knew he did. This was the beginning of what I'd always known could happen.

I watched his eyes drift over my shoulder to Excalibur, secure in its scabbard. There was no mistaking the longing in his expression. At Dennriall's house, he'd demanded I cast the spell and now he wanted to rush off to the Seelie Court. What if he tried to close the veil without the sword or the spell? Would that even be possible?

Dennriall appeared beside me and rested a hand on my shoulder. "Let him go," he said firmly, but kindly.

Why did this feel permanent? Like saying goodbye now was the end. I refused to let that happen without at least a chance for us to say goodbye. I lifted Nibs toward Dennriall, who took the Brownie in his arms. Stepping in close to Aengus, I placed my hands against his chest. "Tell me you will not disappear without seeing me again. On your honor as a knight." He wanted to pull away. "Promise me," I pushed.

Aengus's eyes seemed to go from gold to amber as he wrapped his arms around me and lifted me until our lips met. I could feel the violence simmering below the surface that my blood had only tempered. My stomach fluttered with a touch of fear and a bit of excitement. I slid my hands up and around his neck, meeting his energy. Ignoring the fact that we were not alone.

"Enough," Saoirse ordered. "We leave now."

With a groan, Aengus heaved himself away, and I fought the urge to pull him back down to me. Aengus set his forehead against mine, our noses brushing, our chests heaving. "I will not disappear," he said softly, his warm breath mingling with my own.

His still didn't promise.

Chapter Thirty-Four

I kept leaving people behind. The *ossorians,* my mother, and now Aengus. Grief hovered above me, threatening to smother me if I let it land. Instead, I focused only on my next move, my next action, bouncing my grief continuously away, as if keeping a balloon aloft above me.

Nibs focused on her closet.

The moment we'd stepped through the portal, she'd scrambled down from my arms and dashed towards our room, ripping off the grungy makeshift dress as she ran, tossing it into the air behind her. The house felt right again now that its little menace had returned.

Dennriall, human looking even down to naturally colored eyes, stepped through after me, closing the portal behind him. He looked like the front cover of a romance novel, with his long dark hair and a buttoned-down shirt with sleeves rolled up onto his forearms.

I gave him a questioning look. "Let me guess, Nicholas picked your glamour?"

Dennriall gave himself a once over and then looked back up at me. His brow furrowed. "He told me this was an accurate representation of a human being. Is this wrong?"

I rolled my lips to keep from giggling. "You look very good, Dennriall. No worries."

He didn't seem to believe me. "May I use the phone?" He pointed to the retirement home land line on Everett's desk.

I told him to press "9" to dial out and went to lie down for an hour before the residents woke up.

Asking them for help in breaking the geas on Cathal went remarkably easy and they'd all seemed eager to help. Mr. Friedman even sang off key, "I love going on field trips," as he marched up the back stairs. Even Everett pulled out his cellphone to call and tell his wife that he would be late coming home. I didn't argue, knowing how he felt about his charges.

But my next conversation would not be as easy.

I pushed open the side door on the side of the garage until I viewed a pair of legs stretched out across the concrete floor. I knocked hesitantly. "May I come in?"

"Aye," Fintan answered from within.

Stepping under the harsh florescent light, I found Fintan lounging in an ancient beanbag that had been mine a decade ago before being banished to the garage. Aodh lay on his back on the hard concrete, arms behind his head and eyes closed. Many of the boxes behind them were open and rifled through, clothes hung over the side as if trying to escape. Both men had chosen pieces, but where Aodh had gone with basic pants and a t-shirt, Fintan was definitely wearing one of Grandma's blouses. "I need to tell you both something."

Aodh cracked one eye open.

Fintan sat up as straight as he was able in the recesses of the beanbag. "Of course, but I'll admit I'm not liking the sound in your voice."

Aodh sighed and sat up, watching my movements like I held a bomb.

"Three *ossorians* attacked us today," I said my voice more of a croak. I wrung my hands and tried to keep their gaze, fighting the urge to look at the floor.

"I released them from Leannan, but..." I couldn't finish. All I could see was the mangled body on the beach and the two other *ossorians* standing over it.

"Go on," Aodh said darkly. He got to his feet and Fintan followed.

I rolled my lips and took a deep breath. "Leannan attacked us. The three fought by our side. One fell. They didn't get back up. We were forced to leave the other two behind. The Lady of the Lake, promised to try and save them. I can feel their minds. They're still alive, but I don't know for how long." I couldn't bear to look up any longer and dropped my gaze to the concrete. "I'm so sorry. I don't even know who you may have lost."

Aodh let out a harsh grunt. When I looked up, he'd turned away from me, but Fintan stepped near.

"We thank you. Of the two you released, we'll hope for their safe return. As for the one who fell, we may never know. But their sacrifice will not be forgotten."

"How many were there? *Ossorians*, I mean."

Aodh let out an angry growl of words, "What does it matter? They can never go home. My father stole their lives. I stole their lives." Then he stomped out of the garage, slamming the door behind him.

Fintan cringed at the sound and gave me a half-hearted smile.

"I'm sorry to make this all worse," I said.

He waved away my apology. "Don't mind my brother, it's the guilt you see. My father, the king, ordered all men from all the towns and farms between the ages of fourteen and sixty to join him in allowing Morgana to work her magic. That included his sons. Only our youngest brother, Colin, barely ten, remained free of her curse. Aodh was the one who rounded up all the men. Their mothers and wives screaming and cursing our father and Aodh the whole time for taking their menfolk. And rightly so, seeing as what happened."

"That's horrible," I said, regarding Aodh with a bit more understanding. "So the one who died..." The word stuck in my throat and barely released.

"Could have been any one of the men we forced into servitude."

"I'll try to save as many as I can." I said earnestly. Fintan nodded, but I could tell he held little hope. "There's one more thing. The coven and I are going to see the druid. I want him to make those talismans for you. It might be better if both you and Aodh go with us."

Fintan touched a crooked finger to the middle of his forehead and dipped his head. "Aye, I'll bring him back."

Back in the kitchen, I slumped into one of the dinette chairs and dropped my head into my raised palms. I knew I should search for Geoffrey and tell him about Mira, but I couldn't seem to move.

The absence of Aengus was an aching void and the guilt over leaving my mother and the *ossorians* behind threatened to fill that gaping hole to the brim. Part of me wanted to curl up in my bed and never leave, and the other part wanted to scream and smash something.

Nibs peeked out around the doorframe of the bedroom. I forced a smile onto my face. "You look much better," I told her. Her expression brightened, and she raced across the floor, her delicate sundress flowing out behind her like flower petals floating in the air. She pulled herself up into my lap. "I'm sorry you had to stay in that place for so long."

She nodded sagely and gently patted my cheek. "Let's not do that again."

I stifled a laugh. "No, let's not." A moment passed, and I knew I had to tell her what was going on. "Nibs?" The Brownie folded her arms across her chest when she heard the tone in my voice. "The coven and I are going to see Cathal and the druid. I want you to stay here."

Nibs narrowed her eyes.

I needed to come at it from a different direction or Nibs was just going to fight me. "You're my family. I don't know if I'll see Aengus again. Or my mom. Or even if Geoffrey will stay, but you and me—we are together always and I can't bear the thought of you getting hurt. So for me, will you stay here safe, behind the wards, until I get back?"

Dramatically, she threw her arms in the air. "I'll stay," she said with a sigh.

"Thanks, Nibs, I owe you."

"Six dresses," Nibs negotiated zeroing in on my moment of weakness.

"How about two?"

"Six," she repeated.

"Two and a new swimsuit."

"Three and a swimsuit."

"Fine," I groaned.

"Deal," she said gleefully.

I was never getting out of debt. But who was I kidding? I'd spend anything to keep the little brat safe.

Geoffrey had taken the news of Mira's fate stoically and then had urged Mrs. O'Cleary to come discuss possible spells to remove the geas. I understood perfectly. Taking his lead, I avoided worrying about Aengus by searching the house for anything I could do to help.

Everyone shooed me away, reminding me once again that I may have magic but I had no training or experience, and thus I was practically useless. Frustrated and worried, I went to my room in search of Nibs.

My core tightened and my breath hitched when I opened the door and saw the bed still unmade from my night with Aengus. I sat on the desk chair and tried to ignore the ache his absence caused. I called to Nibs, but she refused to come out from under the bed until her clothes were completely reorganized.

With a huff, I stood up and opened the armoire, grabbing my decorative shoebox from the top shelf. I crawled onto the bed and pulled the covers over me, imagining Aengus was beside me as I thumbed through the few pictures I had of my mom. How many were lost because they had my dad in them, and Grandpa and Grandma had tossed them? I pulled free one of my favorites. In front of a brightly painted Funhouse, Mom crouched next to me, her arms squeezing a laugh out of me. I looked maybe three or four. I don't remember visiting a fair and I don't remember this moment. Staring at the picture, I realize it was likely Geoffrey who took the photo. The best I'd ever get in way of a family photo if Nimue couldn't save Mom.

I leaned and set the box on my chair, not letting go of the photo. At least I had this one. There were no pictures of Aengus and me. I cuddled deeper into the bedding. The next time I saw him we were taking a picture. In fact, before we left I would take one of Geoffrey, too.

Later, when almost everyone had gathered in the front room, I went looking for Geoffrey.

I found him hunched over the desk in Grandma's office. I guess technically my office now, but I usually opted to do the paperwork at the kitchen island. Even after so long, the space still felt like hers. Oddly, my father seemed to fit in there perfectly.

From the doorway, I watched as he circled a phrase on the sheet of paper before him, then double underlined another. It seemed like he and Mrs. O'Cleary had brainstormed some ideas. I pulled out my phone and snapped my picture. I felt bad about disrupting him, but we'd need to get moving soon. "Do you think you know what spell will work to remove the geas?" I asked.

He looked up startled, blinking like an owl. "Hmm? Oh yes." He shuffled more pages. "I've found a few promising ones. I'll need double check them with Mrs. O'Cleary, but I believe if we combine these two" —he pointed down at pages— "we will be able to."

I nodded. There was a long pause. "Geoffrey, I'm sorry—"

He raised a hand to cut off what I was going to say next and came around the desk. He leaned against it, his arms gripping the edge. "You already told me what happened. There's nothing else you could have done, right?" I nodded. "The Lady of the Lake promised she'd try to protect her. We have to believe she did." Hope gleamed in his eyes and almost outshone the sadness.

Inwardly, I cringed as my mind gave me the image of Arthur, Merlin, and Gwynevere bobbing in their tanks, lifeless. Nimue said she had helped them, was my mother helped in the same way? Would we ever be able to bring her home?

Geoffrey left, but before I could follow, Nibs ran in for one last goodbye and to get the answer to the important question: Who would purchase the promised dresses and swimsuit if I died?

Clinging fast to my shirt and spewing a steady stream of chatter, I brought her with me into the front room. The moment I stopped next to Everett she scampered down and ran back toward the kitchen yelling, "I think I'll make cookies!"

"The kitchen is off limits while we're gone!" I yelled after her.

"Not part of the deal!" her voice called back, already down at the end of the hall.

Everett looked over his shoulder then back at me. "She can't really turn the oven on or anything? Right?"

"Maybe you should stay just in case," I reasoned.

"Oh no, we've gone over this before. Those residents are under my care. Where they go, I go."

I shrugged. "Well then, let's get going. The faster we leave, the faster we can return and make sure Nibs doesn't burn down the place."

Dennriall stood in the middle of the front room. Again, all the furniture was pushed up against the far wall to make a space for everyone to stand. He gestured to me. "Genny, I'll need you to stand close and guide me to this place."

I shifted Excalibur in its scabbard more securely across my back and moved around everyone to get close to Dennriall. It was a good thing he remained in his human glamour, there wouldn't have been room for him otherwise. "I only kind of know where we're going. Is that going to be enough?"

"Can you visualize clearly a certain place there?" I thought about the cozy kitchen with its small nook table, the wood stove, and the eclectic canisters across the long peninsula counter. With confidence, I nodded. "Then it should be enough."

Dennriall held out a hand to me and his cool fingers wrapped tightly around mine. With his other, he drew invisible symbols in the air, creating a swirl of color that started small, but grew quickly. When it stabilized, the portal rested floor to ceiling, large enough for two people to walk through side by side.

I turned to Mrs. O'Cleary beside me. "Are you ready?" She dipped her head, but her eyes continued to scrutinize the portal as if trying to deconstruct it.

With a quick pat to make sure the hair scarf she'd tied on was still covering her curls, Mrs. O'Cleary strode toward the portal and stepped through without hesitation. Everett followed quickly after her, and everyone else followed. When Sissy, the last resident to go through, reached the portal, her eyes widened with wonder. She reached tentatively and ran her fingers in the swirling colors like running her hand over the surface of a stream and giggled. With a hop, she disappeared with the others.

Now only Dennriall and I remained. He looked down at me, my hand still linked in his. "I could defy her and come with you."

No doubt he wanted to see if Cathal really was the Seelie Heir and having him with us to create another portal to get home would be nice. Unfortunately, Saoirse had been clear with her order to have Dennriall return to court after he'd portalled us. But maybe he could still make a quick detour. "Thank you for doing this, but no, you should do what she said. Amicus, though, you might want to make sure he isn't getting you in trouble with your homeowner's association."

I knew Amicus wasn't there, and Dennriall knew he wasn't there, but it was an excellent excuse for him to see Nicholas before having to return to court. After everything, he deserved a win.

Dennriall nodded sagely at my suggestion. "The HOA can be quite tiresome. I believe I will make a quick stop."

I smiled as I let go of his hand. "Make sure to tell your husband hi for me," I said, and then followed the rest of the residents through the portal.

Chapter Thirty-Five

The portal snapped shut behind me. The small kitchen barely held all the people within it, and everyone shuffled, looking around, uncertain where to go.

"Come on through," Cathal's voice carried over the crowd from further into the house. I squeezed my way through, finding the familiar hallway and the group followed like one large organism.

Cathal leaned out from the living room archway, his long, dark locks in a messy bun on the top of his head and dressed in a chocolate colored robe that nearly matched his hair and eyes, only missing the gold highlights in each. "Genny, girl, what's going on? It's all well and good to get company, but I must ask why you've come and all at once."

I gestured back toward the retirement home residents. "The coven and I are here to break your geas. Well, not Everett. He's just here to make sure everyone gets home." From the back, Everett raised his head in acknowledgement and Cathal blinked but dipped his in response. Cathal stepped back and out of the way as we all entered.

The room was just as cozy as I remembered, with the morning sun streaming in through the window to bathe all the well-loved furniture in gold. Dan, dressed in a terry robe and fluffy slippers, leaned forward in the threadbare lounger as we filtered in, snapping the footrest closed. He set a steaming mug of hot beverage on the small side table beside him. "Welcome, friends," he said genuinely, but gazed up at Cathal questioningly.

Cathal seemed to measure his words, picking the ones that the spell would not react to. "I didn't expect to see you so soon."

I gave a closed-mouth smile. "Maybe we should just try to break it first, then talk."

He couldn't answer, but his blink seemed to be in agreement.

Mrs. Liu shuffled up to Cathal, sizing him up with a scrutinizing gaze. "You're the ancestor?" Cathal nodded. "Very inconsiderate for you to still be alive. How will Genny pray to you for guidance and protection if you are not beyond to hear it?"

Cathal put a hand to his heart. "Too true. I'd better do my best to help her in the here and now to make up for it."

"See that you do," Mrs. Liu agreed, then made her way to the others.

Everett stepped back as the residents and Geoffrey started pulling materials for the ritual from their pockets.

Dan heaved himself up out of the depth of cushions. "I don't think I like what's happening here." All the congeniality had faded from his voice.

Cathal placed a hand on his arm. "Peace, Dan. They don't mean us any harm."

I nodded, but he didn't look convinced. In a calm, reassuring voice, I said, "I promise we are only here to help."

The druid narrowed his gaze and begrudgingly nodded.

Everett removed a coffee table as Sissy got on her hands and knees to chalk a large circle on the wood floor. Mr. Perez followed behind her, spritzing it with a salt water solution. Mrs. Liu marked four corners with candles and Mr. Friedman lit them. My father took the northern position near a small baggie of garden soil, Sissy took the eastern with a feather at her feet and Mrs. O'Cleary stood at the west with my sticker covered water bottle.

"Genny, take the south," Geoffrey encouraged. I lifted the scabbard off my shoulder and pulled out Excalibur. I tossed the scabbard on the couch across from us and stepped up to the candle twice the size of the other three. The others filled in the rest of the circle.

"Cathal and Dan, would you mind standing over here, please?" Geoffrey asked, gesturing toward the middle of the circle. The way my father said it must not have triggered the gaes, and both men stepped forward as the coven shifted to let them through.

Almost as one, the coven closed their eyes and dropped their heads to their chests. I followed their lead, letting myself fall forward into the chaos of my power, grateful to once again have Excalibur for control.

The chant started low and rhythmic, almost like a heartbeat. Geoffrey said it was the spell for clarity and I just needed to follow the rise and pull of the magic and add my own. I let the power swell, the circle of salt holding it as the pressure rose. My part of the ritual would come after.

At the height of the crescendo, Mrs. O'Cleary lifted my water bottle and removed the lid. She stepped closer to Cathal and Dan, raising the bottle to pour a stream of water over both their heads before stepping back. Streams ran down their noses to pool at their feet.

My turn.

I held Excalibur under my arm as I'd done before at the Unseelie Court and placed my palm under the blade, ready to run my skin along the edge to draw blood.

The front door burst open, slamming against the wall with a crack and guttering the candles.

Everyone startled and fell silent.

Theo, holding a sword, stomped into the entryway, Aurnia behind him. If Aurnia was here, where was Aengus? What had they done to him? Everett moved to block the archway into the living room even as Cathal called for him to stay back. Theo didn't pause. With a lunge, he plunged the sword into Everett who turned just in time to have metal through his side instead of his chest. He crumpled to the floor with a groan.

"Everett!" I cried and would have abandoned the circle if Mrs. Liu's hand wasn't holding my arm like a vise.

Aurnia gazed at the circle. Her eyes widened when they fell on Cathal and Dan, but she quickly rearranged her expression to one of command. "Unless you all wish to die, I'd stop what you're doing. I only want the Cailleach Fae."

Was there anyone in the fae universe who wasn't trying to kidnap me?

Geoffrey covertly motioned Mr. Perez to take his place by the candle. I turned toward him as he stepped out of the circle. He eyes me with a hard stare. "Don't stop," he whispered.

"The scabbard," I whispered back and glanced at it on the couch then at Everett. Geoffrey nodded in understanding.

"Keep going," Mrs. Liu ordered in a low, clipped voice, and the coven nodded.

The chanting began again around me, but I could only focus on Geoffrey. What did he think he could do? Theo canted his head, clearly thinking the same thing. My father reached for the mug Dan had left on the table and flung its contents into Theo's face. The still hot tea hit him and he nearly dropped the sword, trying to wipe the liquid away. That's when Geoffrey barreled into him, slamming him into the wall.

My dad—the bar brawler.

"Genny," Mrs. O'Cleary called, grabbing my attention. "We need the blood."

Aurnia scowled and tried to reach for me, but the circle held. The moment her hand met the wall of magic, a loud pop exploded in the air and the force sent her backwards into the lounger, gaping like a fish.

Biting my lip against the pain, I ran my hand over the blade. The sharp edge sliced through the skin, my body only registering what happened when blood burned its way up through the split. I curled my fingers inward until the pads of fingers sank into the pooling red.

Geoffrey and Theo slammed against the far wall of the house near the couch. Staying too close to allow Theo room to wield his sword, my father snatched up the scabbard and brought it up to block a swing. At least, he'd be healed if Theo managed to get through his defenses.

I reached out to Cathal and raised my bloody fingers to his forehead; he closed his eyes and leaned into my touch as I drew the symbol of the third eye.

There was another crash, and someone let out a broken cry, giving out halfway through.

I glanced over my shoulder. Geoffrey stood skewered against the wall, Theo's sword protruding from his chest. He held the blade, his eyes wide. The scabbard gone. I watched as he slumped to the floor, his head dropping to his chest.

"No!" I screamed.

"You must finish," Sissy bellowed, her voice grabbing hold of me and filled with prophecy. "It is the only way."

Someone needed to get the scabbard to my dad. This couldn't be happening.

My voice broke with every word as tears collected in the back of my throat. I spat out the words to the spell, sending my magic direct and true toward the symbol on Cathal's forehead. The blood sank deep into his skin. He blinked at me, then at Dan. Then he turned a dark gaze on Aurnia, who was extricating herself from the chair.

"Hello, Mother."

I dashed from the circle, just as Theo yanked the sword roughly from Geoffrey's chest. "No!" I screamed again, falling to my knees at Geoffrey's side. Damn it! Where was the scabbard?

"Here," Everett said from where he'd propped himself in the archway. His scrub top shimmered black with blood, but his color looked flush. He held out the familiar jeweled leather. "He threw it to me."

I yanked the scabbard to me. Blood covered the entirety of Geoffrey's front and pooled in his lap. I pushed the leather into Geoffrey's open palms. Nothing happened. "Geoffrey?" I whispered, touching his leg. "Dad?" I whispered and gave him a shove.

With a shaking hand, I lifted his head. His lifeless eyes and bloodless lips stared back at me.

Sadness and anger raged through me, riming my vision in gold. With Excalibur in hand, I was in full control, but control didn't matter. I wanted blood. I gained my feet and swung around toward Theo, ready to devour his life thread whole.

Theo's sword lay at his feet, and he stared down at his hands in horror. Familiar green vines snaked their way under his lavender skin, bursting through like branches from his fingers.

"Bollucks, I'm really dead, aren't I?" Geoffrey's voice came from behind my shoulder.

Chapter Thirty-Six

So many things happened all at once.

Aurnia flew to Theo's side screaming, "What have you done?"

In the circle, Cathal bowed low to Dan, then set his palms against the druid's face.

The coven rushed to Everett's side and marveled at his almost completely healed wound.

And I stared in shock at the ghost of my father standing over me.

The screams coming from Aurnia finally had everyone turning her way. She whirled on me, eyes crazed and hands out like claws. "What did you do?" she demanded again.

"I don't know," I admitted, my gaze lingering on the vines as they wrapped Theo's legs. He whimpered as they moved toward his torso.

Geoffrey answered instead. "I believe when the fae, you know" — he mimicked the stabbing— "he reset the spell. It passes to the victor."

I tried not to think about the body of my father at my feet and only of the solid-looking ghost standing beside me. "My father says Theo reset the Green Knight spell."

"That can't be," Aurnia cried, reaching toward her youngest in a panic.

Cathal stepped from the circle. "Glad to know my memory of who's the favorite son is proven correct."

"Nonsense," she snarled. "I trusted you with my most important duty."

I glared and my anger still pulsed wanting to punish. "Just like you entrusted Aengus? Where is he? What have you done with him?"

Aurnia ignored me and continued to speak to Cathal. "You were the only one who could do what I asked."

"I think it's time to find out what your secret is," I said, stomping back to the circle where Dan stood quiet and still, as if asleep with his eyes open. Cathal leaned in. "I've hypnotized him. If you look, you'll find two life threads connected to him. I need you to find the one that feels the most like Dan and destroy it."

"What," I said, shocked.

"I know you hunger. To break my gaes you used quite a bit of your power. Reclaim it by doing what needs to be done."

"I'm not killing Dan!," I snapped.

"You must do what needs to be done to finish this. To save your man."

To save Aengus? Where was he? What did Aurnia do to him to find out where we were? I wanted to leave and find him, but there was no way for me to get to the Seelie Court without a portal. "Two life threads?" I asked, wanting clarification, but also stalling.

"Yes."

"No," Aurnia cried, but Cathal grabbed her as she flew at me, pulling her arms behind her back and holding her.

"Do it now, Genny," Cathal demanded.

I looked at the faces of the coven standing in a crowd under the archway. They all nodded.

With no other choice, I fell forward into the realm of my magic. Golden life threads swarmed my vision, but I focused on Dan. Cathal was right. Two life threads emerged from him. One felt distinctly like Dan, vibrating with life. The other appeared muted, painted over. Was Cathal right? Would destroying Dan really fix the mess they were in?

What choice did we have? With a heave, I pulled Dan's life thread to me, pulling and pulling and pulling until nothing remained within him. Until I possessed it all. My eyes closed as I shuddered with magic and let out a soft moan. It was so easy.

A body hit the floor.

My eyes flew open. What had I done? I looked for Dan. A possibly human form lay on the floor, but immediately I looked away. The light emanating from it was too bright.

"Bright one," Cathal said as he tightened his hold on Aurnia.

Out of the corner of my eye, the form shifted, and the light lessened enough for a human shape to be seen. The light continued to dim until I could finally look directly at them. It was a cliché, but they truly were the most beautiful thing I'd ever seen. Feminine and masculine weaved into a beauty so intense and stunning I couldn't seem to think or look away.

Nothing that had been Dan existed.

Oh, and they were one hundred percent naked. God prerogative, I guess.

Cathal released Aurnia and dropped to his knees. "Danu, forgive me."

Danu? *The* Danu? "Your alive?" I strained to get out.

The deity ran long-fingered hands over the pristine skin of their arms and their perfectly smooth cheeks. They only seemed to notice everyone when their hands dropped away from their face. "Where is Morgana?" they asked as brightness swelled around them in a rhythmic pulse.

No one answered.

"Where is she?" Danu repeated.

Cathal stood slowly, head bowed reverently. "Apologies, Bright one, we don't know."

I spoke up. "Morgana goes by Leannan now, and she's raised an army to destroy the veil. We think she's here in the human realm."

A heavy, weighted silence hung in the air and then Danu started laughing. "She has not changed."

Cathal smirked. "No, she hasn't."

A roar like a wind tunnel echoed down the hall leading from the kitchen and a gust intense and sudden followed. The sound of multiple feet hitting the tile floor soon materialized into Aengus and Saoirse skidding to a halt at the edge of the chaos.

My voice evaporated with my relief, but Aengus zeroed in on me, plowing through everyone to get to my side. His arms pulled me harshly against him as he buried his face in my hair and neck, breathing deeply. "You're okay," I croaked.

He pulled back and eyed everyone with an almost feral regard. When he recognized the Seelie Queen, he growled.

Saoirse picked her way daintily around the coven and stopped at Theo, now completely encased in vine made armor and seeming to gain height as the moments passed. Soon he wouldn't be able to stand up straight under the low ceiling. Saoirse ran a finger along a trailing vine that ran down his chest. "My Green Knight," she purred. "I thought I'd lost you forever."

"Get your hands off him," Aurnia roared.

Saoirse smiled, one eyebrow raised. "Were they someone important to you?" she asked and then laughed. When she turned she noticed Danu and dropped immediately into a low curtsy. "Bright one, you have returned."

"I have," they agreed.

Aengus tightened his grip around me, his chest hard against the back of my head. "Danu?"

Before I could explain, sand pelted the window, the pinging of grit ringing against the glass. The familiar voice of Leannan reached us from outside. "Cailleach Fae, come on out. I felt your magic. Silly of you to tell me exactly where you are. Now my army has you surrounded."

Chapter Thirty-Seven

I wanted to send the coven home, but even if Saoirse wasn't drained, the coven would have refused. "We won't leave while Genny is still in danger," Mr. Perez said firmly, and Mrs. Liu nodded her head in agreement, along with the rest.

Leannan called again from the yard.

Cathal pushed Aurnia toward the front door. "Come on, Mother. We should at least tell the vengeful lover the full story."

Saoirse squeezed around what had once been Theo and was now the Green Knight. She opened the door, letting in a blast of cold air and gestured for her new minion to proceed her. He hunched, squeezing through the doorframe, as the vines rustled and scraped against the wood. When he finally got through, the Unseelie Queen tightened her side ponytail and followed him.

Cathal dragged Aurnia out with him.

"I'm sure your umm...body will be fine if you leave it," I assured Geoffrey when he questioned going outside as well.

Aengus bent close. "Your father is still with us?" he murmured against my ear. I gave a sad smile and nodded.

The coven, who could see Geoffrey, directed Everett who couldn't as they followed the exodus.

Before Aengus and I walked out, I turned to Danu, still naked and glowing like a meteor. They stood, arms folded tightly against their stomach. They looked nervous. Was it possible for a literal god to be nervous? "I need a moment," they said with a faint smile. I tried to give a reassuring smile in return before we left them behind.

When the winter morning sunlight hit Aengus, he nearly crumpled. "Aurnia didn't feed you, did she?" I said, glaring daggers at the Seelie leader's back.

"I will be fine," Aengus said, his tone strained and his eyes rimmed in red. "But if I am not, just point me in the direction of Leannan's army and run away."

"That's not funny."

Leannan stood front and center with the spear Birga, Janquil beside her as her army of wild fae fanned the area between the barn and greenhouse. There were no other *ossorians* among the group. I hoped again that Nimue had been able to save the two I'd left behind. The *fola tráill*, however, were many and ravenous.

Our ragtag army looked minuscule in comparison.

The horses and cattle in the surrounding fields filled the air with anxious calls. Leannan eyed Cathal and canted her head. "Now, why would you lie about the death of your son, Aurnia?"

The Seelie Leader squirmed in Cathal's arms, but he didn't let go.

Saoirse took a full step into the gap between forces. The Green Knight close behind her. "We can't let you destroy the veil. I don't like how it was used in the past, but the flood of magic would harm this world irreparably."

Leannan sneered. "Traitor. You, of all people, should remember how the Seelie treated any fae not of their court, and yet you stand beside them."

"I'm not on their side. I'm just not on yours."

Leannan rolled her eyes at Saoirse's words.

The Unseelie Queen kept speaking. "Would you like to know the reason the Cailleach Fae used the power that called you here?" Saoirse pointed behind her, toward the house, and as if by command, Danu stepped over the threshold, their entire being glowing like a fallen sun.

A keening wail left Leannan and echoed across the range. She took a step closer. "That's impossible," she whimpered. "I killed you."

Danu walked through our meager line of defense and we gladly parted for them. When they reached Leannan the world seemed to hold its breath. "Only nearly," Danu said gently, breaking the spell, letting the world breathe once more.

"I don't understand." Leannan reached out her fingers barely inches from Danu.

Cathal dragged Aurnia forward. "I think my mother can explain."

Aurnia shrugged off her son's grip and straightened her blazer. "I did what I had to," she snapped.

"Not enough. Tell them everything."

She crossed her arms, refusing.

Cathal sighed deeply. "Leannan, in your anger, you injured Danu greatly. My mother saw an opportunity to get revenge on her husband and gain the power she'd always wanted. She used the last of the great stone circle magic to hide Danu behind the creation of another. She sent this creation to the human realm, and she sent me with them under the power of a gaes. I was to keep watch over Danu, hidden, and both Innisfail and the human realm were to believe they died."

"But why," I asked.

Saoirse's understanding lit up her face as she answered. "So Aurnia could say Leannan was dangerous and all those that consorted with humans. She was the one that convinced us all that the veil needed to be closed. She wouldn't rule the Seelie in Innisfail with her philandering husband. But she could rule here. Completely and without dissent."

Cathal nodded his confirmation. "And by sending me here and taking Theo with her, she denied Oberon his heirs."

Danu slowly raised a hand as if to brush through Leannan's hair. Janquil shifted, snorting through his wide nose. Danu dropped their arm, stepping back. "I would have changed," they said softly.

Leannan's grip on the spear tightened and she narrowed her eyes.

"Eventually," Danu admitted with chagrin. "The druid I was may be gone, but what he learned I still keep. The veil protects the realms, but the gate, my existence, only protected our discrimination. I will support it no longer. If you allow everyone to part ways without bloodshed, I promise the gate will forever remain open."

"What of Aurnia?" Leannan demanded.

Danu looked over their shoulder. "Cathal will take over the Seelie Court in this realm. Aurnia will return to Oberon's side. Saoirse will remain as Unseelie Queen, with the Green Knight and former Seelie prince."

Leannan dipped the spear in my direction. "And the girl?"

This time Danu reached out and captured Leannan's free hand in their glowing one, kissing her knuckles. "What need of her power would you have if you are getting everything you wanted?"

Leannan eyed me with a scowl. "She is dangerous."

They chuckled. "As are you." Danu held out an open palm. "Birga must return to the gods."

Leannan yanked her hand from Danu's and reluctantly laid the spear in their waiting grip. She flashed me a toothy smile. "Keep your power but be careful not to burn yourself out and destroy all you love." She said the words happily with a touch of spite.

I hefted Excalibur onto my shoulder. "It's a good thing I have this."

Danu suddenly focused on both Aengus and I, and I wilted under their godly gaze. "Without my presence, anyone may pass through the gate. You will need to gather more *custos* to encourage those who seek chaos to return home."

Aengus bowed low at the waist. "As you command, Bright One."

I bowed awkwardly too, causing Excalibur to fall from my shoulder, barely missing the deity by a few inches. "Oh my god—goddess—Bright One—I'm so sorry," I yelped stumbling over what to call them as I yanked back my sword.

Danu blinked and patted my shoulder. "You should take some sword lessons from Lancelot here." They threw a wink at Aengus who was definitely biting his tongue. I giggled and nodded, unable to answer.

"Aurnia," Danu called to the Seelie Leader, "come. I'm sure you and Oberon have much to discuss."

Aurnia stepped toward Danu, her shoulders held back, but her face pale. The god made a portal that looked more like a rip in the universe. They stepped through and it zipped closed behind them.

Leannan called to Cathal. "I will leave the *fola* with you. I no longer have a means by which to feed them and I have a feeling you'll decline to let me put them out of their misery."

"You'd be correct," Cathal said.

She then she turned to Janquil, and with a flourish she spun out a portal, she and all the wild fae stepped through.

Saoirse also spun a portal. and she and the Green Knight disappeared through it. In moments, the driveway was more than half empty as only the coven, Cathal, the *fola*, and my ghost dad remained.

"Do you happen to be able to create a portal?" I asked Cathal and he winced.

"I'm afraid I was never very good at it."

I pulled out my cell phone and pulled up a number. On the third ring, Diana picked up. "Hi, funny story. The retirement home residents and I are going to need a ride home." She asked from where? "You know that special house your Grandpa took us to? Yeah, that one. I super appreciate it. I know I owe you the whole story."

Cathal, who had already started letting the starving *fola* take a turn drinking from his wrists, smiled wide. "Would you all like a cup of tea while you wait for the cavalry?"

Cathal herded his hungry horde toward the house and the coven followed. Geoffrey winked at me, following up the rear.

"You should go, too," I encouraged Aengus. The blazing sun seemed to be literally sucking the energy from him the longer he stood outside.

"Soon," he said pulling me into his arms. I gladly burrowed beneath his trench, snaking my arms around his middle.

"This didn't turn out like I thought it would," I said, laying my head against his chest as his arms wrapped tightly around me.

"Much less bloodshed," Aengus said nodding, then seemed to freeze. "Your father. That was callous of me."

"It's okay. I mean I know he's dead, but he's still here. It's complicated and I think my emotions are going to be complicated along with it."

Aengus tipped my head up, his other hand running along my cheek.

I suddenly felt bashful under his unrelenting stare. I looked away. "You won't have to go back to your tomb."

He leaned down and ran his lips along my cheekbone. One, then the other. "No," he murmured against my skin.

"It was a shitty plan," I quipped even as I could feel my whole body tremble beneath his touch. Aengus chortled and pulled back. I looked up at him. "Just think if I'd cast the spell like you wanted, we couldn't touch."

"I will endeavor to follow your advice in the future."

"The future? So you believe you have one now?"

With little effort Aengus lifted me off my feet and against him, my legs instinctively landing around his hips, as his lips found mine. He pulled away only to say, "My future involves staying with you for as long as you will have me, Imogen."

"Oh, well that's good, because I don't plan on letting you go." I smiled. Not a pretty smile, all sweet looks and a curved bow to my lips. No, this smile spread across my face, all teeth, and scrunched nose and my eyes nearly closed.

Suddenly my face fell. "What?" Aengus asked concerned.

"Who's going to tell Nibs she has a to share a room with you, too?"

Aengus pondered my words seriously. "That, I believe, is what bribery is for."

Six Months Later

I giggled as I handed Aengus his morning cup of coffee in my favorite yellow mug with the words "Kiss the Librarian" on it.

"Why do you laugh every time I use this mug?" Aengus asked, staring at it with confusion.

"No reason," I said, giggling again.

As instructed by Cathal, I'd put a drop of my blood in the coffee every morning. Doing this meant Aengus only needed to visit Cathal once a month instead of every few days. The mug was just purely for my own personal amusement.

While holding the mug in one hand and taking a sip, Aengus utilized the spatula in the other, flipping the row of pancakes on the electric griddle. From the top of the island, Nibs supervised, hands on hips. "More chocolate chips," she demanded.

The acts of bribery were ongoing.

My mother in her fuzzy blue robe, shuffled down the back stair and into the kitchen. She scowled as she looked around. "Is your father here?"

I made a show of looking around even though I knew the answer. "No."

"Well, when you see him, you tell him he needs to stop staring at me while I sleep and definitely not while I'm changing. I may not be able to see him, but I can feel his eyes ogling."

"Weren't you guys like almost married?" I asked.

"That's not the point," she answered.

She turned to return upstairs and looked back at me, her eyes glassy. "Your father is still here, right? He hasn't" —she hesitated— "moved on?"

"He's still here," I assured her and she nodded to herself. I hadn't yet thanked Nimue for saving my mother. A few days after everything had happened, our doorbell rang. When I opened the door, my mother stood there with Dennriall and Nicholas flanking her. Nimue had instructed Amicus to deliver her, and the kelpie had done his very best, showing up in their pool.

Nicholas, from his quaffed wave of blond hair to his tailored clothes and perfectly manicured nails appeared to have stepped down off a fashion runway. Nibs was immediately in love. He'd smiled wide, showing off pearly teeth and shook everyone's hand energetically. He seemed so at odds with the reticent Dennriall, but the soft smiles they gave each other could not be mistaken for anything but true affection.

The day of the almost battle, Dennriall had followed his intuition and had not gone home after creating a portal from Cathal's, instead, he'd felt the need to check on his queen. When he found she'd not returned from the Seelie Court he'd portalled there and set both Aengus and Saoirse free from a warded cell.

Saoirse had been so impressed with her seneschal's loyalty that she'd granted them their fae marriage. Merely a formality, but it allowed Dennriall more freedom to be with Nicholas and Nicholas more rights as an acknowledged spouse. It was a situation that benefited everyone.

A flurry of barking vibrated the walls and a fifty pound six-month-old puppy came lumbering into the kitchen. He flew to the island and leaped, placing his front paws on the counter. Nibs squealed with happiness and hissed his wet nose. "You're the best boy, Lancelot."

Aengus cringed, which was the very reason the Brownie had chosen the name.

"Remember dogs can't have chocolate," I reminded her. She made pleading eyes at Aengus.

He sighed. "I will make one without chips."

Nibs clapped her hands.

The bathroom door off the kitchen opened and Fintan stepped out freshly showered, towel barely covering his hips and his silver talisman hanging from his neck.

"Good morning, Ms. Wylde," Fintan said placing a fist against his damp chest and bowing his head at me.

Aengus flopped a stack of done pancakes on a plate, then brandished his spatula toward Fintan like a weapon. "How many times must we tell you to put some clothes on?"

Fintan shrugged, throwing his hands up in defeat. "Send your complaints to the Lady. I canna turn human without water and I canna put on clothes without my hands."

There was a scratch at the back door and I moved to open it. Aodh in his wolf form, jogged in holding a pair of sweats in his mouth. He dipped his head as he passed me and made his way to the bathroom under the glare of Fintan.

"Must you make me look bad, brother?"

Aodh chuffed through the cloth and kicked the bathroom door closed with his back foot.

Nimue had also been able to protect the two other *ossorians*. After I'd altered their spell as well, Nimue had supplied the four with the needed talismans. While wearing them they were conscious, but they need a flow of water to regain human form. The garage now housed them all, but every morning one at a time they trotted in and used the shower.

We were going to need to renovate and add another bathroom soon.

I heard Everett stomp down the front stair and I left the kitchen to speak with him. He'd just settled into his worn office chair at the front desk. I leaned on the edge of the desk as he picked up the digital tablet but didn't dismiss the lock screen. I tilted my head as I asked the same question I'd started asking for the last year, "You find a new job?"

"Not today," he answered as always.

Today I followed up the question. "Honestly, though, why have you stayed? Why haven't you run away screaming?"

Everett laughed. "Truth?"

I nodded.

"Aside from the fact that this job pays well, it's kind of like this old chair. I could get a new one, but my ass fits this one perfectly. Y'all are weird, but you've become *my* weird."

Just then, the residents began shuffling slowly down the stairs, dressed in their gym clothes and holding their yoga mats.

Mrs. O'Cleary pointed at me as she took the last step. "Would you be a dear and go tell Mr. Friedman, it's time to stretch?"

"Of course," I answered.

"Oh," she added and I paused, "and Luttie will be coming this afternoon to handle the books, again."

I pounded the air like a champion athlete winning a gold medal and Mrs. O'Cleary chuckled.

The witches' Discord had found Luttie, a retired accountant whose sister had been a witch so she'd grown up in the community. Now she did accounting on the side to pay for her cruises. A perfect set up all the way around.

I went and poked my head in into the office. Mr. Friedman sat hunched over the computer keyboard, his glasses precariously floating on the end of his nose. Geoffrey stood behind him directing him.

"Found any more *custos* prospects for me and Aengus to interview?" I asked.

Geoffrey nodded with a smile. "There's a young woman in Vancouver that seems promising."

"Oooo, I've always wanted to go there," I said and then added, "It's yoga time, Mr. Friedman and Dad, Mom says stop ogling her." Mr. Friedman gave me a salute and shuffled out the door.

Geoffrey had the decency to look ashamed. "She's just so damn beautiful..."

"Nope, stop there. I promise the next thing we figure out with magic is how to let you both see each other so I can stop being the middle man."

The smell of pancakes and a growling stomach pulled me back to the kitchen as my brain already whirled with plans for our next trip. What time of year was the best to visit Canada? Lancelot happily munched on a plain pancake on the floor. I ducked under Aengus's arm and wrapped my arms around his chest. He kissed the top of my head as he flipped the next batch. With visibly more chocolate chips than batter.

"More chocolate chips," Nibs crowed.

Pronunciation Guide for the
Innisfail Cycle

Aengus – pronounced like Angus
Angusulus – an-G (soft g)US-ah-luhs
Cailleach – Coll-yoch
Cathal – Cah - hall
Cynosure – Sy-na-shoor
Geoffrey – pronounced like Jeffrey
Leannan Sidhe – Lee-AHN-nahn Shee
Saoirse – SUR -sha
Aurnia – OR-neeah
Theophilus – THEE-ah-phi-luhs
Gaius – GUY-uhs
Dennriall – DEN – Ree – all
Innisfail – IN -nis – fail
Ossorians – OH – sore – ree- ans
Fola Traill – FOH – lah TRAY – all
Sul Aos Si – Sool – Ees – she
Tá mo chroí istigh ionat -- Taw mu kree iss-chig uhn-it
Aodh – A (long a sound)
Uisce – ish-cah

Author's Note

Over twenty years ago, I set out to write a King Arthur novel. And for twenty years, I would begin and subsequently abandon it at different stages. Once even reaching "the end" only to put it in a drawer and never return to it. (Believe me, this was for the good of all.) There was even a stretch of time when I wondered if I even wanted to keep writing. Obviously, that didn't last.

What became The Innisfail Cycle is so far from my writing beginning, yet it's very much the culmination of the journey. Both novels in the duology are made up of all the things I love, things I've researched for over two decades, things I didn't even realize were a part of me until I sat down and wrote. This also means it's a crazy melting pot of disparate histories, myths, cultures, and genres. Please forgive me for playing fast and loose—especially with the Gaelic!

No doubt there are things in my novel that did or didn't work for you. And that's totally okay! But I'd like to take a moment and point out a few things I'm rather proud of regarding choices made or references used in both novels. Mostly because I'm a nerdy girl and I desperately want you to think they're as fascinating as I do.

Almost all of the locations and settings in both books are based on real places in Northern Nevada. Sadly Wylde House Retirement Home doesn't exist, nor does the Seelie Court corporate building. Those that are real are used fictitiously, but wherever possible, I tried to describe them as accurately as I could. Yes, there really is a "Batmobile" in the Carson Nugget Casino. There's also a Captain America Motorcycle as well! The historic district in Carson City has 337 historic building/resources and every year in the summer and fall visitors can take a guided ghost walk.

You may have wondered why my "Lancelot" is named Aengus. This wasn't just an attempt to be different. In my research, I read a book written by Norma Lorre Goodrich back in the late 80s. She hypothesized that the name Lancelot was derived from the Latin name for Angus—Anguselus (which I also used in the books). Her line of reasoning convinced me, but I used the older spelling of Angus (Aengus) because honestly, it just looks prettier.

Although, the *fola tráill* are a complete invention (again sorry for my poor use of Gaelic!) I modeled the *ossorians* after an Irish myth—The Werewolves of Ossory. The legend goes that descendants of the wolf-warrior Laignech Fáelad—who became the kings of Ossory in Eastern Ireland—could shapeshift into wolves and raid the surrounding areas. There are several versions of this tale, ranging from the 12th century onward. Some even consider the tale written down by the priest Gerald of Wales in 1182 to be the first werewolf story to be written in the Christian age.

Lastly, Aengus mentions Elaine, his former lover, in both books. As some of you might have guessed, she is a direct reference to a Tennyson poem. As much as it's a product of Victorian misogyny and overt Christian ideology, "The Lady of Shalott" is still one of my favorite Arthurian works. I did, however, apply some modern sensibilities to Elaine's passing.

The entire of story of Arthur and Gwynevere, Aengus's tragic love story with Elaine of Shalott, and the closing of the veil to Faerie is filed away in my head. Who knows, someday I might sit down and complete the cycle by writing it, but right now I'm content to stay in Northern Nevada. There are still so many more stories to tell.

More ways to stay in touch with Angela Laverghetta

Thank you so much for picking up The Hidden Druid. If you enjoyed it, please consider leaving a review. Indie authors rely on reviews and your honest words will help the right readers find it.

If you'd like to get updates on future books you can join my newsletter by going to my website:

www.angelalaverghettabooks.com

You can also follow me on social media—

Instagram, Threads, and TikTok: @angelawithapen

Facebook: Angela Laverghetta

Angela Laverghetta

Angela Laverghetta is a Northern Nevada based fantasy author. She's taken the saying "write what you know" to heart and loves showing readers a different side of Nevada. Almost all her writings take place locally, including her debut modern fantasy novel The Buried Knight published in 2023, and its sequel The Hidden Druid. Other published works include a novella previously published by a small press and two short stories both for The ACES Anthology in 2023 and 2024. When not writing, you can find her handling her zoo of many pets, talking to her youngest son about comics and fanfiction, or curling up in a blanket with a mug of tea and a stack of four or five books in easy reach.

Through it all she found comfort and (more importantly) escape in reading and writing. Her goal as an author is to provide the same comfort and escape for her readers.